LONG LANCE

Chief Buffalo Child Long Lance

From a painting by Leon Gordon

Long Lance

by Chief Buffalo Child Long Lance
[Sylvester Long]

With a foreword by
Irvin S. Cobb

and an introduction by
Donald B. Smith

Banner Books
University Press of Mississippi / Jackson

First published in 1928 by Cosmopolitan Book Corporation,
New York
Introduction copyright © 1995 by the University Press of
Mississippi
All rights reserved
Manufactured in the United States of America

98 97 96 95   4 3 2 1

Library of Congress-Cataloging-in-Publication Data

Buffalo Child Long Lance, 1890-1932.
    Long Lance / by Chief Buffalo Child Long Lance (Sylvester
Long) ; with a foreword by Irvin S. Cobb and an introduction by
Donald B. Smith.
         p.   cm. — (Banner books)
    ISBN 0-87805-829-X (cloth). — ISBN 0-87805-830-3 (paper)
    1. Indians of North America—Great Plains—Fiction. 2. Siksika
Indians—Fiction. I. Title. II. Series: Banner books (Jackson,
Miss.)
PS3503.U2816L66 1995   95-18985
813'.52—dc20   CIP

British Library Cataloging-in-Publication data available

Dedicated to the two White Men
who have guided and encouraged me most
since I have taken a place in civilization:

WILLIAM MORRIS GRAHAM
Commissioner of Indian Affairs
Regina, Saskatchewan

THE REVEREND
CANON SAMUEL MIDDLETON
Missionary of the Blood-Blackfeet Indian
Reservation, Cardston, Alberta

And to a friend of the Indian:
HON. DUNCAN CAMPBELL SCOTT
Deputy Superintendent-General of Indian Affairs

Contents

Illustrations ix

Introduction xi

Foreword xxxv

Introduction to the First Edition xxxvii

I First Remembered Things
1

II "Swear by the Horn"
17

III What's in an Indian Name?
41

IV The Seven Tents of Medicine
46

V The Rite of the Buffalo Head
62

VI Chief Carry-the-Kettle
80

VII An Arrow from White Dog's Quiver
106

VIII The Making of a Brave
120

IX White Foreheads
142

X Sheep, Goats, and Mountain-Lions
156

XI Rock Thunder's Death Song
168

XII Wolf Brother
180

XIII The Ghost Horse
189

XIV The White Man's Buffalo Robe
209

XV The Passing of the Medicine-Man
221

XVI The Carnival of Peace
234

XVII Outlaw
243

XVIII No More Roving
276

Illustrations

Chief Buffalo Child Long Lance
Frontispiece

The famous Horn Society of the Blackfeet at Gleichen,
Alberta
Facing p. 24

Indians with their horse and travois in the Canadian
Rockies
Facing p. 24

Chief Carry-the-Kettle, Assiniboine head chief
Facing p. 84

Mrs. Good Elk, who was stabbed seven times by the
Blackfeet in the Blackfoot Massacre
Facing p. 84

Many Shots, Blackfoot, who has been through the
Sun Dance seven times
Facing p. 130

Sun Dance Camp, of the Northern Blackfeet
Facing p. 130

Woman of the Blood Band of Blackfeet, with
child in moss-bag carrier
Facing p. 186

Wolf Head, famous Blackfoot medicine-man
Facing p. 230

Spotted Calf and Sounding Sky,
parents of the historic Indian fighter Almighty Voice
Facing p. 256

Almighty Voice, Jr., and his twin babies
Facing p. 272

FROM
SYLVESTER LONG
TO BUFFALO CHILD
LONG LANCE

Long Lance's first recollection as a child was the aftermath of a Blackfoot skirmish with the Crows. "Women and horses were everywhere," he wrote in his autobiography, "but I remember only two women: my mother and my aunt." His mother's hand was bleeding. That scene haunted him, leaving "such a startling impression that all during my growing years it kept coming back to me. I wondered what it was and when I had seen that strange panorama, or whether I had ever seen it at all or not—whether it was just a dream." Only when he had "grown into boyhood" did his aunt confirm the details. After he told her his tale she exclaimed: "Can you remember that! You were only fourteen months old then. It was when your uncle, Iron Blanket, was killed in a fight with the Crows—and your mother had cut off one of her fingers in mourning for him, as the women used to do in those days."

Full of arresting detail and so expertly written, *Long Lance,* published by the Cosmopolitan Book Corporation in 1928, became an instant success. Translations into several European languages followed. The book went into further editions in English. Over the years this autobiography of a Blackfoot chief has been quoted by historians and ethnologists for its insights into the last moments of Plains Indian life before the disappearance of the last buffalo herds in the late nineteenth century.

Yet, research in the mid-1970s confirmed that Long Lance was not the author's true name. Rather Chief Buffalo Child Long Lance was one Sylvester Long. Actually, Sylvester had lived a lie since the age of eighteen, from the time he had entered Carlisle Indian School in 1909. His true life story has to do with the inequities of racial segregation and flight from a community that stigmatized him as a Negro. His father was of mixed Native American and probably of European and African ancestry as well. His mother was one-quarter Lumbee Indian and three-quarters white. And, in the climate of the times when Sylvester grew up, he was considered no different from any other "colored" person in Winston-Salem. More significantly he considered himself no different. As far as he was concerned, his life held no more promise than that of any black on the other side of the rope at segregated picnics, who said "Sir" and stepped into the gutter whenever a white man approached him.

Sylvester had grown up at the turn of the century, when the system of Jim Crow racial exclusion flourished. Like all those viewed as "colored," he underwent daily humiliations. It was not just sitting at the back of the streetcar that shamed him or the fact that blacks had to drink out of separate water fountains; it was knowing that the most inadequate white would always be considered superior to the most talented black. His people were sternly reminded of this even in shoe stores. While others could try on as many pairs of shoes as they wanted, blacks had just one chance. They had to go in knowing their exact size and style. But for Sylvester, there was one possible escape from the straightjacket of segregation: he looked like an Indian, as Americans, with their stereotypes, believed Indians should appear.

Sallie Long, Sylvester's mother, was part white, part Indian. In North Carolina, her mother, Adeline Carson, was classified as "Croatan," the name given at the turn of the century to people of mixed Indian, English, and possibly African ancestry, a group now known as the Lumbee, which has since achieved the legal status of a federally recognized Indian tribe. Adeline's mother was an Indian from South Carolina and her own father, Robert Carson, was a white. Sylvester would have known his maternal grandmother for she lived into the 1920s. Sallie's natural father, that is, Sylvester's maternal grandfather, was Andrew Cowles, a local politician, who became a state senator. He died in 1881.

Joe Long's antecedents are not so easily identified. Probably partially Afro-American in ancestry, since he had grown up in slavery, he never knew his parents. His obituary in the Winston-Salem *Journal* of November 16, 1932, simply states that he was born in 1853, a "member of the Catawba tribe of Indians," and, it continues, "as a boy he was taken into the family of the late Rev. Miles Long, serving his young master as a slave."

Whatever the full racial-ethnic background of his parents, Sylvester Long was born in Winston-Salem, North Carolina, on December 1, 1890. On reaching school age in 1897, Sylvester learned what it meant to be labeled "colored." Although there was a white elementary school only three blocks from his home, he had to attend the black school two miles away. By 1904, he had had enough of this. After finishing sixth grade, he left home and joined a traveling Wild West show. He was thirteen years old.

Little is known of his first five years away from home. On the road with other Wild West roustabouts, he undoubtedly passed as an Indian, capitalizing on his high cheek bones, straight, jet black hair, and coppery skin. Gradually he began to think of and identify himself as an Indian. When he returned home in 1909, on August 10, he and his father applied for the boy's admission to the Carlisle Indian School in Pennsylvania. The school had been teaching Indians since a former Indian fighter, General R. H. Pratt, opened it in 1879. Carlisle, in the thinking of American philanthropists, was to inculcate Indian youth with the skills and virtues of Christian civilization. For Sylvester, it served other purposes.

Joe Long honestly could not say from which Indian society he was descended. Thus, in his son's application, he identified him with the best known Native American nation in North Carolina: the Cherokees. Already, Sylvester spoke some of the language. While on the road with the Wild West show, a Cherokee named Whippoorwill began teaching him. Although Carlisle preferred applicants listed as full bloods, all those claiming one-quarter or more Indian ancestry could apply. Sylvester enrolled as a Cherokee.

His early days at Carlisle were painful. The Cherokees were a proud, color sensitive, prejudiced people. Only recently slave holders, they had fought for the Confederacy in the Civil War. Generally speaking, the Cherokee students were anti-black. So, from the first, they refused to accept Sylvester Long as one of them. The youth might pass as Indian among less sensitive whites; the young Cherokees proved a much tougher audience.

A teacher, James Henderson, later recalled in a confidential letter to the Commissioner of Indian Affairs: "The legitimate Cherokees were indignant at his posing as an Eastern Cherokee and a delegation of their number went to the Superintendent and protested his enrollment. I remember well that one of their number indignantly exclaimed, 'Cherokee nigger!' " One of Sylvester's classmates at Carlisle was Emma Newashe, an Indian from Oklahoma. In a memoir about him published in 1933, she recalled how Henderson gave him the name Sylvester Long Lance. Presumably this was to help "Indianize" his identity and to ease his adjustment among his peers in school. At Carlisle, Sylvester found his claim to Indian status being legitimized.

Faced by criticism from his peers, Sylvester refused to back down. He knew that this was his one chance to escape the racial stigmas and the restricted opportunities of rigidly segregated life. He adopted the tactic known as *racial passing*, not uncommon in this era. What distinguished Sylvester Long Lance was that he assumed an Indian identity. For an individual alone to succeed in such a transformation requires an extraordinary demonstration of achievement, and personally securing the acceptance of others. At this, the young man worked hard. *The Carlisle Arrow* magazine noted on October 28, 1910: "Sylvester is interested in everything he does and he knows how to apply himself."

Carlisle provided a combined elementary and trade-school education. It trained its students as carpenters, shoemakers, tailors, and printers. A bright, cooperative achiever, Sylvester won high marks in shop and excelled in the classroom, particularly in English and history. His teachers quickly recognized his ability and he, in turn, found a new self-confidence.

As Long Lance, he went out for football, but his best sport was long-distance running, at which he excelled. In his second year at Carlisle, he made the track team. He later claimed that in three successive races he had defeated the famous Jim Thorpe, a Sac Indian, in the three-mile run. In 1912, Thorpe was selected to represent the United States at the Stockholm Olympics: he picked Long Lance, two years his junior, as his training partner, and they remained good friends until Long Lance died. When Thorpe played baseball with the New York Giants after World War I, he gave Long Lance a picture of himself in his baseball uniform, and wrote at the bottom: "High Chief—Remember the mile runs, was great training for the Olympics."

Carlisle's teachers helped Long Lance develop his appreciation of literature and encouraged him to write. From the other students, he learned much about their nations' customs and legends. An unusually talented, skilled, good-natured storyteller himself, as Chief Buffalo Long Lance he would later use much of this material to enhance his public image and to achieve success.

Sylvester Long Lance, then twenty-one, graduated at the head of Carlisle's 1912 senior class. The school immediately enrolled him at Conway Hall, the preparatory school for Dickinson, a neighboring liberal-arts college. The following year, he won a scholarship to St. John's Military Academy, near Syracuse, New York, where he studied military history, organization, and tactics. In his senior year, he won high marks and played on both the school's track and football teams. In June 1915, President Woodrow Wilson

selected him as one of his six presidential appointments to
West Point. Long Lance was to report to Fort Slocum for
the qualifying examinations the following March.

Long Lance corresponded with his family reporting his
successes. The Longs also heard of his appointment from
their daily paper. As did other newspapers across the United States, the Winston-Salem *Daily Sentinel* carried the
story in late June 1915, on page one with the headline:
"Full Blooded Cherokee to Enter West Point."

The Longs quietly kept their pride to themselves. After
Sylvester had left for Carlisle, not much had changed for
them. Joe continued working as a janitor in the local school
system. Though the fair-skinned Abe and Walter might
have been able to "pass" as white in a northern city, they
stayed in Winston. Their friends and family were all there.
Abe had married a dark complexioned girl, and so would
Walter after World War I. In the city Abe ran a smoke shop
and Walter worked at a newsstand. Walter wanted to
become a policeman but coloreds were automatically
denied this opportunity.

Long Lance knew that if he really wanted to get ahead,
he would have to dissociate himself completely from his
family. West Point would not admit him if the president
discovered his parents were known as colored. It was
Woodrow Wilson, after all, who had introduced into Con-
gress the greatest flood of discriminatory legislation in
American history. He had proposed twenty bills advocating
the segregation of the races in all areas. Although most of
the legislation failed to pass by executive order, Wilson
made Negro federal employees eat their lunches in separate
rooms and use separate washrooms. A colored could never
succeed in Wilson's part of a racially segregated America. As

an Indian, it remained difficult. But Long Lance knew that with "a dash of initiative, grit and determination," as he put it once in an address to some Indian students, he could make it.

As it turned out, Long Lance never attended West Point. The bloodiest war in history then raged in Europe and he decided to prove himself immediately in combat. It was 1916, and the United States had not yet entered the war, so he traveled north to Canada and enlisted in Montreal. As he wrote in *Maclean's* in 1926: "Three weeks after I had 'coughed' and said 'Ah-h' for the medical officer, I was on my way to France on the *Olympic,* as Sergeant B. C. Long Lance, C. Company, 97th Battalion, Canadian Expeditionary force." At the front, he saw "men gutted and lacerated day in and day out." He fought and escaped injury in the terrible battle of Vimy Ridge. But one month later, his luck gave out. As he wrote to a friend in New York: "I am in a field hospital convalescing from a wound in the head received a couple of weeks ago. Nothing serious; only a piece of shrapnel in the back of the head and a broken nose—the latter sustained in falling on my face, I presume. I came through the April 9 scrap (Vimy Ridge) without a scratch. . . . only to get hit a month later on one of the quietest days we have had lately. Such is war!"

Shortly after his release, he was wounded in the legs during another attack. He credited the fact that he was an athlete and in excellent physical condition for his escape from double amputation. Invalided to England, he served with the British Army for a year. Asked where he would prefer his discharge, he chose the last Canadian province to be settled, distant Alberta, by the Rocky Mountains of Western Canada.

After demobilization, Long Lance joined the *Calgary Herald* as a cub reporter, and during the next three years, he covered every beat: police to sports to city hall. To enhance his image in town, he told those who inquired that he had won the *Croix de Guerre,* and he promoted himself from sergeant to captain. When asked his tribal identity, he said he identified himself as a Cherokee from Oklahoma.

With his customary enthusiasm, Long Lance became involved in the community around him. He refereed boxing matches at the YMCA, coached football, and helped at the Calgary Stampede. Then, in the summer of 1921, he began to visit the Indians on reservations around the city.

As a rule, Indians were treated despicably in the 1920s. In 1921, farmers around Calgary paid European immigrants $4 a day for harvest work, but Indians only $2.50. The federal government regarded them as a dying race and did little for their welfare. All too often, proper health services were denied them. Their average life span remained less than half that of the national norm. School history texts, portrayed Indians as filthy, childlike, cruel, and constantly at war. Looking around him, Long Lance felt it was time the true conditions of modern Indians were revealed.

On June 11, 1921, his first article on the Blackfoot appeared in the *Herald.* The title of the piece left no doubt about his convictions and determination: "Blackfoot Indians of this District Have in the Last Fifty Years Evolved from Savage Hunters into an Industrious People. Struck like a Thunderbolt with White Man's Civilization, These Indians were Forced Overnight into a Complete Change of Perspective—Have They Benefited by the Civilization? White Man's Evils Caused Them No Little Handicap."

Long Lance mentioned he obtained much of his information about modern conditions on the Blackfoot reserve from the Indian agent, George Gooderham. Their first meeting proved embarrassing. Long Lance handed Gooderham his card, but the agent was too preoccupied to read it. From his visitor's dark complexion, Gooderham assumed he was a *West* Indian. When Long Lance said he wanted to write an article on the Blackfoot, Gooderham showed him around the reserve, explaining everything simply, thinking Long Lance had never seen an Indian before. There was a long, polite silence; finally Long Lance identified himself. Despite this awkward beginning, they became close friends.

As Gooderham later recalled, Long Lance had "a wonderful ability to write imaginative stories from what he had known and seen, something that would appeal to the Whites." As far as the Blackfoot were concerned, the agent frankly felt Long Lance "didn't know much about Indian life, but he did in many, many of his writings go to the very rock bottom and get the correct story of the life of whatever Indians he was writing about. He was a fantastic man. He could do anything."

During the summer of 1921, Long Lance visited other reservations. In July, he called on the Sarcees or Tsuu T'ina near Calgary. He found them in horrible condition. As the headline read, the tribe was "Gradually Dying Off Owing to Ravages of Tubercular Trouble." The Sarcee population had fallen from 300 in 1877 to 155 in 1921. He wrote in the *Herald* of July 23, 1921: "The plight of the Sarcee is a real tragedy. Little do the people of Calgary realize that they are daily witnessing the passing of a nation as dramatically as any that have been depicted by the pen of J. Fenimore Cooper."

In August, he traveled south to the Cardston to visit the Bloods, where he met Rev. S. H. Middleton, principal of St. Paul's, the Anglican boarding school on the reserve. The two men became friends. Indeed, Long Lance came to consider the priest as his closest friend and named him sole executor in the will he signed on March 30, 1929. At Middleton's suggestion, the Bloods, in February 1923, adopted the Indian newspaperman, giving him a new name—Buffalo Child.

Howard Kelly was a Calgary friend who, at the age of nineteen, was sports editor of the *Herald*. Years later, Kelly remembered his Indian colleague: "Long Lance used to come to our home a lot, and have meals at our place. In any social get-together he always became the focal point in conversation because of his laughter, his merriment."

There was much anti-Indian prejudice in the Canadian West in those days, but what riled Long Lance most was being seen as black, as occasionally happened. The veteran journalist Fred Kennedy, who worked with Long Lance on the *Herald*, recorded one such incident. In his book, *Alberta Was My Beat*, Kennedy recalls the time when he was assigned to cover a regimental reunion dinner at the Palliser Hotel. There he found himself at the same table as Long Lance, who held the rank of militia captain in the 50th Battalion.

After dinner, Kennedy, Long Lance, and two others walked across the street to McCrohan's restaurant. They sat down at the horseshoe counter. About ten minutes later, two men entered. Kennedy wrote: "The waitress motioned them to stools alongside our group. They moved forward, stopped and then I heard one of them exclaim, 'I am not sitting alongside any Nigger.' The remark was obviously directed at Long Lance." The target of these slurs paid no attention, so the man repeated it—louder. "Long Lance excused himself and then, turning to the man who stood there glowering at him, he said, 'Were you addressing me, Sir?' 'I sure as hell was.' Long Lance's left didn't seem to travel anymore than eight inches but when it connected with the man's jaw, he went out like a light."

In spring 1922, Long Lance became restless. For months, he had covered city hall; since the previous fall, he had been given no more Indian assignments. So he decided to liven up the municipal meetings with a mock terrorist attack. Donning a mask, he slipped into the council chamber and placed inside the door of the mayor's office a gas inspector's bag that looked suspiciously like a bomb, the fuse attached sputtering sparks. City commissioners and the mayor ran for their lives, the mayor colliding with his secretary in a jammed exit door. One commissioner dived under a table. Another leaped through layers of storm window glass, then jumped ten feet to the ground. Over the next several days, the rival newspaper, the *Albertan,* played this prankster story for its laugh value. But the *Herald* was not amused: Long Lance was summarily fired.

That proved a blessing in disguise: it forced him into what became a profitable freelance career. In May, he left for the Pacific Coast, where he convinced the *Vancouver Sun* to let him write a series on the Indians of British Columbia. He visited Native communities throughout the province, and his several articles attracted the attention of editors of both the *Regina Leader* and the *Winnipeg Tribune.* After four months in British Columbia, and several months in Saskatchewan with the *Leader,* he joined the *Tribune,* writing about the Indians of Manitoba. Buffalo Child Long Lance, Blood Indian, was now his byline.

On the Assiniboine reserve at Sintaluta, just east of Indian Head, Saskatchewan, Long Lance met Chief Carry-the-Kettle, one of the few noted war chiefs still living in 1922. This aged warrior was then 107 years old. He had led his people to war when Sitting Bull, Crowfoot, and Big Bear were still in their infancy. Although ill and enfeebled, Carry-the-Kettle insisted on walking a hundred yards unsupported so he might greet Long Lance in the manner becoming an Assiniboine chief of his fame and standing. "He was being visited by a chief of a former enemy tribe," Long Lance later wrote, "and—as his people told me later—he would have walked that hundred yards had he known that it would have cost him his life." "Chief" Buffalo Child Long Lance continued: "Though Chief Carry-the-Kettle had killed more than one hundred men on the warpath, there was something in his face that was truly spiritual—a remarkable gleam of human goodness that made him bigger in my eyes than any man I have seen. When he had to refer to his killings on the warpath he did it with a whimsical air of apology which made it evident that it was distasteful to him. In spite of his destructive record, Chief Carry-the-Kettle was one of those men in whose fearless hands a person would gladly place his life, if it depended on a matter of fair judgment and the kindness of human nature."

On February 16, 1923, four months after their visit, the old Assiniboine chief died. In his memory, Long Lance wrote: "If there is a Heaven and Chief Carry-the-Kettle did not go to it, then I want to go where he went."

During the fall of 1923, in what Long Lance described as "a beautiful stretch of bush-dotted prairieland," twenty miles northeast of Duck Lake, Saskatchewan, he visited Sounding Sky and Spotted Calf, parents of the Indian martyr Almighty Voice. They still lived only four miles from the bluff where, twenty-six years earlier, their son made his last stand against the Mounties. Long Lance reported how he spent a week with them. Within two days, the old people, who had refused since 1897 to talk about their son's death, started to discuss the tragedy. They told him about their son's arrest for killing a government range steer, and his imprisonment in the Duck Lake guardhouse. As Long Lance explained in *Maclean's* on January 1, 1924: "I had not been there two days when the old mother asked me to exchange names with her and become her adopted son. Under these friendly relations, the old people without my asking, volunteered to tell me the whole story of their son's career."

Long Lance continually felt impelled to embellish his stories. Almighty Voice apparently escaped from the jail at Duck Lake after a police officer, by mistake, left the key in the prison door when leaving one evening. Long Lance, though, improved on these events, claiming the corporal in charge, through an interpreter, jokingly told Almighty Voice they were "going to hang him for killing that steer." In Long Lance's words, "hardly did the corporal realize the terrible effect which this innocent little joke was going to have on this untutored young Indian." The young Cree escaped and shot dead the first Mountie to track him down.

Then began the greatest manhunt in the history of the Canadian West. For two years, Almighty Voice, "famed throughout the region as a runner, hunter, a man of indomitable courage and independence," evaded pursuit. When finally tracked down, it was because he wanted to be found. Joined by two relatives, he had decided that he would die in one last defiant stand. The determined trio chose a thicket in a half-mile clump of bush lying on rolling, open prairie land.

The large force of police and volunteers charged twice, Long Lance reported. One of Almighty Voice's comrades was hit and died, but he and the other Indian shot down the postmaster of Duck Lake and two more Mounties. The police and their deputies called for reinforcements. Mounties came from Duck Lake, Prince Albert, and Regina, and hundreds of volunteers rode to the scene. That night, Almighty Voice, still unconquerable, shouted off the bluff to the troops: "We have had a good fight today. I have worked hard and I am hungry. You have plenty of food; send me some, and tomorrow we'll finish the fight." All night his mother chanted to him from a nearby hill, urging him to die the brave that he had shown himself to be. Now and then Almighty Voice would yell back through the darkness: "I am almost starving. I am eating the bark off the trees. I have dug into the ground as far as my arm will reach, but can get no water. But have no fear—I'll hold out to the end."

By the next evening, "the field guns were in place—a nine-pounder and a seven-pounder—and at 6 o'clock the first shells were sent thundering into the thicket." For three days, the Indians had not eaten, drunk, or slept. The besieging force kept up the barrage for hours. When they stopped shooting, they heard Almighty Voice: "You have done well, but you will have to do better." That night, sensing the inevitable, Almighty Voice's mother changed her chant to a proud lament: a death song for her son.

"At 6 o'clock the next morning," Long Lance wrote, "the big guns began belching forth their devastating storm of lead and iron in deadly earnestness. It was obvious that no living things could long endure their steady beat. At noon the pelting ceased." Almighty Voice was dead. "The bluff where he and his two companions died," concluded Long Lance, "marks the spot where the North American Indian made his last stand against the white man."

Long Lance had a tremendous vitality and zest for life; his prose moves along at the same rapid pace of his own life. How he loved it! In the early 1920s, he covered the world heavyweight boxing matches, traveling across the continent for a number of Western Canadian newspapers. Life was exciting, significant, fully dimensioned, especially at ringside, "where crushing blows are swishing through the air like nine-pounders, where bulky frames are tottering like giant buildings in an earthquake."

These were his salad days and he knew it. His friends in Calgary and Winnipeg remember him as a manly, happy-go-lucky fellow, full of fun. He would accept any dare. When challenged by a fellow reporter to duplicate a feat of the "Human Fly," a successful stunt artist of the day, Long Lance stood on his head on the parapet of a Winnipeg skyscraper. He boxed, played lacrosse, snowshoed, and everywhere he went succeeded with women—married or otherwise.

One woman at a resort in the Canadian Rockies almost caused his downfall. In the summer of 1926 Long Lance worked at the famous Banff Springs Hotel as the Canadian Pacific Railway's press representative for Western Canada. At the hotel, he met a Chicago lawyer's wife. She, her husband, and their houseman were spending the summer in a rented home nearby. The lawyer went to bed early, the wife late. The couple's houseman took violent exception to his employer's wife having an affair with an Indian. One night he rushed at Long Lance with a razor. The Chief saw him in time and with all his great strength smashed an iron poker over the servant's skull, almost killing him. For days, it appeared the assailant might die and Long Lance would face a murder charge. The man survived, but the Chief lost his job again.

But this time, Chief Buffalo Child Long Lance had no cause for worry. He had already acquired a name through his articles in major Canadian periodicals and newspapers such as *Maclean's* and the *Toronto Star Weekly*, as well as in equally prominent American magazines like *Mentor* and *Cosmopolitan*, even *Good Housekeeping*. And he had an ace in the hole—a story so sensational he knew he could sell it for almost any price. *Cosmopolitan*, then a general interest magazine, swallowed his latest fanciful tale whole and published it.

In July 1927, "The Secret of the Sioux" hit the newsstands. After interviewing several old Sioux warriors living in Canadian exile, Long Lance claimed General George Armstrong Custer was not killed by Indians at the Battle of Little Big Horn. He did not die with a revolver in each hand, his golden locks bravely waving in the wind, besieged by thousands of Sioux and Cheyenne—as portrayed in the famous Budweiser tavern lithograph. He made no courageous "last stand." Instead, Custer took a coward's exit—at the height of the battle, the man popularly portrayed as one of America's great military heroes committed suicide.

The protests of American patriotic groups did Long Lance no harm. Thanks to the publicity, he became an overnight celebrity. The Cosmopolitan Book Corporation of New York asked him to write a book for boys, so he stayed in New York to round it out. First, the gifted jour-

nalist reworked several of his published articles on the
Blackfoot—even slipping in the Carry-the-Kettle and
Almighty Voice stories, then drafted new material on growing up among the Blackfoot. Much of his raw material was
gathered from Mike Eagle Speaker, a young Blood student,
then studying at the agricultural college at Claresholm,
south of Calgary. Long Lance met Mike earlier through the
Rev. S. H. Middleton. By late 1927, he completed the
book, all 72,000 words, and he presented his publishers
with his fictionalized account of Blackfoot life before the
Indians settled on the reservations. Later, Long Lance told
a friend, "They thought it was too good for a boy's book,
and forthwith decided to run it as my autobiography." *Long
Lance* appeared in the fall of 1928, brazenly described as his
life story.

The celebrity status brought by publication of *Long
Lance* made him the target of many journalists' interviews.
The acid test for the Chief came in early October when
Gladys Baker, New York correspondent for a daily paper
that proclaimed itself "the South's Greatest Newspaper," the
News-Age-Herald of Birmingham, Alabama, interviewed
him. Now, the Sylvester Long behind the public Long
Lance had to be especially cautious. He certainly had not
forgotten the scars of his childhood in Winston-Salem.
One slip on his part could lead to exposure.

Gladys Baker and Long Lance met in a small French
restaurant on Eighth Avenue. It proved a "no contest"
engagement. The Chief impressed her on all counts—first
because of appearance. In her article for her southern read-
ers, she described him as "distinguished" looking, making
what she considered the supreme compliment, "were it not
for his straight black hair, which is cut close to his head,

and his skin, which is not red but more the color of ivory-toned parchment, he might be taken for a Wall Street broker." She loved his conversation and his manners. "His voice is low, harmonious and dramatic. He speaks without a trace of an accent. His words attest a wide and tastefully acquired vocabulary. His gestures are broad and simple, his manner one of ease and gallantry."

Not just Miss Baker, but all New York celebrated the Blackfoot writer. At first, Long Lance loved the attention and excitement. On June 8, 1928, he wrote his Calgary friend Howard Kelly about house parties on Long Island: "You know the kind we've often seen in the movies, but never in practice. Well, I can tell you now that they exist." While in New York, he became a close friend of the Kaiser's former daughter-in-law, Princess Alexandra. After the war, this noblewoman left the Kaiser's son to become an artist in New York. In the Crystal Room of the Ritz Hotel, he danced with Rudolph Valentino's exotic ex-wife, Natasha Rambova (born Winifred Shaughnessy). "A social lion of the season is an Indian—Buffalo Child Long Lance—who has been invited everywhere" (wrote one New York columnist). The New York society gossip writer Walter Winchell once encountered him at play. In his syndicated column, Winchell observed, "Chief Long Lance, the Indian lecturer, and the first Mrs. Guy Bolton are uh-huh. . . . "

For "the Beau Brummell of Broadway," as his friend and writer Irvin S. Cobb called him, there was only one more world to conquer: Hollywood. Soon, he signed a contract for a leading role in a film titled *The Silent Enemy,* to be made in Canada by Douglas Burden, a producer associated with the American Museum of Natural History. Paramount distributed the film about Indian life in North America before Columbus, the "Silent Enemy" in this case being hunger. Long Lance played the lead, Baluk, who saves his people. When released in 1930, *Variety* warned: "*The Silent Enemy* is interesting, educational, and a fine study anywhere, but it has not the commercial draw exhibitors look for." *The Silent Enemy* suffered at the box office also, because it was a silent film just when the talkies were capturing the market. But Long Lance received praise for his screen performance. *Variety* endorsed him: "Chief Long Lance is an ideal picture Indian, because he is a full-blooded one, an author of Indian lore, and now an actor in fact." And the public loved him. *Screenland* reported in its issue for October 1930, that "ever since the picture was released, Long Lance, one of the few real one-hundred-percent Americans, has had New York right in his pocket."

But success would not stay sweet, for in 1930, Long Lance's past caught up with him. Unknown to him, his father had been dangerously ill all year. He was in the hospital more than once and needed a major operation. How could the family possibly pay for it? His brother, Abe, was then working as the manager of the colored section of a Winston-Salem movie theater. His other brother, Walter, thwarted in his attempts to join the police force, had opened a detective agency in the black community. But in that second year of the Depression, business for both was terrible. Pushed to the wall, they had only one option left. One of them would have to ask Sylvester for help. They had followed his career, with what mixture of pride, perhaps resentment, we can only guess. They knew where he was. On December 31, 1930, Walter left for New York.

The brothers met in Manhattan during the first week of January. Sylvester had not seen Walter for twenty-two years, since the morning he left home for the Carlisle Indian School. After the meeting, Sylvester lay awake most of the night. "I have never," he later wrote Walter, "been torn like this before." Then he promised: "I am going to try to make some money now, so that I can help lift the burden." From then until shortly before his own death, Long Lance regularly sent home hundreds of dollars. At the same time, he forwarded money to his old friend, Jim Thorpe, who was also going through hard times.

The forty-first and last year of his life was unhappy. Long Lance took up flying and performed the extraordinary feat of soloing after only five hours and twenty minutes of instruction in the air (and then made three loops for good measure). He began parachuting, and even earned his commercial flying license. But his old zest for life had gone. He had spent twenty years building himself into a superhuman, not simply a successful, accomplished Indian, but a walking, talking image of the Noble Savage. Then, he saw Walter again and was pulled back by his roots, the troubles of his family. Suddenly, an agonizing lesson was driven into his thoughts. While he had achieved phenomenal public success in two countries—as athlete, soldier, author, bon vivant, and actor, his brothers and family still experienced the degrading absurdities of racial segregation.

All Long Lance had wanted was to fulfill himself as a human being, to achieve personal goals blocked by the social accidents and circumstances of his birth. To do that, he had to become more of an Indian than he really was; but he paid his dues. By his own demonstrated achievement, in his successful career, in his book and articles, he had tried to strike down many of the ridiculous notions prevailing about Indians. But now, what could he do? If he went home, the world would discover his parents were identified as "coloreds," and his public identity and writing might be discredited. At the same time, knowing how badly his family needed him, he could not endure the guilt of staying away.

Finally, Long Lance decided in May 1931 to leave New York for Los Angeles, where his friend Jim Thorpe lived. There, he found employment as the secretary and bodyguard of Anita Baldwin, daughter of a rich mining magnate, for her forthcoming European tour. For years, this wealthy woman had been interested in North American Indians; she owned a large collection of books on the subject. Much impressed by this extraordinary Plains Indian, following their return from Europe, she paid for his additional flying lessons at the neighboring Glendale airport. She also allowed Long Lance, whenever he wished, to use the library at her mansion at Arcadia outside Los Angeles. He often did so.

But these fresh adventures did not still his anguish. On Saturday, March 19, 1932, he talked to his dentist of suicide. That night he went to a movie, then returned to the Glendale Hotel and began drinking. When he came down into the lobby from his room, the desk clerk noticed he carried a pistol. Then he was seen entering a taxi, which carried him to Anita Baldwin's estate, arriving about midnight. Anita Baldwin, reading in her library, heard him arrive and greeted Long Lance at the door. His behavior startled her, as she later testified in a written statement read at the coroner's inquest: "He acted in a manner that I had never seen before, being quite abrupt, very depressed and non-communicative." She left him on his own in the library.

He sat alone with his thoughts for nearly two hours. The

complex and introspective Long Lance, tortured by his lies and deceptions, finally placed the muzzle of the new .45 caliber Colt against his right temple and pulled the trigger. When the police arrived, they found his body slumped on a leather settee at the end of the library, the revolver clutched in both hands.

So much of his earnings, royalties, and fees he had given away; after his death he left almost nothing. Once his personal effects were sold and bank accounts closed, only about $700 remained. He was buried in the British Empire veterans' section of the Inglewood cemetery, Los Angeles.

What was his contribution? The meaning of his life? On anyone's terms, Long Lance was a survivor and an achiever, in an era when it was difficult for non-whites merely to exist with dignity. He employed his newly adopted identities, his position, and his skills to advocate the rights of Native Americans during the troubled 1920s. While the assumed persona of Chief Buffalo Child Long Lance certainly nourished the wants of the man born Sylvester Long, the man beneath the image had used it as an instrument to serve the needs of others.

Perhaps his lasting contribution is his "autobiography," too full of journalist license to be cited as a factual source, but still an exciting fictional account. The contemporary assessment of anthrologist Paul Radin in his review of the book in the New York *Herald Tribune* on October 14, 1928, strikes the right note: "I cannot think of any work that could act as a better corrective of the ridiculous notions still prevailing about the Indians than this autobiography of Long Lance."

NOTES

Adapted from "From Sylvester Long to Chief Buffalo Child Long Lance," in James A. Clifton, Editor, *Being and Becoming Indian: Biographical Studies of North American Frontiers*, pp. 183-203, Copyright 1989 by James A. Clifton. Used by permission of Waveland Press, Inc., Prospect Heights, IL (reissued 1993).

Much of the material in the essay originally appeared in my two-part article on Long Lance in *The Canadian Magazine*, February 7 and 14, 1976 (my thanks to Alan Walker and David Cobb for their assistance with its presentation). The fullest treatment of the "Chief" is given in my biography, *Long Lance: The True Story of an Impostor* (Toronto: Macmillan, 1982). The University of Nebraska Press published an American edition of the work in 1983. The National Film Board of Canada has produced a one-hour documentary-drama about his life, *Long Lance*, which was released on film and on video in January 1987. It is available in the United States from Films Inc., 5547 N. Ravenswood Avenue, Chicago, Illinois 60640. The film in which Long Lance starred, *The Silent Enemy*, can be obtained on video from Milestone Film and Video, 275 West 96th Street, Suite 28C, New York, New York 10025.

Foreword

It was altogether another and a different book that my friend Buffalo Child Long Lance might have written. He might have written to tell how he won scholastic and athletic honors at Carlisle and at Manlius; of how, while mastering the white man's tongue, he learned half a dozen tribal languages other than his own; of how, having received a presidential award of appointment to West Point, he threw away that most cherished dream of his—the dream of being a full-blooded Indian officer in the regular army—to cross the line in 1916, and at the first call for recruits for overseas service, to enlist in the Canadian forces; of how, going in as a private, he came out at the end of the World War as a captain of infantry, his body covered with wounds and his breast glittering with medals bestowed for high conduct and gallantry; of how he fought as a sniper, as a raider, as a leader of forlorn hopes in the trenches and across No Man's Land; of how his own people conferred upon him the chieftainship of one of the four principal bands of the Northern Blackfeet; of how, beginning as a reporter on a Western Canadian paper, he has earned for himself distinction as a writer for magazines.

He might have told these things, but, being an Indian, he didn't. And I for one am glad that instead of writing the book he might have written, he has written this one. For here, sinking his own engaging personality, his own individual achievements into the background, he depicts graphic phases of a life which has altogether vanished, of a race which rapidly is vanishing. I know of no man better fitted than Chief Long Lance to write a true book about the true American Indian and I know of no book on the subject which better reveals the spirit of the Indian in the years that are gone and the spirit of times the like of which will never be seen again.

I claim there is authentic history in these pages and verity and most of all a power to describe in English words the thoughts, the instincts, the events which originally were framed in a native language.

And I claim the white man will owe him a debt for this work of his and that his people the Indians already owe him a debt for having performed it.

IRVIN S. COBB

Introduction to the First Edition

The Indians of whose experience I have written in this book were the last tribes to encounter the white man. The region is the Far Northwest: northern Montana, Alberta, Saskatchewan and British Columbia. Until 1905 Alberta and Saskatchewan were known as the Northwest territories, a wild untamed region of North America, which had seen its first white settlers only twenty years before. The Indians of this vast stretch of high rolling plains still remember the first white man they ever saw. Before that they were a restless, aggressive people who lived as fighting nomads, traveling incessantly from the Missouri River in Montana up eight hundred miles north into the Peace River country; and from the Rocky Mountains east into what is now Manitoba.

The ruling tribe of this wild domain was that of the Blackfeet, known as the "Tigers of the Plains." Upon the signing of the last Northwestern Treaty they became permanently divided, and now they live half in the United States and half in western Canada—Montana and Alberta. The four former bands of the one big tribe of powerful Blackfeet are now erroneously known by the white man as four different tribes. They are the Blood Indians, living at Cardston, Alberta; the South Piegans (American Blackfeet),

at Browning and Glacier Park, Montana; the North Piegans, at Brockett, Alberta; and the Blackfeet, at Gleichen,
Alberta. Their most deadly enemies were the Sioux, the
Crees, Assiniboines, Crows and Kutenais, with whom they
carried on ceaseless warfare up to the coming of the white
man.

This dramatic period, the period leading out of the old
tribal conflicts into that marking the coming of the new
white race, constitutes what is perhaps the most colorful
period in the history of the North American Indian. And it
is of the experiences of this period that I write, the experiences of our old warriors who are still living, but who cannot tell their own stories because they do not speak the
white man's tongue.

I want to point out two things more: The Royal Northwest Mounted Police are the best friends, brothers and pro-
tectors that the Indians of the Northwest ever had; and the
conflict that I mention herein is one of the only two fights
they ever had with our people—both of them were against
individual Indians. And the Crow Indians were the highest
type of foe that the Blackfeet ever fought—the Crow and
the Sioux.

This is a book which my friends of the Northwest have
urged me to write ever since I returned from the World
War. They and my publishers have persuaded me that it is
an interesting narrative. And, so, here it is.

Buffalo Child Long Lance

Blood Indian Reservation
Cardston, Alberta
July 1, 1928

Long Lance

LONG LANCE

I

FIRST REMEMBERED THINGS

THE first thing in my life that I can remember is the exciting aftermath of an Indian fight in northern Montana. My mother was crying and running about with me in my moss bag-carrier on her back. I remember the scene as though it were yesterday, yet I was barely a year old. Women and horses were everywhere, but I remember only two women: my mother and my aunt.

My mother's hand was bleeding. She was crying. She handed me to my aunt and jumped on a pony and rode away. My infant mind told me that something tragic was happening, and though Indian babies seldom cry, I cried for my mother when she ran away and left me. It seemed that I should never see her again.

That scene left such a startling impression that all during my growing years it kept coming back to me. I wondered what it was and when I had seen that strange panorama, or whether I had ever seen it at all or not—whether it was just a dream.

One day, when I had grown into boyhood, I asked my aunt about it. I described the scene to her and told her the position in which she was standing in relation to the pony, where my mother was standing and how she handed me to her; I gave her a word-picture of the whole circumstance as it was so indelibly inscribed on my memory. As I talked, I could see my aunt's features gradually taking on a look of wonderment. And when I was through she looked at me in great surprise and exclaimed:

"Can you remember that! You were only fourteen months old then. It was when your uncle, Iron Blanket, was killed in a fight with the Crows—and your mother had cut off one of her fingers in mourning for him, as the women used to do in those days."

After this remarkable awakening of early memory I went back into the mystic sleep of infancy again; I do not remember anything more until I was four. And then I came to life again one day in mid-air. I was in the act of falling off a horse. I do not remember sitting on the horse's back, but I remember falling through the air, hitting the ground and lying there on my back, looking up in bewilderment at the spotted belly of the black-and-white pinto as it stood over me. Then the strong arms of my elder brother grabbed me and lifted me up to the back of the horse again, and he hissed into my ear:

"Now, you stay there! You are four years old, and if you cannot ride a horse now, we will put girl's clothing on you and let you grow up a woman."

From this incident on, I remember things distinctly. I remember moving over the prairies from camp to camp. As I close my eyes now and allow my memory to drift back to this early nomadic existence, a life which has vanished forever in North America, the first thing that comes to me is a color—a dull, deep bluish gray. That was the color of my early world. Everything I saw was tinted with this mystic grayness. It represented danger, mystery, and distance. We were not yet entirely at peace with our ancient enemies, the Crows, the Assiniboines, the Sioux, and the Crees; and stories of a new peril which might spell our doom—the White Man—were being whispered about our camp-fires. Danger lurked everywhere, even in the animals from which we secured our food.

Mystery pervaded everything. In addition to the natural mysteries attendant upon early youth, we had also to grope under the weird mysteries of Indian cult and superstition. And our fathers themselves were facing a big mystery which they could not fathom: the mystery of the future in relation to the coming of the White Man.

Then there was that great mystery of distance, which so fascinated us youngsters. Over the flat bosom of the plains we could see as far as the human eye could reach, yet always we wondered what was beyond. We heard that there were "big waters," bigger than the plains themselves; that there were thousands of White People living in another world across the big waters where there were no Indians at all. They traveled about in "big houses," which swam the waters like fish. And they had another "long house," which spat fire and smoke and raced across the ground faster than a buffalo could run. These things came to us as legends from other tribes. They even told us of "black white men" who lived under the sun, where it rested when it went under the horizon, and who were "scorched" until they were black.

Through all this mystery we lived a life of uncertainty, ever on the move, traveling from camp to camp; sometimes building fires in our teepees and then going out on the open plains and rolling up in our blankets to sleep, lest we should be slain in our slumber.

And we used to be hungry, too. We could not put by anything for the winter, because of the scarceness of the vanishing buffalo and our wandering existence. It is hard to be hungry. I remember being so hungry once that all of us boys got together

and slipped into our mothers' teepees and took the
rawhide bags which they carried their meat in and
roasted them over the fire and ate them. That was
during the "year of the big snow," when we all came
near to starvation. Our fathers went over the plains
picking up buffalo heads that had been killed early
in the fall and were frozen; and they took their
axes and chopped off the skin at the top of the heads
and cooked it for food. Finally, we came upon a
herd of mountain-sheep which had been driven down
into the foot-hills by the big snows, and we slew
the entire herd and ate them on the spot. We ate
so much that we went about camp as though we were
drunk.

We could not travel much during the winter, because of the depth of the snows. We would select
a good wind-break in the bosom of a large coulée—
prairie hollow—and make our camp and cover the
buffalo-hide teepees with tree bark to conceal them
from the view of prowlers and possible enemies.
And there we would remain until snow flew. We
would keep our spirits up during the long dark winter evenings by singing around the camp-fire in the
big council lodge.

Always, winter and summer, we would keep a
close watch on the actions of the animals and birds.
If the antelope and buffalo grazed quietly we knew
that all was well. But if the birds or animals showed

any excitement in their movements or calls we knew that there were prowlers abroad; and we sent out scouts to cover the camp. The Indians always attacked just at the break of day, when everybody was tired and brains were slow to think. Therefore, every morning before dawn two of our spies would leave the camp under the cover of darkness and climb upon the highest eminence in the district, and lie there until daybreak. They would then peer out over the surrounding country to see if any of our enemies were camping on our trail or preparing to raid us.

During the long winters in the far northern zones, when the days were just a few short hours, our mothers spent a good deal of their time each day teaching and training us youngsters into the ways of the Indian. Like the white boy, we had to take our schooling during the winter. Our mothers spent about two hours every day teaching us how to speak our tribal language correctly. This is a very important point with the Indian—his language —as his social status in later years depends on his ability to handle his grammar properly. Any Indian allowed to grow up without being able to speak his language with absolute correctness is relegated to the rank of an outcast in the tribe; and he is never allowed to speak in public, lest his linguistic defects should be passed on to others—and especially the children—and thus defile the tribal tongue. Therefore, since we had no books nor written language, our mothers had to spend many hours drilling into us the ancient grammar of our tribal speech—which is very elaborate, having nine conjugations, four genders and eighty forms.

Our fathers looked after our physical training, which was very rigid. Their main idea was to harden our bodies, make us strong and courageous and able to stand any amount of pain. The Indian's only profession was that of a warrior and hunter. Hence, outside of our linguistic and moral teaching, our sole training was to make us brave and stoical, and good and courageous fighters.

To toughen our bodies, our fathers used to whip the boy members of each family as we arose in the morning. After they had whipped us they would hand us the fir branches and tell us to go to the river and bathe in the cold water. If it was winter they would make us go out and take a snow bath. And every time it rained we all had to strip off and go out for a rain bath. All of this was to harden our bodies.

Far from disliking this sort of treatment, we youngsters used to display the welts on our bodies with great pride. Sometimes we actually would ask for more. When we were in winter camp we would get our fathers to erect a whipping-bar for us in the council lodge. Two poles would be sunk into the ground and a bar stretched across their tops at the height of an average boy's reach. And then on extremely cold days when we could not get out of doors to go through our games and contests, we would all get together and ask our fathers to give us "the whipping of the brave."

One by one, as the tribe looked on, we would bare our backs and walk up to the bar and take hold of it. Then the "whipper," who had been chosen by our fathers, would step up and start to flog us heavily with a bunch of stout fir branches. When we could stand it no longer we would let go the bar, which was the signal that we had had enough, and the flogger would stop. The more stout-hearted among us would sometimes stick it out until the flogger had completely worn off the switches. Then he would stop and hand us the stub, which we would keep and display with considerable pride during the rest of our young lives.

I well remember my first introduction to the icy morning plunge. I must have been five years old. One cold morning my big brother came over to my sleeping nest and grabbed me out of my bedding and raced down to the river with me under his arm. I was squirming and yelling and kicking at him, trying to get away. It was very cold, and I was wondering what he was going to do with me. I was not long in finding out. When he reached the stream he kicked a hole in a thin coating of ice and hurled me into it, and the shock nearly took my breath. When he reached down and pulled me out I fought him, but he proceeded on back to the camp with me under his arm as though nothing had happened.

When I got back into the warm teepee and got my breath again, I asked him why he had done that; and he said that my father had told him to do it. I went to my father and asked him why he had told my brother to do that to me. He said:

"You will have to do that yourself every morn-ing from now on, unless you want to be a girl—then we will put dresses on you." I assured him that I did not want to be a girl, and he said: "All right, then, we will make a warrior of you."

That pleased me; and so I never kicked after that. Soon I grew to like my morning plunge, and I still like cold water to this day.

But on leaving my father's teepee, he said to me: "Hear me. If you want to get even with your brother for what he did to you this morning you go into his teepee tomorrow morning before sunrise —I shall awake you—and you will find him lying on his back asleep. Pull back the blankets and you will see his big, naked chest lying beneath you. Go out of doors and get a good big chunk of ice and place it on his chest. Then you will be even with him."

I did as my father told me to do, and my brother awoke with a yell that startled the whole camp. He grabbed me before I could get out of the teepee and gave me a whipping that I have never forgotten. When I told my father what happened he laughed lustily, and patting me on the head, said:

"That is good, my son; so now you know what it feels like to be whipped early in the morning—from now on you will be whipped at dawn. You are not going to be a little girl and cry: you are going to be a brave." And so it seemed.

By the time I was six years old I was beginning to enjoy the rougher games of my elder brother and playmates. I remember one funny game we used to play on cold, blizzardy afternoons when we could not go out of the teepee. We used to burn one another and see who could stand the most pain. We would go out and get some dry fir needles and come back into the teepee and sit down in a circle around the fire. Then we would light the fir needles and place them on the back of our hands and see who could stand to allow them to burn down to ashes. When our hands were all burned raw, sometimes we would pull up our buckskin shirts and allow the other fellows to place the needles on our backs and let them burn down. If there was anyone among us who could not stand the pain, we would ridicule him.

On occasion we would take the sharp bone needles which our mothers used to sew the skins with, and make little rips in each other's legs until they bled. Then we would wash them with fresh water. Our fathers told us that this would let out the bad blood and prevent us from having sickness, or becoming tired in our strenuous games during the summer months.

Our moral training was entirely in the hands of our mothers. They would tell us about our Great Spirit; and they told us that when we grew older the Great Spirit would appoint some other good spirit in the spirit world to be our guide and look after us. This spirit would give us our "medicine"—lucky charm—our medicine-song and our death song; the former to be sung at all times when in trouble, the latter when we were called on to die.

We had no Bible as the white boys have; so our mothers trained us to live right by telling us legends of how all of the good things started to be good. We had a legend for everything—from the care of our feet to the "great shame" befalling those who tell lies. Many long winter afternoons we would sit around our mother as she made skins into clothing, and listen to the magic stories of righteousness which she was passing on to us from the dark, unknown depths of our history.

Some of the legends would have a humorous turn

to them, such as the one which taught us to take care of our feet. According to this legend, an Indian warrior was once being chased by a large number of the enemy, when suddenly his speed began to slacken. As he ran he invoked his feet to put on speed. His feet told him to invoke his head; and so the warrior sat down and talked to his feet. He said: "I shall be killed if you do not help me."

But his feet replied: "Talk to your head. You always anoint your head after every meal and take good care of it, but you never anoint us; you neglect us." (It was the Indian's habit to take his greasy fingers and rub his scalp after every meal.)

"But," said the warrior to his feet, "if I am killed the enemy will have great rejoicing with my scalp at the war dance; they will dance around it and honor it, but as for you, feet, you will not be noticed; they will dismember you and throw you around the camp, and the dogs will scrap over you."

At this juncture of the warrior's beseeching, his feet suddenly started kicking on their own account. They kicked so hard that they carried him forward with great speed, and ultimately accomplished his escape. And, so, said our mothers, ever since that time the old people warn the young ones to take good care of their feet; to anoint them and rub them every night, and to hold them to the fire to supple them when tired.

Every Indian has from six to ten wolf-dogs in his camp, and to teach us to be kind to our dogs, our mothers used to tell us this legend:

Once upon a time a warrior and his camp left the main tribal camp to go out hunting. In one of the teepees of this warrior's camp was a dog with a litter of puppies. She was an ugly, woolly little dog. One evening about dusk this little mother dog went out to a near-by slough to get a drink of water. She came back and went among her pups, but instead of lying down and feeding them, she nosed them about and looked at the occupants of the teepee and then nosed them again.

Suddenly the dog spoke. She said: "I love my little ones because they are ugly, and I should hate to see them come to any harm."

The warrior was alarmed. He said: "Now that you can talk, tell us what you mean."

The dog said that while she was out drinking at the slough someone struck her in the ribs, and she saw a bunch of enemy Indians.

"If you tell us what you know, your puppies will live; we will save you from the enemy," said the warrior. The dog told him where the enemy was camped, and said that they were hidden away in a near-by thicket of trees. The warrior took the dog and the puppies and the whole camp and hid them away in an adjoining thicket and then set out on his pony to race back to the main camp and notify them of the presence of the enemy. They returned just as the enemy was launching an attack on those left behind, and swooping down upon them, the warrior and his tribe wiped them completely out. Since then, said our mothers, the Indians have been kind to their dogs.

We had a legend for everything that was good, and the more we youngsters lived up to the legends which our mothers told us the more highly respected we were in the tribe. We tried hard to remember each legend and to live out the moral that it taught us.

Our mothers spent a good part of the winter making all of the family clothing, while our fathers were out hunting and bringing in the skins. Every evening we youngsters would scramble around our father as he came in, to see what he had bagged that day—and we hoped that he had been able to catch a lynx kitten or a baby coyote for us to play with for a while and then turn loose. Among the skins he would bring in would be muskrat, otter, deer, coyote, lynx and black and gray wolves.

Our mother would take these and bury them overnight in ashes to remove the hair. Then she would rub them with buffalo brains or rotten wood to prepare them for their final dressing. After all the hair had been removed from the skins, and they had become soft and dry, she would then polish them off with a smooth, round bone and bleach them to a brilliant white by rubbing them with a white, chalky stone.

Then she would get her dyes ready, with which she would dye porcupine quills and work them into the skins in beautiful Indian designs. The only natural colors we had were red, yellow, black, white, and blue. We never saw any greens, browns, pinks, or purples. We obtained our colors from the ocher beds found principally in the foot-hills of the Rockies—iron deposits on the ground, which gave us reds, blues, and yellows. We secured our white by cooking "prairie dust," and our black by cooking a piece of wood that had lain at the bottom of a running stream for several years. When our father wanted a grease paint to paint the family "medicine" designs—or heraldic bearings—on our teepees, he would boil the above powders with bone marrow or buffalo brains. For thread our mother used dried muscle sinew.

All of our buckskin clothing was gaily decorated with ermine tails and dyed porcupine quills or beads. If we were good youngsters and lived up to the tribal customs and legends, we were allowed to wear roaches on our heads, made of badger hair dyed yellow and red. This was a sign of distinction among youngsters not yet old enough to wear the eagle-feather trophies awarded to those who won distinction on the warpath. For trousers we wore buckskin leggings tied to a belt, with no seat in them. Instead of a "seat," we wore breech-cloths between our legs, which were drawn through the belts so that they would hang down in front and behind. And over the whole we wore buckskin shirts, which were worked with colored porcupine quills or beads.

We had no matches in those days; so we had to make our fires by striking white Indian flint or by filling a piece of buckskin with dry, rotten wood or tree-canker—touchwood—and then rubbing it up and down a sinew bow-string until it got hot and started an ember in the touchwood. We had a professional "fire-man" with the tribe, a man whose business it was to carry fire with him from camp to camp and sell it to the members of the tribe when they got ready to make their fires. He carried the fire in a hollow birch log about two feet long. He would start an ember and then put in a lot of touchwood and strap the log to his horse and carry it for a day or so without having to bother about it again. We youngsters used to like to see him open it; it looked like a quiet, glowing little furnace, as he placed himself in the middle of the camp and started to dole out embers to those who wanted to start fires.

II

"Swear by the Horn"

OUR greatest joy as youngsters was to see the
first touches of spring after the long, cold
winter had lost its grip on the country. The Northern Lights would start to dart across the sky, and
the wild geese would honk far above the tops of
our teepees at night on their journey into the Arctic. We knew that it would not be long before we
should be striking camp and starting out on our end-
less wandering over the sunlit prairies of the Northwest.

We would soon be at our summer games, running about naked, with nothing on but a breech-cloth
and moccasins. Our hearts leaped at the thought
of some of the adventures we would meet with.
We would perhaps have a fight with the Crows or
the Sioux or the Crees. We young fellows would
come upon youngsters of other roving Indian tribes,
and we would pit our strength and skill against
theirs in the many games and contests which we enjoyed during the long, lazy summer days, when we
were allowed to run as wild as the antelope.

17

On our last night in winter-quarters, the night before the big movement, our fathers would hold a
big war dance which lasted all night, and no one
would go to bed but us youngsters. We could stay
up and watch the dance until about ten o'clock; but
our fathers and mothers would dance and feast all
night—and wake us at four and tell us to get our
clothes on. Right after supper we would hear the
drummers tuning up the big war-drums and the
singers trying out their voices. Our fathers would
be painting their bodies in beautiful colors, and our
mothers would be braiding their hair and putting
on their best buckskin finery, ornamented with many
quills, beads, bear-claws and ermine tails.

We youngsters were dressed up and allowed to
paint our faces that night, too. Our mothers would
smear our faces with war-red, and tell us to sit
quietly and watch our fathers, and learn all we could
about the war dance. This big dance was held to
thank the Great Spirit for allowing us to survive the
winter and to steel our tempers for any trouble or
fights that we might encounter during the turbulent
summer season.

If anyone had died during the winter his relatives would bring to the war dance many sacrifices in
the form of fine buckskin garments, buffalo robes,
blankets and choice breasts of meat, to be burned on
the big fire, so that they might be transformed into

"spirit matter" and be taken up for use by the spirits of the deceased, who were supposed to be present.

Boom, boom, boom, boom! Four thundering beats on the big war-drum would announce that the dance was to start. Then, boomboom, boomboom— the regular cadence of the war dance would be taken up by the drums, and the singers would start their dolorous, haunting chant, which would last all night. "Hie-hie, hie-yeh, hie-yo-h, hie-yoh." And our fathers would come prancing into the crowded lodge, stripped to their breech-cloths, painted all over, and uttering short, gruff grunts as they stamped their feet —thump-*thump*, thump-*thump*—and proceed to circle around the glowing blaze in the center of the lodge.

At first they dance mildly, with much dignity and grace of movement. Then, as the chanting and beating grows louder and wilder, they start to work themselves up into a warlike frenzy, shouting, "Ee-h-whoop, hy-hyuh," and gradually jumping higher and higher as they circle the booming tom-toms. A wild, strange light comes over their features. Their bodies weave up and down like fighting roosters; their teeth gleam in the firelight; and their eyes, beaming a sinister smile of destruction, look far past the heads of the spectators and on into the eternal depths of tradition which lie behind the terrible spirit of the war dance.

That spirit is born in the Indian blood. Even we youngsters could feel it tingling our blood to action as our fathers jerked their shoulders and chanted: "May we have an easy victory. May the enemy sleep long and deep."

Then they would throw into the air big chunks of wood, and catching them on their lances they would shout: "May we thus act with our enemies; may we toss them as brush on our spear-points!"

And so, as the night went on, our fathers would continue to dance the dance of death; and we children would be put to bed with the wild, haunting music of the war-song surging through our beings and urging us on to the adventures that our fathers had experienced.

Long before daylight the next morning we would hear the "camp crier" going through the camp shouting: "It is the word of your chief. Move! Move! Move!" That was the signal to strike camp. We youngsters were the first ones up. Out under the cold, starry heavens we would dash, helping our mothers to remove the skins from the teepee and roll them into big round bundles, to be packed on the backs of our horses.

By the time the first streaks of dawn commenced to shimmer in the eastern skies we would be well on our way—leaving the foot-hills and the snow-white peaks of the Rockies behind us in the west and making our way out onto the great open expanses of the land we loved so much: the high rolling plains of the Northwest.

My small brother and I were always carried in the travois behind the horse on which our mother rode. This travois consisted of two long poles crossed over the horse's shoulders and dragging on the ground behind. A little hammock made of skins was stretched between these poles under the horse's tail, and it was in this hammock that my brother and I rode along with some of the "household" effects which were packed under and around us. We used to have great fun laughing at one another when the horse would suddenly swish his tail and strike us a violent blow across the face. Sometimes it would almost blind us and leave big, red welts on our faces, but we never cried nor complained to our mother, lest we should be ridiculed in the eyes of the others.

We measured distance in those days by "camps." A place "one camp" away would be thirty miles distant—and "two camps" would be sixty miles. On our first day out from the winter-quarters in the foot-hills we would always make "two camps," in order to avoid having to camp in the deep snow in the region of the mountains.

Sometimes as we journeyed across the prairies we would sight another tribe moving toward us.

They would approach us cautiously, and then they would stop and make a sign to us in the sign language. Each with the finger tips of his right hand would rub the top of his left wrist, and then draw the right hand away and work the fingers up and down from under the thumb, with palm up and hand jerking interrogatively from right to left and back. Touching the wrist meant "Indian" (brown skin), and the wiggling ·of the fingers and hand meant, "What kind?" That sign always asked us what tribe we were. Our chief would make the sign for the Blackfeet, and then point toward the country in which we lived. He would always follow this by raising his right arm into the air, hand open and palm facing the strangers. This meant peace—an ancient symbol showing that he had no weapon in his fighting·hand.

Then the two chiefs would dismount, and walk out to meet one another half-way between the two tribes. They would exchange gifts of tobacco, offer their lighted pipes to each other, and then return to their tribes and resume their journeys.

Though most of the northwestern tribes had already signed peace treaties with the governments of the United States and Canada, there was one tribe of Indians with whom we were not yet entirely peaceful. This was what our band called the *Okotoks* band of the *Isahpo*—the Rock Band of the

Crows. Ancient feuds between us were still harbored by our older people, and many times when we came upon this band on the plains, there was trouble. While there was peace between us and the other bands of this splendid tribe, there was also an indifference which bordered on hatred.

Whenever we passed through the Crow country they always followed us until we were entirely out of their territory. As we camped at night we could see them camping upon our trail in the distance. They mistrusted us and we mistrusted them. And all through the night we could hear their spies signaling to one another from the neighboring buttes, by mimicking the night calls of the coyote or the night-hawk. Often by day, as we traveled across the Crow country, some of us youngsters sitting in the travaux would see a bunch of eagle feathers appearing above the horizon behind us, and then we would see a brown face and two eyes looking at us. We would tell our mother what we saw—and she would say, "Sh-h—keep quiet—they will not harm you."

But a very queer thing happened one day while we were camping along the upper Missouri River, where we had stopped in the heart of the Crow country to have an afternoon meal. After the lunch one of our braves, Rattling Track, was sitting on the bank of the river cleaning his muzzle-loader with a rod. Another brave, Flying Bow Boy, came past him and looked down at him and remarked jokingly:

"What are you cleaning that gun for? You can't shoot anything with it."

"I can use it better than you can," said Rattling Track.

"Put your fire-bag on that," said Flying Bow Boy, throwing down his own ornamented fire-bag as a wager, "and we shall see who is the better shot."

Rattling Track took his fire-bag from his belt and threw it down on the other's, and said:

"All right. Do you see that bit of log floating out there in the middle of the stream? Watch it!"

He raised the old muzzle-loader, took a bead on it and fired.

As the gun cracked, a thing happened which caused the two men to jump and hold their breath in startling suspense. As the shot pierced the log it leaped forward like a lizard, and two human arms came splashing out of the water on either side of the log and beat the water furiously for a second— and then dropped back out of sight. As the log continued to float aimlessly down the river, Rattling Track threw off his blanket and jumped into the water and swam out to it. Our whole band was on the river-bank when he struggled back and pulled the log ashore.

THE FAMOUS HORN SOCIETY OF THE BLACKFEET,
AT GLEICHEN, ALBERTA

INDIANS WITH THEIR HORSE AND TRAVOIS
IN THE CANADIAN ROCKIES

It was not a log at all. It was a hollow cylinder of birch bark with a man's head inside of it. When the man was taken out he proved to be a Crow spy. He had been floating down the river spying upon our camp—swimming with his body below the water and his eyes peering at us through two holes in the side of the cylinder of bark. We struck camp and moved from the spot at once, and it is doubtful if the Crows ever knew what became of their spy.

We went north after this happening. We were on our way up into the Cree country, in Assiniboia, to see if there were any buffalo left in that region.

One day as we were making our way through the Cypress Hills we came upon a band of Crees who had never been back to their main tribe since it signed peace with the government of the Northwest Territories. But they gave us the "peace sign"; and when our chief advanced and held a council with them they told him that though they had had a skirmish with the Northern Blackfeet, since their tribe had signed peace, they were willing to make peace with us on the spot if it was agreeable to us. They belonged to Chief Piapot's tribe of Crees, who lived up in the Calling Valley of Assiniboia.

Our chiefs and councilmen accepted their proposal, and it was arranged to hold a big feast that afternoon to celebrate this unique event.

While we were eating at this feast one of our braves, Six Killer, kept gazing hard at a Cree warrior who sat in front of him eating his food quietly. Six Killer never said anything, but not once during the meal did he take his eyes off this Cree, whose name proved to be Brown Moccasin. Brown Moccasin noticed the stare but said nothing. This Cree, Brown Moccasin, was wearing a string of buffalo teeth, and our brave Six Killer was looking at this.

When the feast was over Six Killer addressed the Cree for the first time. He asked him if he had made that string of buffalo teeth himself. Brown Moccasin rubbed the teeth up and down on his chest with the palms of his hands and threw his head back and laughed loud and long. Then between his chuckles he said:

"No, I did not make them: I took them off a Blackfoot I killed a few years ago." And he continued to laugh.

Our warrior Six Killer asked him if we, the Blackfeet, had killed any of their number in this battle. Brown Moccasin said: "Yes, one Cree and fourteen Sioux who were fighting with us."

Six Killer arose from his seat and went over to our chief. And, pointing to Brown Moccasin, he shouted into the chief's ear: "There is the man who killed your son. He wears his necklace around his neck!"

The chief looked quickly at Brown Moccasin and the necklace, and then he threw his arms into the air and roared that he was going to kill Brown Moccasin right there on the spot. He was wild with rage, and everyone thought that we were going to have a big fight right there. But fortunately the chief was the only man in our tribe who got angry, and after some of our men of good counsel had talked with him, they all agreed to let the country have peace and not to fight any more. Everyone felt friendly right away, and we have been good friends of these Indians ever since.

These Crees were so elated at the outcome of our meeting and our peace pact that they asked permission to go along with us down into Montana, so that they could make peace as they went with all of the other tribes with whom they had fought in the past.

We visited the Sioux, the Gros Ventres, Cheyennes and one band of the Crows who were friendly to us. Huge feasts were prepared for them everywhere by their former enemies. And everything went well until we came to Standing Bull's camp in Montana (American Sioux). Just as we arrived there Chief Standing Bull became enraged at hearing the cries of the Sioux children as they were being packed off to a mission school by some of the missionaries, who were protected by an escort of cavalrymen; and he wanted to call off all of the peace treaties and start a new period of warfare by starting in on the massacre of the Crees whom we had brought with us. Our chiefs intervened, and after a while Standing Bull cooled down and shook hands with the Crees—and gave them a feast.

We had trouble with the north band of Crows, too. Their chief was friendly toward the visiting Crees, but he could not hold his braves back, who were all for starting a war dance and killing the Crees. They set up a guard around them so that they could not escape, and then started their dancing with their weapons concealed beneath their blankets. The presence of a young Assiniboine in the Cree party, who could speak Crow, saved the situation and averted what would have been a terrible massacre. This young Assiniboine took his life in his hands by stepping out in the center of the dancers and making a masterly speech, in which he pointed out the need for peace among the Indian tribes and told the Crows that they would act like cowards if they killed the Crees who had come to them in good faith—seeking peace and not war.

"If you massacre these defenseless people," he said, "you will be laughed at by all of the other tribes of these plains—and there will not be a brave among you in the eyes of other Indians—they will all look upon you as old women."

That was too much for the Crows; they called off their war dance and ordered their women to start cooking a big feast—and they said: "Your talk is good. Now we no longer want to kill the Crees; we want to honor them." And they did.

They were a brave little band, these Crees; and many of them are still living up in the Calling Valley—now Qu'appelle Valley of Saskatchewan.

During our wanderings in the summer we often stopped at certain points on the prairies to hold a week of sports and keep ourselves in condition. Our tribe would do this every two or three weeks, and we children enjoyed the period of recreation perhaps more than our elders; for now we could play our games and practice our mimic warfare.

While our elders raced their horses, ran long-distance races, and pitted their strength against one another in wrestling, weight-lifting and weight-throwing, we youngsters were given the freedom of the entire prairies on which to carry out our little games and our "fights." Our mothers never worried about us from morning till night; we could go and come as we chose.

We knew the game of Indian warfare almost as well as our fathers; for it was the Indian custom for noted warriors to relate and reenact all of their famous battles at the Sun Dance—and we boys had memorized most of our tribal conflicts in every detail.

Sometimes when we were camping in the neighborhood of one of our historic battles with the Crows or Gros Ventres, we youngsters would leave our camp early in the morning, taking along with us a large bag of pemmican for our lunch and our bows and arrows, and go to this spot to "fight." We would divide ourselves into two tribes, and we would look up the old landmarks we had heard our fathers talk about, and station ourselves in the exact positions from which the original battle was fought. Lucky were the boys who were chosen to be the chiefs and medicine-men.

When the "chiefs" had got their warriors lined up in their positions, they would hold separate councils of war, to go over their line of attack. Then we would all strip ourselves as our fathers did when they fought, and paint our bodies the color of the local landscape so that we could not be easily seen by the "enemy." And when the signal was given we would start our battle.

We had little arrows, made by our mothers, with blunt, round balls on their striking ends, and whenever a fellow was hit by one of these he was "dead," and had to fall in his tracks and lie there. Our mothers had also tied locks of black horsehair in our hair so that we could be "scalped" when "killed."

When we were at our war games we did not rush at one another blindly as I have seen white boys do.

We took the battle very seriously, hiding ourselves as much as possible, and creeping upon one another unexpectedly—as the Indian fights. Our fathers made us do that, so that we would be good warriors when we grew up. Our battles sometimes lasted for an hour or more. When the big fight was over, the fellow having the most scalps was the "big brave" of the entire camp of youngsters, and remained so for many days afterward.

Following our battles we would hold a big victory dance, as our fathers did, and we would make the first five boys holding the most scalps our heroes at these fêtes. As we danced our dance of victory we would provide five special seats for these distinguished "warriors," and make the lesser braves wait upon them and feed them, as they sat stolidly and viewed the dance in their honor. When we returned to our camp in the afternoon and displayed our five "biggest braves," our elders would pat them on the back and tell them that some day they would be great warriors like their fathers; and we youngsters used to take this very seriously. Our mothers and fathers encouraged us to take part in games of war, that we might grow up to be "men of honor."

When we were not out on our war skirmishes we were contesting our strength and skill against one another in camp. We were never idle; we played incessantly.

One of our favored contests was "throwing the stone," to see who had the best back and arms. We would take a sizable stone and grasp it with both hands, and then bend forward and hurl it backward between our legs. We would play this game all afternoon, trying to extend our marks farther and farther; and the fellow who had the longest mark won the "arm-and-back" championship of the tribal youngsters. But it did not mean that he was the best athlete; for we had yet to try out the legs. Strength with the Indian is measured in arm-and-leg power—not in wind and endurance; for every Indian is born with that, naturally. To strike down the enemy with the lance and the battle-ax, one had to have powerful arms; and to run after him and leap upon him, one had to have legs equally strong.

Therefore we had many foot-races to decide who was the fleetest. We youngsters seldom ran more than two or three miles in our races, but our elders ran as high as 150 and 200 miles in a single race. A favorite race of the Northern Blackfeet, on sports days, was from Blackfoot Crossing, now Gleichen, Alberta, to Medicine Hat and back. That was a distance of about 240 miles. They would start one morning and return the next day—non-stop and on foot.

We always ran our foot-races barefoot, not caring to wear out our moccasins, and at the same time wishing to strengthen and toughen our feet. We would tie a buckskin band around our heads to keep our long hair out of our faces, and pull off everything but our breech-cloth, and we ran with our hands down at our hips. It was undignified and a sign of weakness to bend the elbows and run with the hands seesawing back and forth across our chests. After our races we always plunged into the cold river for a swim.

The first thing we youngsters did whenever we stopped for our days of sports was to take our ponies and go out on the prairies and look for a big *okotoks* —stone. We would take the largest stone we could find in the prairie country and throw our lariats around it and drag it back into camp with our ponies. Then we would place it on the ground beside a red peg, and see who could carry it the farthest. We each had a stake painted in such a way that we could identify it, and wherever we dropped the big stone we would drive this stake into the ground. Then four or five of us would roll the stone back to the red stake, and the other fellows would have a go at it. Many times we spent whole days trying to beat our own marks and those of the others.

Abstinence from overeating and overindulgence in physical comforts was very rigidly enforced on us by our parents, whose sole aim with us seemed to be to keep us tough and fit. We were never allowed to stand close to the fire, lest our bodies should get overheated and make us lazy. And our parents never allowed us to eat fat meats of any kind. That, they said, would make our stomachs soft.

We youngsters were given daily lectures on how to live, by twelve of the oldest men of the tribe. Because they had lived to such remarkable ages it was considered that they knew better how to live than anyone else. Every morning just before sunrise, while the camp still lay on their pallets in their teepees, one of these old men would take his turn in getting up early and walking through the camp shouting out his lecture on how to live to be old and his advice on morals, courage, and personal bravery. His voice would awake us, and we would lie still and listen intently to every word he said. At that time of the morning, just as we had awakened from a night's rest, his words seemed to pierce deep into us; we remembered every word he said, and all during the day his advice would keep coming back into our minds, and we would try to live up to it.

All of these men were great warriors who had many scalps to their credit, and we respected our old people above all others in the tribe. To live to be so old they must have been brave and strong and good fighters, and we aspired to be like them. We never allowed our old people to want for anything, and whenever any one of them would stop as he made his silent, dignified way through the camp, and put his arm across our shoulders and utter a little prayer for us to the Great Spirit, we would feel highly honored. We would stand quietly, and when he was through we would remain in our tracks, respectful and silent, until he had disappeared. We looked upon our old people as demigods of a kind, and we loved them deeply; they were all our fathers.

This respect for the aged was so deeply bred into us that to this day I have not the courage to dispute the word of an old person. To me old people still are demigods to be heeded and reverenced at all times.

Each morning at sunrise every boy and young man in the camp would race to be the first up and into the river for the morning plunge—we always camped near a river for our water supply. The boy or young brave who most often attained the distinction of being the first up and outside, just as the sun peeped over the eastern horizon, was the model man of the camp.

Any youngster who chose to follow his own inclinations, or loved his bed too much, was relegated to the position of an "also ran." His name was never allowed to be called out in public. He had no significance in the social scheme of the tribe whatever.

Our tribe was divided into "camps," each camp headed by a minor chief; and whenever one camp invited another to come over and smoke with it that night, the host would take a position in the center of the main camp and call out by name all those who had distinguished themselves by following the tribal precepts; and then he would add a general invitation to "the rest." "The rest" were those who were laggards. Special seats at the front of the assemblage would be provided for the young men of merit, while the slothful were appointed to perches near the door. "That is nature's place for them," said our old men. "Nature provides a place for its own. The laggards would be late anyway; so we place them near the door where they will not disturb the distinguished when they enter." This seating arrangement had a rather humorous consequence, too. When the pipe was lighted by the chief and started around the big circle, those distinguished young braves seated around the chief would get all of the sweet smoke, while those who liked to be last in everything got nothing but the strong tobacco juice.

On rainy days when we could not play out-of-doors our parents used to encourage us to hold Indian dances. They would put up a council lodge for us and instruct us in all of the famous dances of our tribe: the War Dance, the Eagle War Dance,

the Ghost Dance, the Medicine Dance, the Chiefs'
Dance, the Pony War Dance, the "I Saw" Dance
and the Scalp Dance.

We favored the Eagle War Dance more than
any other, because it had a spirit of contest at the
end of it. Whenever we wanted to hold this dance
we had to go out onto a bluff and find an eagle nest,
and then cut down a small tree and lug them both
back to camp with our ponies. We would then skin
the tree, paint it red, and remove all of the branches
except a few at the top. In these remaining branches
we would tie the eagle's nest and leave it dangling
at the end of a small string. Then we would plant
the tree in the center of the lodge and make a
square around it with the branches.

Now we would dig a hole inside this square, and
the boy giving the dance would get into it with his
tom-tom. When the dance was ready to start this
boy would commence pounding his tom-tom and
singing. He would sing slowly for a time, and
then when he started to sing fast we would all come
into the lodge dancing and holding our bows and
arrows above our heads.

We danced around and around the tree until the
boy in the hole suddenly stopped singing; then we
all raised our bows and started shooting at the string
holding the dangling eagle's nest at the top of the
tree. And when the eagle's nest fell to the ground

we rushed at it, yelling our tribal war-cry; and the first three boys who touched the nest each got a feather to wear in his hair. This was like the "first," "second," and "third" honors which our fathers got when they killed an enemy in battle— all of the warriors would rush forward when a man fell, to be the first to touch him. We liked this dance because it was the only dance or game we had which gave us eagle-trophy feathers to wear in our hair, like those which our fathers wore.

In all of our games, in all of our playing, I would say that *honor* was the outstanding characteristic. None of us ever disputed the other fellow's mark, the other fellow's record or the other fellow's word. Our parents taught us that lying was the "great shame"; that it was the "battle-shield behind which the coward hid his shame." We believed them, and seldom did we have occasion to assert our truthfulness to our playmates.

If, however, we *were* ever doubted by our playmates, we would "swear by the Horn," and that would always settle the argument. No one would ever swear falsely by the Horn. It was the same oath that our fathers took; and it means that we will swear by the famous Blackfoot Horn Society that what we are telling is the truth.

Of all my boyhood life, I remember only one occasion when any of us youngsters was doubted enough to be called upon to "swear before the Horn." That was when one of two pet coyotes which had taken up with our dogs and become pets in our camps was killed by somebody. One of our playmates, a boy named Star Wolf, was blamed with the killing of this coyote. He claimed innocence, and his father asked him to "swear before the Horn."

The Horn Society has a limited membership of twenty-five of the most upstanding men and outstanding warriors in the tribe. These men are members for life and no one can be admitted until one of them dies. It is said that this society strongly resembles the Masonic Order of the white man; and being limited to a life-membership of only twenty-five honorable men, its secrets are more strongly guarded than those of any other society known to the Indian.

On the occasion when young Star Wolf was called upon to swear before the Horn, all of us youngsters were admitted to witness the incident. The twenty-five Horns were all seated in a circle, dressed in their ceremonial regalia and guarded by armed braves.

Star Wolf was led to the center of the lodge, and he stood there quietly while the Great Head of the Horns slowly filled the great medicine pipe with tobacco and then put in a wad of hay on top of the tobacco. While he was loading the pipe he was talking in a mysterious way, now and then warning Star Wolf that he was "about to swear before the Horn—to consider the truth deep in his heart; for death would follow if he should speak with a crooked tongue."

When he had filled the pipe he lighted it four times, and each time he lighted it he looked at Star Wolf through the flames of his fagot and uttered a word which we could not understand. Then, with a flourish of the medicine pipe to the four corners of the earth, he got up and walked over to Star Wolf and held out the medicine pipe, saying in stern, deliberate tones:

"Brother, smoke if you are telling the truth. If you *lie, don't smoke!*"

Star Wolf "took" the pipe; and no one doubted him after that.

It is said that if anyone lies before the Horn he will die within a half-year. And it is claimed with authority that instances of death from this cause have been known.

III

What's in an Indian Name?

IN the civilization in which we live, a man may be one thing and appear to be another. But this is not possible in the social structure of the Indian, because an Indian's name tells the world what he is: a coward, a liar, a thief, or a brave.

When I was a youngster every Indian had at least three names during his lifetime. His first name, which he received at birth and retained until he was old enough to go on the war-path, was descriptive of some circumstance surrounding his birth. As an instance, we have a man among the Blackfeet whose name is Howling-in-the-Middle-of-the-Night. When he was born along the banks of the Belly River in southern Alberta, the Indian woman who was assisting his mother went out to the river to get some water with which to wash him. When she returned to the teepee she remarked: "I heard a wolf howling across the river." "Then," said the baby's mother, "I shall call my son 'Howling-in-the-Middle-of-the-Night.'"

This birth name of the youngster was supposed to

be retained by him until he was old enough to earn one for himself; but always when he grew old enough to play with other children his playmates would give him a name of their own by which he would be known among them, no matter what his parents called him. And this name often was not flattering; for we Indian boys were likely to choose some characteristic defect on which to base our names for our playmates—such as Bow Legs, Crazy Dog, Running Nose, Bad Boy, or Wolf Tail. Instances are known where these boyhood nicknames have been so characteristic of the youngster that they have superseded his birth name and stuck with him throughout his life, if he was not able to earn a better one on the war-path.

But the real name of the Indian was earned in the latter instance: when he was old enough to go out for his first fight against the enemy. His life name depended on whatever showing he should make in this first battle. When he returned from the war-path the whole tribe would gather to witness the ceremony in which he would be given his tribal name by the chief of the tribe. If he made a good showing, he would be given a good name, such as: Uses-Both-Arms, Charging Buffalo, Six Killer, Good Striker, Heavy Lance, or Many Chiefs. But if he should make a poor showing his name might be: Crazy Wolf, Man-Afraid-of-a-Horse, or Smoking-Old-Woman. Thus, an Indian's name tells his record or what kind of man he is.

But a man was given many opportunities to improve his name as time went on. If he should go into some future battle and pull off some unusual exploit against the enemy, he would be given a better name. Some of our great warriors have had as many as twelve names—all good names, and each one better than the one that preceded it. No matter how many names were successively given to him, all of his past names belonged to him just the same, and no one else could adopt them. These names were just as patently his as if they had been copyrighted; and even he, himself, could not give one of them away. Indian names were handed out by the tribe, not the family, and no man could give his name even to his own son, unless the chief and the tribe should ask him to, as a result of some noteworthy deed his son had performed. I know of only three or four instances where this has happened, and it is the rarest honor that can befall a person—the honor of assuming one's father's name. In my day every son had to earn his own name.

The foregoing is the reason why no old Indian will ever tell you his own name. If you ask him he will turn to some third person and nod for him to tell you. The reason for this is that he is too modest to brag of his exploits on the war-path. His names are like decorations in the white man's army, and the Indian has a certain reticence against advertising his bravery by pronouncing his own name in public.

There are certain "Chief Names" among the Indians which the original owners made so distinguished that the tribe never allows them to pass out. These names are perpetuated in successive generations, and after a while they become a dynastical name, such as "Ptolemy" in the Egyptian line of rulers. One of my names, Chief Buffalo Child, is a dynastical name and title among the Blood Band of Blackfeet living at Cardston, Alberta. The original Chief Buffalo Child was killed in battle, in what is now Montana, more than eighty years ago; and years ago when I became a chief of this band his name was resurrected and perpetuated in the present holder of the title—thanks to our war chiefs, Mountain Horse and Heavy Shields, and to the Blood Missionary, the Reverend Canon S. Middleton.

I have four other names: Night Traveler, Spotted Calf, Holds Fire, and Long Lance. Of these latter four I value Spotted Calf the most, because it was given to me by my adopted mother, Spotted Calf, wife of Sounding Sky. They were parents of the famous Indian outlaw, Almighty Voice—whose lone-handed battle against the Royal Northwest Mounted Police has become a conspicuous page in northwestern history. This wonderful woman,

Spotted Calf—daughter of the renowned Chief One Arrow—who stuck to her son throughout his sensational siege and shouted advice to him through a rain of bullets, is still living (1928) on the One Arrow Indian Reserve at Duck Lake, Saskatchewan. I think her name ranks with those of great warriors, and that is why I value it, and her motherhood.

IV

The Seven Tents of Medicine

WHEN I was a youngster the ambition of every Indian boy was to be a medicine-man; for this mystic being was, and still is, often more powerful in the tribe than the head chief, himself. There may be several chiefs in a tribe, there may be many councilmen, but there is only one medicine-man, and he guards the secrets of his cult more zealously than he does his own life. The medicine-man has a triple office in the tribe: he is the doctor, lawyer, and priest. He cures the sick, gives advice and counsel on tribal matters and on the outcome of future events, and prays for those at the point of death—often effecting miraculous recoveries through some strange mental influence which he wields over those who come under his "power."

Before remarking upon a few of the uncanny things which I have seen the medicine-man do, I shall first explain how he is chosen in the tribe.

The medicine-man, himself, has always chosen his own successor. He chooses a boy about twelve or thirteen years old, for the training which he must go through is a long and tedious course, extending over some ten or fifteen years. The medicine-man picks out some youth in the tribe who has shown extraordinary qualities of the mind and body and in the spiritual realm—especially a boy who is a leader among his playmates, who "gets things" easily and who has a keen understanding of human nature. He goes to this boy's parents and asks their permission to take him away with him and train him for a medicine-man. Since this is about the highest honor that can befall a young Indian, the parents are proud to hand the boy over to him.

The medicine-man then takes the boy away with him and remains away about six months. He takes him into the wilderness of the Rocky Mountains or out to some secluded spot on the vast sea of the plains, and there during the long months of his first trip, he instructs the boy in the primary secrets of his mysterious cult.

The first step in the course of training is to teach the boy to make his mind stronger than his physical side—to make his mind master of his body, as it were. This is accomplished by making him go without food for many days at a time and by having him to undergo voluntary physical torture without flinching. When the boy returns from his first trip he looks and acts differently, and he is never the same again to his playmates.

To us as youngsters such a boy seemed to have learned some great secret which he would not tell anybody, not even his own parents.

On succeeding trips into the mountains the medicine-man continues the mental strengthening process and gradually adds to this a severe course in physical training; for, according to him, a strong mind and a "strong heart" (courage) cannot exist in other than a strong body.

This training of the will-power and the body lasts for about three years. At the end of this period the boy's body is as hard as steel, and his will-power is developed to such a high degree that he can stand the severest forms of pain without any apparent suffering. The young man now acts like his tutor. His body is a thing apart from himself and its sensations are to be ignored. For instance, he never scratches himself when a fly bites him or a temporary itching sensation occurs on his body. He ignores it. His mind has gained the ascendancy over his physical self, according to the medicine-man, and soon the boy will be able to control others with his mind alone.

But first he must go through a long, strenuous course in "medicine." This "medical" training consists of learning the art of conjuring, of learning the healing power of the various herbs, of learning to see into the future and of developing the "power to get in touch with the spirits"—whence all of the information concerning the future is supposed to come to the medicine-man.

The boy must go through seven "tents" of medicine, each tent consisting of a year's course and dealing with a different division of the medicine-man's art. For each "tent"—which is a teepee—the young man must train a year; then at the end of that year he "goes through the tent." That is, the medicine-man erects the medicine-teepee and lays out all of the paraphernalia that are to be used, and then for a number of days he sits alone in the teepee and watches the boy go through the various things he has taught him during the year. It is like the annual examination following the white boy's school year, though slightly more weird, perhaps; for we youngsters used to gather around and hear some of the strange sounds which came from this teepee, and they awed us.

Following the completion of five "tents," or years, the boy must go through two "tents" of "bad medicine" in order to master the power to "throw spells" on people—even unto killing them by some strange mental process, which has often been done; as I shall show with proof. "Bad medicine" of the kind that kills is seldom used by the medicine-man, and when it is, it is supposed to be for the purpose of ridding the tribe of some person whom the medicine-man deems undesirable to the tribal welfare. But the "throwing of spells" on people is still used among certain tribes of the Northwest.

Upon the graduation of the young student he becomes the medicine-man's assistant until the latter's death, and then he steps into the medicine-man's shoes. To prevent the possibility of a vacancy in this important post, there are always two acolytes —one in training and one graduate assistant.

Often, as youngsters, we used to stand at a distance from the medicine-teepee and listen to the pounding of the big *Miteyawin* medicine-drum; and we hoped in our breasts that some day the medicine-man would ask our parents to let him have us for his craft.

We heard that they "did queer things in there." Sometimes we would see a person walking about the camp with one side of his face paralyzed and sagging in a swollen heap over the side of his jaw. The under-lid of his eye would be drawn down grotesquely, and the corner of his mouth would be drooping away down near the edge of his jaw. We would ask our mother what was the matter with him, and she would tell us that the "medicine-man had cast an evil spirit into him."

There were one or two old women in the tribe who could undo the work of the medicine-man. Though they could not cast spells themselves, they could "cast out the evil spirits" and cure the person whose face was distorted in the above manner. We used to watch them do this. They would take some sort of herbs and place them in an earthen bowl and set them on fire. Then they would tell the suffering person to bend over this bowl and breathe in the fumes from the burning herbs. After several minutes the patient would feel something in his mouth. He would run his finger into his mouth and pull out a long hair, sometimes nearly a foot long—and then his face would gradually straighten up to its natural lines. Where this hair came from, no one has ever been able to tell, though one Indian who had been afflicted told me that he found it between his gums and his cheek. He thinks the medicine-man slipped a poisoned hair into the stem of his pipe.

But the most weird and interesting part of the medicine-man's practices was the sensational rites which he would carry out when "getting in touch with the spirits." Whenever he wanted to get a forecast of the future, get the outcome of some future event or cure some sick person who was lying at the point of death, he would hold this rite in the big medicine-teepee, and the entire tribe would be allowed to witness it. I often watched this as a youngster, and to this day I am puzzled over what I saw. I have never seen any old Indian who could explain it.

An hour or so preceding one of these medicine lodges the camp crier would go through the camp crying out the news that the medicine-man was "preparing to talk with the spirits." This caused great excitement in camp. The entire tribe would go early to the medicine lodge in order to get seats; for only about one hundred could get inside of the lodge, and the rest had to stay outside and listen to the uncanny ceremony. Our mother would take us children with her and bundle us close to her on the women's side of the lodge.

As we sat and looked on with eyes agape, the medicine-man's assistant would erect four poles in the center of the big lodge and tie them together at the top in tripod fashion. Under these poles there was an area about twelve feet across. In this area the assistant, with the help of four men, would drive into the ground a series of sharp pegs, placing them at intervals of about an inch until the entire area was covered. These pegs were so sharp at the top that they would go through a man's foot if stepped upon. In the center of the twelve-foot area a little square was left clear, a place just large enough for a man to stand in. The only way one could reach this area over the sharp pegs was to jump into it, and that seemingly would mean serious injury or death.

The medicine-man would now enter with four

men. These men would undress him, leaving only his breech-cloth on his body, and then lay him down on his back. They would place his two hands together, palm to palm, and with a strong rawhide thong they would bind his two thumbs together so tightly that they would sometimes bleed. They would place each pair of fingers together and bind them together in the same way. Then they would go down to his feet and tie his two big toes together, pulling with all their strength to bind them as tightly as they could.

Now they would take a hide about the size of a blanket and roll it tightly around him from head to foot, like a cigar wrapper. Around this wrapper they would twine him up from neck to ankles with a stout rawhide thong, winding it tightly around and around his body at intervals of every inch down the length of his form until he was securely bound. And still another hide was wrapped around him, and another rawhide thong was wound tightly around his motionless form. Now, as he lay helpless on the ground, he resembled a long brown cigar. Literally, he could not move a finger.

The assistants would now raise the medicine-man to a standing position and carefully balance him on the soles of his bare feet. He would stand there for a while like a post. Then gradually he would begin slightly to bend his knees and draw them up again, and after a while each bend of the knees would take the form of a short jump. These jumps would keep increasing in length until finally he would be leaping around and around the four poles with startling speed, resembling some ghostly post bobbing up and down through the air so fast that the eye could hardly follow him.

Then, suddenly, with a huge leap, so quickly executed that no one could see how he made it, he would dart through space and land with a thud in the one-foot clearing in the center of the area of sharp pegs. He had leaped six feet over these dangerous spikes and landed safely in the little clearing, which was just big enough to hold his two feet—truly a remarkable exploit in itself.

But he has not yet started the real thrilling part of the ceremony.

As he stands there in the center under the poles, still bound securely, he commences to sing his medicine song, accompanied by the boom of the big medicine-drum in the hands of his assistant.

What I am going to describe now may seem strange; it is strange, but it is precisely what happens. How and why, no one knows.

Presently, as the medicine-man stands there singing his weird chant to the spirits, voices from above are heard; voices which seem to emanate from the opening away up at the top of the big medicine-teepee. As everyone can see, there is nothing up there but the night air and the stars above. Where these voices come from no Indian has ever been able to explain. But, according to the medicine-man, they are the voices of the spirits—the spirits with whom he is trying to get in touch. The mystery of it is that no one has ever been able to prove that they were anything else.

These voices speak in a language which we cannot understand. Even the medicine-man cannot understand most of them. All he can say is that they are speaking in foreign tongues, and that they are not the spirits that he wants. There were only four spirits whom our medicine-man, White Dog, could understand. I remember the name of only one of them, and that was "First White Man." And that name had been with our medicine-men for years before our tribe knew that there was a white man in existence.

As these voices keep moaning down into the lodge, the medicine-man rejects them one by one, and continues to ask for one of the four spirits whom he can understand. Sometimes it takes him many minutes to do this. I remember one or two times when he could not get hold of one of them at all, and he had to end the ceremony without accomplishing his aim.

But when he did get hold of the spirit whom he

was seeking he would become excited and talk away so fast that we could hardly hear what he was saying. It seemed that he had to hurry to get in what he wanted to say before the spirit departed. If it was a cure he was after, the dying patient lying there in the medicine lodge would also become excited; and we have seen such get up and walk. If it was information the medicine-man was seeking, he would make his inquiries in short parables of his own, and he would be answered by the spirits in these same unintelligible parables, which later had to be explained to us. It was our language, but it was phrased in a way that we could not understand. And, furthermore, it was the ancient method of speaking our language—the way it was spoken a long time ago—and only our oldest men could understand some of the phraseology and old words.

But the part of the ceremony which made us youngsters afraid came at the conclusion of the medicine-man's interview with the spirits.

These interviews ended in many exciting ways, but always the final scene was accompanied by a howling wind, which would start to roar across the top of the lodge as the spirits ceased talking. The big medicine-teepee would rock and quiver under the strain of this wind, as it screeched through the poles at the top of the teepee and caused us to shake with fright. It was a startling climax. A chaotic

medley of noise would come down to us from above
—from the round opening at the top of the lodge
where the teepee poles jutted out into the night air.
Strange voices shrieking in weird pandemonium
above the wailing of the winds; the clanking and
jingling of unknown objects, and then a sudden
jerk of the entire lodge, a flicker of the flames, a
terrifying yell from the medicine-man, and then—

He would disappear right in front of our eyes.
But in that same instant we would hear him yelling
for help. And looking up in the direction of his
voice, we would see him hanging precariously by one
foot at the top of the Lodge, stripped as naked as
the day he was born. The only thing that held him
from falling and breaking his neck was his foot,
which seemed to be caught in between the skin covering of the teepee and one of the slanting poles
which supported it.

. . *"Kokenaytukishpewow!*—Hurry!"* he would yell
frantically.

And the men would rush for long poles with
which to remove him from his dangerous, dangling
perch at the roof of the lodge, lest he should fall
and break his neck.

How he got there, no one knows; but he said that
the spirits left him there on their way out. But
the greatest puzzle to us youngsters was how he got
stripped of all those stout bindings!

I have seen some miraculous things done by the old-time medicine-men. I have seen them send messages for a distance of many miles merely by going into their teepee and sitting down, "thinking the message" to the other camp. There were quite a few old Indians who could "receive" these messages. I have seen them cure dying people, and I have known them to foretell with accuracy the outcome of future events.

Lest it might be assumed that I am a little overcredulous of the medicine-man because I am an Indian, I am going to relate an incident which happened to the missionary on the Blackfoot Indian Reserve some time ago. This missionary, the Reverend Canon Stocken, who is still in charge of the Indian Mission on the Blackfoot Reserve at Gleichen, Alberta, had always doubted the stories the Indians told him about the strange doings of their medicine-men. And he had for years preached against medicine practices before these Indians, and tried to instil in them the same doubts he had as to their effectiveness. But to me and others this reverend gentleman has had to admit that he is still marveling over the following incident which was brought to his own door.

One day, a few years ago, Canon Stocken was sitting in his mission study preparing a sermon, when a knock came at his door. He opened the door and found the renowned Blackfoot chief, Crow Shoe, standing silently in front of him.

In the Blackfoot language, which the canon speaks fluently, he said to the chief:

"Hello. What has brought you here?"

"I want you to take my picture," said Chief Crow Shoe.

The canon thought this was very strange; for he had never before seen an Indian of these parts who would not refuse to have his photograph taken—through superstition.

"Why, what for? Why do you want your picture taken?" inquired the canon with surprise.

"I am going to die," replied Crow Shoe nonchalantly, "and I want my people to have my picture."

"Going to die?"

"Yes—Wednesday morning."

"Who said you were going to die!"

"I have just come from a visit with the Crees up on the Red Deer, and their medicine-man held a *Miteyawin* and told me that a ghost had shot a poison dart through me, and that I am going to die Wednesday morning."

"You are foolish to believe such nonsense," admonished the canon. "Go home to your people and forget that; you are not going to die."

"Yes I am—and I want a picture taken so that my people can remember me."

Crow Shoe spoke with such assurance that Canon Stocken was at a loss to know what to do. He tried every persuasion he could think of to get Chief Crow Shoe to go home and forget about the Cree medicine-man, but the chief stood stanchly in his tracks and refused. So, to satisfy him, the canon finally got his camera and took his picture standing in the doorway of the mission—a superb figure, more than six feet tall in his moccasins, his braided hair flowing in two glossy streaks over his buckskin shirt and his long, muscular arms folded evenly across his chest.

Then the canon took him by the hand and said: "Now, go home and forget all you have told me. I shall drive over to see you next week."

But the canon never went to see Crow Shoe; for he died three days later—on Wednesday morning.

One day when we were camping on the Milk River, one of the half-breed traders who used to come up to trade with the Indians from Fort Benton, Montana, rode into our camp and asked for our medicine-man. He told him that one of the kegs of liquor which he was taking up north to trade for buffalo robes had been stolen the night before, near our camp, and he wanted to know if the medicine-man could tell him anything about it, offering him money if he could.

Our medicine-man, White Dog, held a medicine lodge, and when it was over he told the trader to walk nine hundred paces west, when he would come to a grove. He told him to turn into this grove and walk three hundred paces to the right, when he would come upon an "old man." Between the legs of this old man he would find the liquor. The trader did as he was told, and at that point he came upon a tree whose two huge bottom roots resembled the legs of a man. He searched between these roots and found his keg of liquor securely hidden there beneath the ground. The way the medicine-man referred to the tree as the "old man" illustrates the queer phraseology which I mentioned a few paragraphs back. The old man in this case was a very ancient tree whose roots had been bared with age.

V

The Rite of the Buffalo Head

I SHALL never forget the first time I witnessed the medicine-man's startling incantations over the dead buffalo head, which is a special ceremony performed when out on war parties. I was young, and I was so scared that I ran. We were camping at Shell Creek, south of the Milk River in Montana, when one night the band of Crows whose spy we had killed, caught us off guard and crept into our camp and drove away our entire herd of horses. The next day our band decided to chase the Crows and avenge this raid. Our aim was to recapture our own ponies and to take all of the horses possessed by the Crows, if we could.

Whenever a war party of this nature was to start out, the leader always first consulted the medicine-man to find out what sort of luck the party would have. The chief would go to the medicine-man and "offer him the pipe." If the medicine-man "accepted" the pipe—smoked it—that meant that he would accept the responsibility of advising for or against the party and that he would go with it. And the chief would give him the names of all those who were to be on the party. The medicine-man would then instruct the chief to meet him at a given place on the following night, and he would tell him "what the spirits said" about their luck.

After the chief had left, the medicine-man would hold his incantations with the "spirits" and secure his "vision" as to the outcome of the venture.

When the chief called the next night the medicine-man would tell him how many we should "take"—kill—and how many the enemy would "take," and if we were to "take" many more than the enemy, he would advise the chief to go ahead and have the fight.

The medicine-man accompanied every war party; and on every fourth night out, while they were looking for the enemy, he would hold another communion with the "spirits" to see if luck was still with them.

To get in touch with the "spirits" while out on the war-path, the medicine-man had to have the head of a freshly killed buffalo. I was very young when we went against the Crows on this trip, but I can remember it, because I was so badly frightened at what happened.

On the fourth night out the medicine-man White Dog told some braves to go out and scout around for a buffalo and bring back its head. It was early afternoon. The men were gone for several hours, but when they returned they said that they could find no buffalo. The buffalo were fast disappearing from the plains then, and it was only when in the north that they could be found.

White Dog received this news with no apparent sign of worry. He said he would have a nap in his teepee. But he was not in there long. He came out a little while afterwards and said that he had had a dream. He said: "You braves follow this river up for a distance of 'six buffalo arrows' [about one mile] and then cross the river and climb over a butte which you will find on the other side. When you come up on top of the butte you will see an antelope grazing in the distance. It will be getting dark. Crawl as close as you can to this antelope, and then look sharply and you will see a lone buffalo grazing 'two buffalo arrows' away. Work your way toward this buffalo under cover of the antelope, gradually driving it toward the buffalo; and then when you are close enough, kill the buffalo."

The braves went out, and they returned after dark with a dripping buffalo head swinging on a long pole over their shoulders.

That night they put the buffalo head outside of the camp and built a big fire; and the men formed around it in a semicircle, facing the direction in which we were traveling. Afterwards the medicine-man, White Dog, came out and took a position in the center of the semicircle and began to sing. When he started singing the coyotes started to sing, too, setting up a mournful howl all along the river-bank. After he had sung his first song he told the rest to keep their eyes on the buffalo head and see "if there were any unusual signs." If so, he said, it was good, and they must give thanks.

Then he started to sing a second song, and when he came to the part where he mentioned the buffalo head, sparks came out of the left eye, then the right, and then the left again. And next the buffalo head started to wag from side to side, just like a buffalo that had been brought down by a bullet. Smoke came out of its nostrils, and it panted.

We youngsters were supposed to be in bed, but two of my playmates and I had slipped out of our pallets and were standing behind the men, unknown to them. When we saw the sparks coming out of the buffalo's eyes we were at first too scared to move. But when it started to snort and move, we let out a yell and turned on our heels and ran as fast as we could out into the darkness of the prairies. We did not know where we were going; we just tore away with all the speed we had. Had the men not run and overtaken us, we probably should have been lost.

When we got back to camp the men told us not

to be scared; for the buffalo head had told us that our venture against the Crows was going to be successful. Our mothers laughed at us for being scared, and then put us to bed again. As they tucked us back under our buffalo robes, they made us angry when they said: "After this we shall have to watch our 'little girls.'"

The next morning White Dog interpreted to the tribe the "vision" he had received over the buffalo head. He said that the spirits still spoke favorably of our prospects against the Crows. He said that we were going to see the enemy on the following day, and that we were going to "take" four of them.

On the following morning when we resumed our journey we saw quite a commotion ahead of us—lots of moving objects. When we went closer we saw that they were a huge herd of jumping deer—several hundred of them. They were in a big circle a hundred feet across. This circle was four feet deep. The antelopes had eaten the black earth down to that depth. We had no horses with us—the Crows had all of them—and so we had to go back to the old Indian burden-bearer, the dog. We had all of our camping effects packed on the backs of our dogs or trailing behind them on the travaux. It was almost impossible to get our dogs across this deep area of black earth. They were packed so heavily that we had to roll them over the boggy portions, lest they should stick in the mud up to their bellies and stay there. We had to roll them over logs, too.

We passed Shell Creek and struck out for the "High Hills"—the Rocky Mountains. We came to the foot of a mountain which we called "Snow Never Melts." When we arrived at the foot of this mountain, our medicine-man told us to lie down at the foot of the rising slope and keep still; for he saw a hunting party going home with meat. They were *Sahpos*—Crows!

We lay there until the hunters disappeared beyond a ridge, and shortly afterward a buffalo bull appeared from the ridge and came in our direction. It stopped about two hundred yards from us and stamped its feet and stuck out its tail. Among Indians this is a signal for the Indians to walk back and forth on their horses. The buffalo did this twice, and came to within about a hundred yards of where we were lying. Suddenly it disappeared over the brink of another ridge, and White Dog shouted, "Shoot him!" But it was too late.

This buffalo was nothing more than two Crow Indians disguised in one of their "spying suits." Indians often disguised themselves as wolves, buffalo and antelope. This "buffalo" was trying to find out what we were; what tribe. And when we did not give it a signal they knew that we were an enemy.

We followed in the direction in which the hunters had gone, and when we thought that we might be close enough to be in danger, our war chief Going Soul sent out three scouts to find where the Crows were going to camp for the night.

We stopped, and White Dog said that we had better hold a "Snow Dance." Whenever Indians intended to raid for horses they always held a "Rain Dance" or a "Snow Dance," to pray for wind and storm under which to cover their raid.

We all crowd around the medicine-man as tightly as we can, and while he goes through his incantations and prays for rain, we join in a ceaseless chant which beseeches the elements to let loose rain or snow. There is not much noise to this dance, but it sometimes lasts for several hours, everyone concentrating his thoughts on rain or snow with each beat of the drum. "Ta-plum, ta-plum, ta-plum"— goes the drum. "Give rain, give rain, give rain"— go our thoughts.

When the scouts returned they told us that it was the band of Crows whom we were seeking. They were camped at a distance of about "twenty buffalo arrows" from where we were—about four miles— (one "buffalo arrow" was about 350 yards, or the longest distance at which our tribe had killed a buffalo with an arrow). The scouts said that the Crows were camped in a large coulée along the edge of the foot-hills (of the Rockies); and it was evident, they said, that the Crow spies did not suspect that we had recognized their presence in the buffalo hide, for they were entirely off their guard.

Owing to the fact that we had not dared to do any hunting, lest we should disclose our presence to the enemy, we had nothing to eat that night; so Chief Going Soul said that we would kill a stray horse which we had picked up earlier in the day— one that had evidently got away from the Crows— and have a horse feast. Indians did not like to kill their mounts, but they were forced to whenever they were caught out without food. We killed the horse, and we were all given pieces of it to roast on the end of long green sticks. We built our fire in a ravine along the river-bank and stretched some buffalo robes over it on four poles, so that its smoke would not glow as it went up into the skies.

After our meal the chief made all of us strip off and go into the river and wash ourselves thoroughly, using for soap the fine black silt at the bottom of the stream. We scrubbed our bodies until they glowed, to remove all odors of the horse flesh we had eaten. If any of these odors should remain on us the enemy's horses would stampede when it reached their nostrils in the darkness. Horses are frightened at the smell of their own flesh, especially horse fat, and they go wild when they scent it. As

we had to sneak upon the enemy's camp and take
their horses while they were asleep, we could not
risk a disturbance in the herd while we were at work.

That night we followed our scouts to a point on
a high butte where we could look down upon the
camp of the Crows.   It was situated in a large
coulée—ravine—and was enclosed on all sides but
one by the surrounding buttes and foot-hills.   We
crept down to the open end of the camp under the
cover of darkness and lay there for what seemed several hours, waiting for the Crows to go to sleep.
There was a water-hole near us, and we could see
the Crows coming and going from this hole with
their water bladders.   Out of revenge some of our
men wanted to crawl down to the water-hole and
sneak off a Crow scalp, but White Dog and the chief
would not allow them to.   They said that we had
come not to shed blood but to take back our horses
and those of the Crows, to teach them a lesson.

After midnight Chief Going Soul whispered the
order to crawl into the Crow camp.   The braves left
the women and us children where we were, with
instructions to seek safety in the opposite direction
if we heard the "bay of a gray wolf twice."   That
was our signal—we had men in the tribe, scouts,
who could give the call of these animals so perfectly
that the most experienced ear could not detect the
difference.

Our mothers allowed some of us boys to creep along behind our fathers to the edge of the camp, so that we could watch what they did. When our fathers saw us they told us to lie on the right side of the camp entrance, and when the horses came down that way to rise on our feet and wave our arms, and "sh-sh" them the other way; and they told us to be sure to run back to our mothers before they got back.

As we lay there we watched our fathers crawl away from us on their bellies, pushing their muzzle-loaders in front of them and rustling the undergrowth once in a while to let the horses know that they were coming, so that they would not be frightened. Now and then one of them would get up and stand still for a moment, to let the horses see him and to ease the fear of the dogs in the camp.

The Crows had a log corral for their horses, and the camp was set up all around it except on one side, the south; so our fathers made for this side, and as we lay there we could see them removing the logs from a section of that side. When some of the Crow dogs set up a chorus of barking, two of our scouts set up a duet of coyote "yipping" to make the Crows believe that the dogs were barking at these. We heard a baby start crying in one of the Crow teepees, and it seemed that the mother put her hand over its mouth. One of our boys said in a loud whisper: "If I had a gun I would shoot into that teepee and quiet that little gopher—bad dog Crow!" We told him that if he did not keep his tongue in his mouth we would tie his hands and feet and leave him there—and he was quiet after that.

The Indians always tied their favorite saddle-horses right at the doors of their teepees, so that they could mount them quickly and be after anyone who disturbed their camp; and also to protect them in case anyone should try to raid their horses. Our men were bold that night; for we could see them sneaking upon these special mounts at the teepee doors and unloosening them. There were two fine black-and-gray pintos in front of the chief's teepee, and they got these, too, all bridled and ready for riding.

Pretty soon we heard the thumping of horses' feet coming our way, and this boy who had spoken about the Crow baby got up and ran—he was afraid that we were going to tie him. Just a few horses came by us, and we kept waiting for the others, but in a moment we saw our fathers coming and we ran. When we got back to our mothers our fathers told them that the Crows had built a double corral— with a partition in the center—and that they had found this out too late to get at the other horses which were next to the camp. All of their best horses were in that side, and we had got the poorest of the lot, which must have been their aim in case they were raided.

But our braves had fooled them in one respect: they had been bold enough to undo those prize mounts at the teepee doors and fetch them back with their Indian bridles and saddles already on them. Our chief laughed at this; for he said that if the Crows should awake and find their horses gone they would have to make bridles before they could chase us.

We made our way eastward rather leisurely, considering what we had done, and daylight was on us before we had got very far from the Crow camp. In the early hours of dawn we could see the big camp lying back there in the coulée. In the soft brown moonlight of mid-dawn it looked like a big snow-bank. When we got up on a ridge from which we could watch the camp, we made a halt, and White Dog and our older men smoked. Our spies could detect no movement in the Crow camp. They must have thought that we had not seen them on the afternoon before; for they had evidently taken no precautions against us.

When we started on again we abandoned the ridge and rode down into the river valley where the traveling was easier. We had not gone more than three miles when we heard a noise, and we looked up— and there were the Crows firing at us from the top of a big cut-bank ahead of us. They had been smarter than we thought they were. They had sneaked out of their camp right behind us, and headed us off, evidently using the few bridles they had left and allowing the other horses to follow the leader—guiding them with their knees in the Indian fashion.

White Dog yelled for the women and children to make for the river-bank, and he and our braves rode ahead to meet the Crows. White Dog, who had been riding ahead of us, had been hit in the chest by a bullet, and blood was running from his mouth.

Fortunately, some of our men had continued traveling along the ridge above us, and the Crows did not know this; for they were taken by surprise when they came riding down upon them. As they assailed the Crows from their left, White Dog and our chief raced around the edge of the cut-bank and struck them on their right. The Crows were willing to fight it out, but their horses were not. They became frightened at the gun-fire, and their riders having no bridles to hold them in, they began to buck. They bucked and swapped ends in all directions, as the Crows tried to level their muzzle-loaders and fire at us. The Crows fought bravely, but aiming and shooting and riding a bucking horse at the same time proved too much for them; and one by one they were thrown to the ground and were forced to retreat afoot.

Several Crows who had bridles on their horses turned and followed the rest on horseback, and our men wanted to chase them; but our chief said that we had had enough bloodshed and he ordered them to keep with the band.

When the excitement was over three Crows were lying dead upon the cut-bank, and trails of blood told that others had been hit. We rounded up all of their abandoned horses, and we now had more horses than we did before the Crows raided us.

The bullet which had struck White Dog in the chest had only bruised his skin—it had struck his breastplate of round elk shin-bones and flattened out and dropped down into his fire-bag. But the blow of the bullet against his chest caused blood to come out of his mouth for several hours.

After we got out of this predicament we traveled till late that night, and then we stopped and slept all of the next day. The next morning our men went out and killed some antelope, and we had our first good meal since leaving home.

But while we were eating White Dog said: "Hurry up; we are not the only people around this district." Sensing that something was wrong, the braves struck camp and we resumed our journey eastward across the plains.

We had gone about a half-mile when we crossed the bed of a dry creek. A ridge crossed the creek at this point. White Dog was riding at the head of our party with two others, Thunder Face, a scout; and Chief Going Soul. As they came to the top of the ridge, we saw White Dog signal to his two companions to stand back while he peered over the ridge alone. As soon as White Dog looked over the ridge he jerked himself back quickly and said something to the other two, and they waved their blankets at us, crossways, signaling that something was ahead of us. Then they came down and tied their ponies at the bottom of the dry creek, which was a signal for us to do likewise. After fastening their ponies our men went up and joined White Dog and the chief and the scout, leaving us youngsters back with the women. Soon we heard a lot of firing, and we knew that there was a fight.

When our men came back they told us that they had ambuscaded a party of forty Crows who had evidently been out looking for us. The Crows were struck with bewilderment when our fire hit them; they stood still and could not tell where it was coming from until half of them had been hit. Then, realizing that they were hopelessly at the mercy of a superior force, they crawled to the river-bank and disappeared over its edge into the darkness of the night that had already overtaken us. When our men started to follow them, our chief said: "No, let them go back to the Crows and tell them what happened to their party, that they may be taught that we cannot be trapped."

White Dog, the medicine-man, went out onto the field and pulled in four dead Crows and stretched them in a line on the ground in front of us. Then he started to sing one of his medicine songs over them. And while he was singing he said that there were going to be four shots, and on the fourth shot we were all to turn right-about and start for home. We did that, and before we had gone a hundred yards a blizzard broke suddenly upon us. We rushed back to the field and searched it for all the Crow blankets we could find; for though it was still early spring, we were not prepared for this. Our men ran down to the river-bank and found all of the blankets of the Crows who had escaped. They had piled their blankets and buffalo robes on the river-bank and swum across, evidently intending to return and get them. We took these and others from the dead Crows.

When we started off a lot of Crow horses, riderless and with their bridle-reins dangling in front of them, came up to us through the howling darkness and followed us like dogs in the blizzard. A few moments before they had been wild, kicking broncos. Now, awed by the screeching elements, they sought human contact rather than face the blizzard alone. When our braves went up to them to remove their Indian bridles, so that they could join our herd without stumbling and breaking their necks, they stopped dead still and pushed their bodies back on stiff, trembling legs, and stood, wild-eyed but trustful, while our men gently removed their rawhide bridles and grass-mat saddles. Then they kicked up their heels and whinnied and joined our own herd.

We wound all of our heavy robes and blankets around us and faced the blizzard as White Dog had told us to. He said that it was the belated storm which he asked for in his "Snow Dance," and that the Spirits had perhaps sent it late to protect us from some unknown danger. The snow-laden northern winds howled at us mercilessly and stung our eyes to the quick with blinding chunks of snow, but we kept on. We traveled without a halt until it broke early the next morning. Then we all stopped and dug into the snow and pitched our camp. As we dug our beds into the snow and curled up to sleep, we wondered if the Crows had got home alive without their blankets and horses.

When we awoke many hours later we discovered that one of our warriors, Roving Night Eagle, was missing. His wife said that he had not been with us at any time during the storm, but she had thought that he was with the horses. Roving Night Eagle was the best marksman in our tribe, a brave of great renown on the war-path. Now the Crows had got him. Some of our braves were angry at this; for, they said, White Dog had told us that we were going to "take" four of the enemy and that we were not going to "give" any of our number to the Crows. White Dog ordered them to stop the discussion, saying that the "Spirits never spoke falsely" to him, and that if they had told him that, it was right.

It was the first time White Dog had ever given out a forecast that did not come true! And some of our older men said that his medicine powers must be waning, and that he ought to go out into the wilderness alone and train for several months, to recoup these powers. (Medicine-men always did that when they found their medicine growing "weak," and then they would return to their people and sweep everything before them.) But White Dog insisted that the spirits were still "with him," and no one could convince him otherwise.

VI

CHIEF CARRY-THE-KETTLE

THIS was the last blizzard of early spring. When we journeyed on and reached the upper Missouri River (Montana) the ice was breaking, and we decided to wait until the floes had passed before risking our horses and our lives in the swift-flowing, ice-jammed torrent. White Dog and Going Soul decided that we should go down the river a little way to look for a good camping-place. To do this we had to "travel high" to keep out of the slush; so we went back up the south butte again and made our way slowly eastward.

It was mid-afternoon when White Dog stopped his horse and signed back to us to halt. He and Thunder Face, the scout, came back and said that there was a big camp of Indians on the river-bank ahead of us; and they called a council of the chiefs and councilmen to decide what to do. From the paintings on the teepees they could not make out what tribe they were, but the council decided that they were sure we had left all of the hostile band of Crows west of us. And so they decided that the best thing to do would be to ask the Indians who they were, before approaching them.

So White Dog rode up on the ridge and shouted, "Ho-h!"

And then in the sign language he asked them to sign back the name of their tribe. They signed back that they were Gros Ventres and North Assiniboines all camped together; and they asked us who we were. White Dog signed back that we were Blackfeet. This did not seem to put them at ease, for they signed back, asking, "Which Blackfeet?"

White Dog and Going Soul were at a loss to know what to tell them; for our band had in it members of all four of the Blackfoot bands—the North Blackfeet, the South Blackfeet, the Bloods, and the Piegans—and White Dog was not sure which of these bands might be held as enemies by the Assiniboines, who were Northern Sioux of Assiniboia—now Saskatchewan—and were strangers along the Missouri. So he finally decided on a ruse. He stood up and made the sign of the Crees, and then he walked a few paces to the right and made the sign of the Kootenays. Then he stepped midway between these two points and indicated that we lived between these two tribes. The Gros Ventres and Assiniboines signed back that they did not know any Blackfeet who lived between these two tribes; so we "must be all right," they said. And they invited us to come into their camp.

We rode into their camp and paraded before them all of the horses we had taken from the Crows; and they said that we must be great warriors. And they were pleased; for they, too, were enemies of the Crows.

Before our warriors got off their horses we saw the Assiniboine chief going around the mounted group, looking at all of their shields, which were tied on the shoulders of the mounts. And soon he went up to our chief and held out his hand and said: "It seems that we are not enemies. I have looked at all of the medicine paintings on your shields, and I do not remember seeing any of them in any of our battles with the Blackfeet." They shook hands, and we all felt friendly right away.

All of the chiefs and .councilmen and medicine-men of the three tribes got together and held a council. When it was over they sent a "camp-crier" through the big camp to notify everyone that we were all going to have a big feast and hold an "I Saw" Dance that night. An I Saw Dance is a dance in which all of the most renowned warriors of the tribe relate their most famous exploits on the war-path; and after they have related it the drums start to beating, and then they dance and reenact the fight as it actually happened—selecting others to be their victims.

Naturally, we youngsters looked upon this with

great favor; for with us in that massive camp we had some of the most noted Indian warriors who ever graced the American plains. Most famous among them was Chief Carry-the-Kettle, head chief of the Assiniboines, who was then an old man but who lived to pass the century mark and died only in 1923 on the Assiniboine Reserve at Sintaluta, Saskatchewan, at the age of 107.

We also had with us the famous Assiniboine scout Runs-with-Another, who was General Nelson A. Miles's personal scout in the Nez Percés war against Chief Joseph, and who was later decorated for his valor by President Grant. Then there was Chief Atsistamokon, famous Blackfoot chief and medicine-man, who had the most unusual fighting career of any Indian within historic times.

But the most unique character at this historic assemblage was Mrs. Good Elk, a famous Assiniboine beauty who had been stabbed seven times by the Blackfeet in the Blackfoot massacre, "one camp" north of Saskatoon, Saskatchewan, a few years before. Here she was for the first time facing some of the warriors who killed her entire family and who stabbed her and left her for dead on that memorable battle-field. Unknown to the Assiniboines at that moment, we had in our band a number of the Northern Blackfeet who took part in that conflict against the Assiniboines. In fact, Chief Atsistamokon was the Blackfoot medicine-man who led the advance party against the Assiniboines.

Mrs. Good Elk was a very beautiful woman who had two tattoo marks running down from the corners of her mouth to the edge of her chin, and our Blackfoot warriors recognized her at once; for she had been famous among all tribes of the plains for her unusual looks. When they espied her among the Assiniboines these Blackfoot warriors went over and crowded around her and gave her the Blackfoot greeting of pleasure used when one has not seen a friend for a long time. They raised their right hands and said: "Hie-hie-hie-hie-hie!" Far from resenting the presence of her former enemies, Mrs. Good Elk was pleased to be greeted by them. She looked at them one by one and smiled and nodded her head. And she asked if the fellow were there who stabbed her.

"What did this fellow look like?" asked Chief Atsistamokon.

"*O-waya-washtay!*" she exclaimed, sweeping her two hands down her face. "Very good-looking!"

"What would you do if you should see him here?" the chief asked.

"Throw my arms around him and kiss him," she replied, carrying her arms through the motions of an embrace.

But Mrs. Good Elk's sister was very angry and

MRS. GOOD ELK
Who Was Stabbed Seven Times by the
Blackfeet in the Blackfoot Massacre

CHIEF CARRY-THE-KETTLE
Leader of the Assiniboines for Forty Years
at the Age of 107

insensed at the presence of the Blackfeet. She went into her teepee and sat down and began to sharpen a big buffalo knife. She scolded and threatened us youngsters when we went into her teepee with some Assiniboine children, and we went to our elders and told them what she was doing—sharpening her knife "to get a Blackfoot for every member of her family who had been killed."

Some of the Assiniboines heard of this, and they went into her teepee and tried to talk her into friendship with the Blackfeet. But she was implacable, and when her sister, Mrs. Good Elk, went into her teepee she handed her the knife and told her to "use it on her enemies." Mrs. Good Elk strapped the knife around her waist and came out of the teepee, sending us youngsters scurrying away with fright. We thought she was going to start a fight. But, instead, she went back to the group of Blackfeet and resumed her conversation with dignified friendliness.

Mrs. Good Elk married one of the Blackfoot warriors; and she is still living—on the Assiniboine Reserve at Sintaluta, Saskatchewan. Though nearly eighty, she is still very handsome.

There was one other Assiniboine who was raging in his teepee to get at the Blackfeet. His name was E-ah-chee-cha—Queer Talker—and he refused to come out of his teepee to greet us. He lay there in his teepee in a reclining position, uttering muffled threats to any of us youngsters who should go too near him. It was Queer Talker who had chased the wounded Blackfeet in their battle with his tribe, and killed them one by one along the trail—and he still had nothing but the bitterest hatred for us. Chief Path-Maker, a fine young Assiniboine minor chief who still rules his tribe, volunteered to take charge of these two Assiniboines and prevent them from carrying out any of their hatred against the Blackfeet; for the rest of the Assiniboines were very friendly toward us.

We children were very happy in the big, massed encampment of the three illustrious tribes of Assiniboines, Blackfeet and Gros Ventres. The teepees of the huge camp were all thrown in a large circle more than a half-mile around. These teepees were painted in all colors of the rainbow, each painted differently and bearing the "medicine" crest of the family that occupied it.

The sun of early spring shone brightly on our big, happy camp as we ran back and forth between the teepees and the river, playing games and getting acquainted. We could not talk with one another except through the sign language, but we shouted our glee just the same.

We had heard our fathers talk so much about the fights between the Blackfeet and Assiniboines that

we youngsters wanted to hold a "play battle" with
the Assiniboine youngsters, but our older people
would not allow us to do that. They were afraid
that some of us would inflict accidental injury on
some of the young Assiniboines and start a fight
between the tribes. So we had to content ourselves
with wrestling, throwing heavy stones, and riding
bucking colts, to show off our prowess.

Our mothers sat out in front of their teepees,
keeping a close watch on us to see that we conducted
ourselves properly in front of the "stranger Indians," and to make sure that we did not start a
contest that might hurt one of our hosts and start
a fight.

But if they had only known it, fighting was the
last thing in our minds. We were all so glad to
see some other youngsters like ourselves that we
looked upon them as our brothers, and we did everything possible to be friendly and get acquainted, so
that we could laugh at one another in our pranks—
of which the Indian boy is so fond.

The older braves seemed to be happy, too. They
busied themselves constructing the huge council
lodge in which we were to hold the I Saw Dance
that night. They were taking down a lot of the
smaller teepees and stretching them over poles and
turning them into one big enclosure, where we could
all seat ourselves for the dance. Our mothers and

sisters, like all Indian women, sunny and happy in all circumstances, sat around their teepees enjoying with placid cackles the unique situation and the crowds and the bustle which so delights Indian nature.

We feasted that night on buffalo pemmican, which no other tribe can make better than the Assiniboines. Pemmican, the chief article of food of the Indian during winter, is made of dried buffalo meat cut into bits and mixed with saskatoon-berries. After it has been put into buffalo bladders and hot fat has been poured over it, it will keep for months and years without spoiling. It is the Indian's only "canned" food; the only food he can lay by for the winter months.

After the feast we all filed into the big council lodge and seated ourselves for the I Saw Dance.

Five of the most renowned warriors of the three tribes had been selected to reenact their most famous exploits on the war-path. These fifteen stalwarts came into the lodge after we had been seated, and they took their seats on the right and left of the chiefs, who sat facing us in a semicircle at the far end of the lodge.

All of these warriors were stripped down to the breech-cloths and the feathered war decorations which adorned their heads. They all had their old war wounds freshly painted on their bodies, according to the custom of Indians on festive occasions. Some of these wounds were so cleverly reproduced that one could not tell them from the original gaping wounds over which they were painted. They also had the terrible scars of the Sun Dance reproduced on their chests in all their bloody detail.

It was an imposing assemblage of old-time warriors. There were "three-feather" men and "four-feather" men and "war-bonnet" men; there were chiefs and medicine-men galore. A three-feather man was one who had killed three men in battle and was entitled to wear three eagle feathers tipped with red horsehair dangling from the crown of his head. Those who had killed more than four men on the war-path were wearing their war-bonnets of many eagle feathers made into an elaborate head-dress. The warriors wore other feathers in their hair to show how many times they had been wounded. One eagle feather split down the center meant that the wearer had been wounded once by an arrow. An eagle feather with a red ball painted on it meant that the wearer had been wounded once by a bullet. Some of the warriors wore a lot of these feathers, showing that they had been wounded a number of times.

All of the fifteen warriors who were to take part in the I Saw Dance had many of these "wound" and "scalp" feathers adorning their heads; and their bodies were covered with old wounds, which had been touched up with paint to make them fresh again. We boys sat and counted them, and we tried to figure out among ourselves which was the greatest hero. Indians always permitted their youngsters to witness these warlike displays, that they might inspire us to emulate the bravery of our fathers and encourage us to be great warriors.

Chief Carry-the-Kettle, being the oldest war-chief present, was the first to be called upon to relate his exploits in the I Saw Dance. I shall not forget the impressive dignity of this wonderful gentleman of the plains. The hero of a dozen escapades that would set at naught the wildest dreams of the imagination, Chief Carry-the-Kettle was leading his people to war when Sitting Bull, Crow Foot, and Pound Maker were still in their infancy. And yet he survived until 1923, when Sitting Bull and the rest of the frontier chiefs had become little more than mythical figures of history.

Though Chief Carry-the-Kettle had killed more than a hundred men on the war-path, there was something in his face that was truly spiritual—a remarkable gleam of human goodness that made him bigger in my eyes than any man I have seen. When he had to refer to his killings on the war-path he did it with a whimsical air of apology which made it evident that it was distasteful to him. In spite of his destructive record, Chief Carry-the-Kettle was one of those men in whose fearless hands a person would gladly place his life, if it depended on a matter of fair judgment and the kindness of human nature.

This great chief of the Assiniboines was known throughout the plains in the old days as a master runner. We had many times heard of the time when he had led the Blood band of Blackfeet into the belief that they were surrounded by an overwhelming number of Assiniboines by one of his feats of speed. By running around a superior number of Bloods under cover of the surrounding hills and bobbing up at intervals so that they could see him, Chief Carry-the-Kettle made the Bloods believe that they were completely surrounded by the Assiniboines; and thereby he turned into victory what otherwise would have been the complete annihilation of himself and his handful of Assiniboine warriors. We had often heard this story related around our camp-fires—how the Assiniboines once fooled our tribe into defeat. And now, as it happened, we had the great chief himself here to tell us how he had done it. But we will let the chief go on with the story.

As the war-drums boomed softly to the accompaniment of four tribal singers who were seated in the center of the lodge, chanting the dolorous tune of the I Saw Dance, Chief Carry-the-Kettle arose and planted his long, feathered scalp-stick on the ground in front of him, holding on to it with his right hand. He stood silent for several seconds, looking meditatively at a scalp which hung in the middle of the stick. Then lifting his head firmly and looking over toward the Blackfeet, he began:

"*Hanh-h!* I am going to tell you about something that happened down here in your own country, to your own tribe, the Weh-winchasta Seehasapa (Blood-Blackfeet). It is the story you asked me to tell—the time I ran and fooled your people. You know it, Blackfeet!"

"*Agh, agh, agh!* (yes, yes, yes)," affirmed the Blackfoot warriors, as they bent forward and turned their heads to listen.

"This was years ago when I was a chief of twenty-two winters," continued the chief. "I brought my people, the Assiniboines, out on the war-path to seek revenge on the Blackfeet for an attack they had lately delivered on us in Assiniboia. We came down here and had crossed the Milk River [Montana] when early one morning we saw you for the first time. I was traveling a little ahead of my party with my brother Hide Scrapings, when we saw lots of moving objects ahead of us. It was a hazy morning, and the objects danced up and down and changed their form like an *itowapi*—mirage. We could not tell what they were, but they looked like neither antelope nor buffalo. We stopped, and while I was trying to figure out what they were, I saw two buffalo two hundred yards away, grazing toward a knoll in the distance. My brother wanted to shoot one of them, so that we could have a meal of raw buffalo kidneys, but I restrained him. I warned him that the objects in the distance might be the enemy.

"I told my brother to watch these bobbing forms while I crawled out on the flat under cover of the two buffalo and tried to make my way to the knoll ahead of us, whence I could get a better view of these queer moving things. After a hard crawl I made the top of the knoll. With care I peeped slowly over its shoulder—and then I jumped back quickly. I crawled down out of view and waved my blanket and signaled to my brother that it was the enemy dancing one of their dances out on the open prairies.

"My brother passed this signal back to my tribe, who had been trudging along with no knowledge of what we had seen. They all ran up to my brother and asked him what was the matter. I could hear them talking loud, and I wanted to get their attention so that I could tell them to keep quiet. But I could not catch their eyes until I got right up to them. Then I heard one of my men, a man of good counsel, saying that I, their chief, did not want to open battle because we were a small party. Another of my braves, a man of much mouth and poor counsel, was arguing that they should all run up and attack the enemy and not wait for me to return.

"They did not see me until I came upon them. Then they looked at me for orders. I told them to stop their talking and to retire a short distance that we might hold a war council in safety.

"We went back to a small coulée. Then the brave with much mouth wanted to know why the brave of good counsel did not want to fight. I told them that I would answer that question. I said to them:

" 'You are all of distinguished parentage, and I should not like to take the responsibility in case any of you are killed. There are only eight of us against many times that number of the enemy. Your chief has spoken.'

"Then the man of mouth turned to me and said:

" 'What did we come here for? Did we not come here to fight? Are you now going to back out?'

" 'No, I am not,' I said, 'I want you all to die like braves—fighting, not running away. And we shall do that. Your chief has spoken for the last time.'

"The man of mouth said nothing more; and I ordered my men to strip themselves for battle, paint their bodies, line themselves along the coulée for an ambuscade, and then leave the rest to me.

"You know it, Assiniboines!" exclaimed the chief, looking over toward his own people.

"*How, how, how!*" came the response.

"Then I threw off my clothes and started to run," continued the chief. "I ran ahead along the coulée for about a half a mile and then raised myself above the horizon in full view of the enemy—the Black-feet. They were now dressing an antelope—and they saw me.

"You know it, Blackfeet!"

"*Agh, agh, agh!*"

"Then I pulled myself out of view and ran bent like this as fast as I could, and soon—a quarter of a mile farther—I raised myself and looked over at the Blood-Blackfeet. I saw now that they knew they were being watched; for they had all concealed their weapons beneath their blankets and were keeping close together so that they could not be counted.

"You know it, Blackfeet!"

"*Agh, agh, agh!*"

"Then I bent low and put on speed again—this time on, on, on, to a point many hundreds of yards away—then up again—then more speed—and up again. I went clear around them three times, coming up so fast that they thought I was many men looking at them from all sides.

"You know it, Blackfeet!"

"*Agh—Awk-see!* (Yes—Bravo!)"

"When I looked over at them the last time I came up close so that I could see them well. They were all big, tall fellows, all wearing buffalo jackets —and I knew they were Blood-Blackfeet. They were beginning to be alarmed now—they thought they were all surrounded by the Assiniboines. But they were brave, and they were not daunted. They started a war dance.

"The sun would soon be setting; so I ran speedily back to my warriors, and I told them that we would have to fight now; for the Bloods had already started their dance. I told them to throw off their blankets and lie there on the side of the coulée, still, and not to move until they saw me fire.

"Pretty soon we heard the Bloods moving into action. They were going where I wanted them to: against a false front where I had led them to believe that most of us were. As they came over the knoll and the mouth of another coulée, as I had planned for them to, I picked out their leading chief and fired at him.

"But just as I had fooled the Bloods, they had fooled us, too. Instead of having ten guns, as I had counted, every one of them had a weapon; and they had been wise enough to conceal them between their bodies and their blankets. They opened up on us with a rain of bullets and arrows. I saw an arrow coming straight for my brother, who lay beside me, but just when my mouth opened to warn him the arrow sank into his back.

"Our fire from this unexpected coulée so bewildered the Bloods that they retreated to the southwest. They expected us to be hundreds, and thought we would follow and attack them. But the Assiniboines had accomplished what they wanted. We had saved our lives and upheld our honor.

"When the Bloods had retreated over the shoulder of the coulée all of our Assiniboine braves rushed out to touch the one Blood who had been killed, so that they could get first, second, and third honors. Then we took our Assiniboine who had been killed, my brother, and gave him a warrior's funeral and buried him on the spot. We dug a round hole in the ground and sat him down in this hole facing the rising sun, according to the custom of the Assiniboines.

"Our scores were even. We had 'taken' one Blood, and the Bloods had 'taken' one Assiniboine," said the chief, again looking meditatively at the scalp in the center of his stick. Then in measured words, he continued: "And here is the scalp I took from your people. We are friends now, and I will give it back to you, that you may take good care of it until you get home, and then give it a warrior's burial.

"Carry-the-Kettle has spoken. Carry-the-Kettle has said that we are friends as long as the sun shines and the waters flow. Carry-the-Kettle has never broken his word.

"You know it, Blackfeet!"

"*Agh, agh, agh!—Sokah-pse! Akai-sokah-pse!* [Yes, yes, yes—Good! Very good!]"

The soft booming drums that had accompanied the chief's narrative suddenly broke into a wild rhythm, and then the chief and his companions proceeded to go through the famous ruse that he had just related, while some of the Bloods who were actually in the encounter looked silently on.

When his I Saw Dance was over Chief Carry-the-Kettle walked up in front of the Blackfoot chiefs and said:

"Already I am becoming an old man. I may never see any of you again. And before we break this camp I want to tell you the story of one of your chiefs who saved my life and caused me to be here tonight. I do not see him here, but some of you may know him. If you do you must, when you go again to the Northern Blackfoot country, tell him the story I am going to tell you now.

"This happened in the year of my twenty-sixth winter. You were camping on the Milk River in the country of the Northern Blackfeet [now Alberta]. All of the Blackfoot bands were camped there: the Bloods, Piegans and Siksika [Blackfeet proper].

"I was a young chief then, and I was not wise. With my half-brother, Nompa Winchasta (Two Men) I took the Assiniboines against your people to raid your horses.

"We found you one night camping on the Milk River after we had been out seven days looking for you.

"Next to your camp there was a small coulée filled with brush, and I told my half-brother that we had better leave the tribe behind us some distance and crawl into this coulée and watch you for a while before attempting to take your horses.

"We crawled upon our stomachs to within a hundred yards of your camp, and lay there in hiding, trying to find a way to get my tribe into your camp without being seen. It had grown very dark, and we were about to crawl back and order an attack, when one of the Blood horses broke away from the camp and came walking right toward us. We made small noises and tried to shoo him in another direction, but he did not hear us. Then we saw a tall Blood coming after the horse, but he did not see us in the darkness. My brother, lying alongside me, pointed his arrow at him and was going to pull the string, but he did not have the courage. In the darkness the Blood bumped into him, and I heard a grunt and a big scuffle. The big Blood soon had my brother helpless, and I saw him taking him back to camp, holding his hands behind him. I watched them closely, and I saw the Blood take my brother into a teepee in the center of the camp. It looked like the chief's lodge.

"I did not know what to do. But I knew that I must save my brother. I took off my clothes and put my blanket around my body, with my gun concealed beneath it. And I hid my face under the blanket and crept up toward that teepee. I saw a man at the door leaning against something. I was very scared, but I thought that I would have to die some time—and I was wondering what was happening to my brother. So I had to do something.

"I got so close to the fellow that I could touch his face. He jumped when he saw me; and I asked him what he had done with my brother. He took hold of me and led me to his own camp. I had lost all fear by now. I knew I had to die; so I threw my gun away.

"This fellow took me to a teepee with a fire inside of it and pushed me through the door, and came in after me. When he got inside he said something to his wife, and she took some meat and began to cook it on the coals. I had had nothing to eat for seven days; I had been on the war-path all that time—and I was shivering.

"When his wife put the meat before me I grabbed it like a dog with both hands and ate it greedily.

When I got through eating two strangers came in and said something to the other people; and then these two strangers took me outside and through the darkness to another teepee; and when they pushed me inside I saw my brother sitting there. Several others were in the teepee, and they were all very angry. They wanted to finish us quickly; and I wanted to be killed right away.

"While they were holding a council, discussing the best way to kill us, a man came into the lodge and sat down beside me. He was an American Piegan (Blackfoot) who could speak Assiniboine. He told me that a lot of horse-raiding had been going on from the Sioux and the Assiniboines, and he said that the Blackfeet were very angry about this raiding, and that we would be killed in a short while by the whole tribe. He said that they had already sent out word that they had two Assiniboines to kill, and everybody was very excited.

"Soon all of the men began to go out of the teepee, but the fellow who fed me stayed inside. He gave me back my flint-lock gun with a ball in it but no powder. I went over and sat with my brother and talked with him in Assiniboine.

"While we were talking we heard the tribe all gathering outside and making a lot of noise, as if they were much aroused.

"This big fellow took my brother outside and

left me there alone. I loaded my flint-lock with some powder I found near the door, and made up my mind that I would get a chief if I could pick one out. I made ready to bolt; I was going to dash right into the crowd outside and get as many of them as I could before they got me. But just as I ran through the door of the teepee two fellows grabbed me and held me so that I could do nothing. All of the three bands of Blackfeet were before me with their knives bared—and they began to whoop and shout when they saw me. I could not understand what they were saying.

"These two fellows took me down into a steep coulée and into a thicket. When I got there I saw the big fellow who had fed me, holding my brother. Then this big fellow handed my brother over to another fellow, and then got on his horse and began to drive the crowd back. I saw who he was now: he was the head chief.

"After he had driven the crowd away he turned around and drove me and my brother into a clump of bushes. He had on a fine buckskin suit, worked all over with porcupine quills. He took this off and handed it to me and told me to put it on my naked body—it was cold and I had left my clothes in the bush and was shivering—and the chief took my blanket and covered his own body with it. Then he took hold of my arm and said to me:

" 'You will find two ponies tied at the end of this coulée. Now, go! If you live long enough, when you are an old man you will be able to tell the story of the Blackfoot chief who spared you when you should have been killed.'

"That is the story I had to tell you," said Chief Carry-the-Kettle, looking kindly over toward the Blackfoot chiefs. "I am getting to be an old man now; and if that chief is still living, I want you to tell him that I told you that story. And though he and his people have always been the enemies of my people, I want you also to tell him that I have prayed for him at every Sun Dance the Assiniboines have held since that night. *Amba-wastaytch Seeha-sapa* [Good-by, Blackfeet]. That is all I have to say."

When the chief sat down, one of our chiefs, Chief Niokskatas, arose and said:

"That chief who saved your life was my father. We were all boys then, but every one of our chiefs here has heard that story from my father's lips, and we well remember the night it happened on the Milk River. You owe your life to your own bravery. My father said that he left you in the teepee with the gunpowder and the ball in your gun, to see what you would do. You had been brave enough to give your life for your brother; and when he saw that you would fight even though you would die for it, he said that you were too brave to kill. It is a law among the Blackfeet that a person must give his own life to save that of a relative. You did that, Carry-the-Kettle, brave warrior and chief of all the Assiniboines."

Chief Niokskatas went back and talked for a moment among the Blackfoot chiefs. Then he stood up again and said:

"If my father were here, I know what he would do: he would want to give you his name, Niokskatas, the highest name in the Blackfoot nation. You have a son with you. We, the Blackfeet, are going to bestow that name on your son; for even the Blackfeet do not believe that they could improve the name which you, yourself, bear and which you have made illustrious among all tribes of these plains."

"Hanh-h-h-h-h-h-h," came the deep, nasal grunt from all the Assiniboines, as they smiled and looked at one another with pleasure written over their features. It was plainly evident that they were deeply pleased and somewhat moved by this Blackfoot gesture of friendliness.

Chief Carry-the-Kettle's son, living on the Assiniboine Reserve at Sintaluta, Saskatchewan, still bears the name Niokskatas—Crow Foot.

The next time I saw Chief Carry-the-Kettle was in 1922—on the Assiniboine Reserve at Sintaluta. He was then 107 years old, and he was totally blind. Though lying ill on his pallet in his teepee, he insisted on getting up and coming out into the sunshine to meet me in the open—standing on his two feet—as befits a chief when greeting another chief from a former enemy tribe. He threw back his aged shoulders proudly and raised his blinded face to me in all the hauteur of his younger days—and he said:

"Tatonka Wahunkeza-honska [Chief Long Lance], I greet you in the name of the Assiniboines. You are the first member of your tribe I have seen since I was out in your country many years ago. Your great chief Niokskatas is dead; I have heard it. And so is Mekasto, your other great chief. When they were born I was leading the Assiniboines as their chief. Now they have come and gone, and still I am spared. I do not know why. I was a bad fellow when I was young. I killed many warriors. We were all foolish then"—the chief meditated a moment and then concluded—"but I suppose it was just our way."

Four months later, on February 23, 1923, Chief Carry-the-Kettle passed into the Great Unknown. And he was laid to rest with military honors by the Royal Northwest Mounted Police. If there is a Heaven and Chief Carry-the-Kettle did not go to it, then I want to go where he went.

VII

AN ARROW FROM WHITE DOG'S QUIVER

AFTER holding our big I Saw Dance with the Assiniboines and Gros Ventres we left them the next day with "good feelings in all our hearts"— as our chief expressed it in his farewell speech to the camp—and we started down the river to a point where the Assiniboines had told us that they had crossed without any trouble. We crossed the Missouri and bent our steps northward to see if we could find any buffalo in the "Chinook Winds."

We had been trekking northward for three days, when one night, near midnight, we were all awakened suddenly by a strange noise. Startled, we sat up on our pallets and listened in silence for several seconds, then turned and looked at one another in the dimness of the flickering fire, and wondered out loud. It was a strange, weird noise; yet we knew it. It was a song—a death song! "Who can it be?" we asked in fearful whispers. "What can it mean? What has been going on while we were sleeping?"

"Hoh! It is White Dog—our medicine-man!" said my father, jerking himself to his feet and standing for a moment with his ear turned attentively towards the teepee door.

Then he swirled his blanket about his body and dashed out of the teepee and disappeared in the darkness.

We heard the soft patter of moccasined feet dashing hither and yon through the camp, and we knew that something tragic was on.

We sat silently for about ten minutes—nobody spoke. Then my father pulled back the teepee flap, stooped and entered, and pulled himself up gravely and folded his arms across his chest. We could see that he was under emotion; that his "feeling" was expanding within himself, and that his outward calm was controlled only by the stoicism of our race.

My mother threw a splinter of wood on the embers and said:

"*Tsanistapi? Tsanistapi?* [What? What?]"

Without taking his eyes off the coals, my father said, in a voice that I had never heard before:

"White Dog is dead."

My mother opened her mouth wide and clapped her hand over it, in the Indian gesture of horror.

"Yes—he is dead," repeated my father, as if he were trying to assure himself that he was saying the truth.

My mother's breast heaved with emotion, but she said nothing for a time. Then she turned her eyes toward the dark, windy door, which my father had left up, and said:

"How?"

"His wife doesn't know," said my father. "She awoke and he was singing his death song—and there was blood coming from his mouth. He spoke no words. . . . He died singing."

Then, as if he suddenly remembered something terrible and blasphemous, my father uttered two words:

"*Sahpo! Sahpo!*

It was the Crows! My father had said it.

White Dog had died from the Crow bullet which had flattened itself against his chest.

These two words had no sooner left my father's lips than a long, lone wail, like that of a baying wolf, went echoing through the camp. It was White Dog's widow. This solitary lament was taken up by a hundred female voices; and from then on until dawn the camp reverberated with this mournful volume of primitive wailing—the Indian women's elemental way of expressing their grief at the death of a relative or a great warrior.

When we youngsters were allowed to get up early in the morning, all of the women in the camp had their faces painted black—in mourning—and a dozen of White Dog's female relatives had cut off a finger and thrown them into a big pot, or gashed themselves in the thigh with their buffalo knives. This was all in keeping with the tribal way of mourning the loss of one of its illustrious chiefs; for though only a medicine-man in name, White Dog was really a great leader of his people—more powerful in the tribe than some of its minor chiefs. Like Sitting Bull, his medicine powers had elevated him to an eminence of power which made his people look upon him really as their head chief.

It was our custom to bury our dead very quickly and to burn the death teepee as soon as the body had been taken out for burial. This was to prevent the evil spirits that caused death from lingering in our camp.

Therefore, early the next morning White Dog's body was dressed in his best regalia and then laid out on a number of large skins and buffalo robes. His flint-lock gun and his best bow and arrow were broken and laid beside him—they were broken so that they, too, would "die" and their spirits could go along with him to the Hunting Ground. All of his most cherished possessions were also placed around him, and then the whole was tightly wound with the robes and skins and bound with rawhide thongs.

We marched a distance out on the plains and laid his scaffold on the highest point of land—a butte— that our eyes could see in the vicinity. Just be-

fore we left him two men took White Dog's favorite
pony, one of the two gray-and-black pintos we had
taken from the front of the teepee of the Crow
Chief, and led it up to the body and shot it. The
pony was frightened of the body and would not be
led near it; so the men had to tie a fire-bag around
its eyes, to blindfold it.

That was the sad end of our great medicine-man
White Dog. Nevermore would he charm us with
his mysticism; nevermore would we hear his deep
guttural voice shouting to the spirits who had so
unexpectedly come and taken him away from us.
But he had a worthy successor in the Blackfoot man
of marvel known as Mokuyi-Kinasi, who soon was to
wield over us his famous "Power of the Thunder,"
which has become renowned in the history of the
Blackfoot nation. And, now, with our heads still
bent in mourning, we resumed our journey in quest
of the buffalo we had heard of.

Several days later, as we were making our way
northward, we came upon a "buffalo stone" lying
on the prairie; and we decided to stop and hold a
Buffalo Dance, to see what luck we were going to
have in our quest of buffalo, which were becoming
scarcer every day on the plains of the Far Northwest where they were fighting valiantly to survive
the slaughter being waged against them in the country south of us—of which country we knew little,

but of which we heard much from the lone half-breed traders who came among us with their kegs of whisky. They offered the Indians a pint of liquor for every buffalo robe they could produce, and soon the buffalo robe became known among the Indians as "a pint of fire-water." But our chiefs were strongly against "fire-water," and they counseled our braves not to accept any of it, as it would "destroy their hearts and make them cowards."

Where we used to sit on the sunny plains and watch the buffalo grazing by the thousands, we now traveled for days in order to see one or two lone buffalo feeding nervously at the bottom of some out-of-the-way coulée. Now and then we would see as many as ten in one herd, but never more. Chief Apa-anistau of the Piegan band of Blackfeet had told our chief that the frightened buffalo had wintered in the Far North that year, and that we could find them if we journeyed far enough in that direction.

We youngsters liked the Buffalo Dance, because we could all take part in it. The "buffalo stone"—a peculiar-shaped red stone—was always extremely rare on the plains. No one ever knew where these stones came from. They were just found lying on the prairie, about a foot long and shaped something like a buffalo, solely by the hand of Nature. Whenever the Indians came upon one of them they stopped forthwith and held a dance over it; for it was considered a sure sign that buffalo would be "taken." A peculiar angle of the Buffalo Dance was that if more females took part in the dance than males, it meant that we would get more cows than buffalo bulls—and we liked the cows much better.

Five days after we had held the Buffalo Dance— when we had gone a good distance north—one of our warriors, Kitsiponista, noticed some buffalo-birds over to our right, which kept flying up into the air and then disappearing again into what seemed to be a coulée. It was the habit of these birds to live on the buffalo, gaining all of their food by sitting on the backs of the buffalo and eating off the ticks. So Kitsiponista drew the attention of our chief to these birds, and said that he believed that there were buffalo in that direction.

The chief told us to make a halt long enough for him and two scouts to ride over and see what was behind those buttes. After a while they came galloping back from another direction—the north—and they told us that they had sighted the largest herd of buffalo they had seen in several years. The buffalo had scented them and had broken off from their grazing and were heading north up the valley.

The chief ordered the camp to make ready for a big hunt right away. Our mothers took the travaux off the horses and told us youngsters that we would

have to ride ponies along with them. Some of the
children were so small that they had to be tied to
the backs of their ponies, and we older boys had to
ride along with them to see that they did not come
to any harm.

We did not have saddles in those days—just Indian saddles, which were bags made of hide and
filled with grass or buffalo wool. It was more of a
cushion than a saddle; for it had no stirrups, and it
was fastened on the horse's back merely by two rawhide thongs, which were carried around the horse
and tied under his belly. Our bridles consisted only
of a long loop of rawhide which was tied to the
lower jaw of the horse, and it was meant only to hold
the horse in; we guided them with our knees.

The best of our warriors would not use these
saddles. They said that they were meant only for
women, and they preferred to show their hardi-
hood by riding bareback always.

All of the smaller children, except those in the
carrier bags, were put on ponies by the mothers, who
told us boys to tie them there while they got out their
buffalo knives and sharpened them for the hunt.
We took the feet of the little ones and pushed them
under the cinch-band, so that they were held tightly
against the horse's withers; and then we took a piece
of rawhide and tied them there so that they would
not work out when the horse should trot.

Our fathers gave us boys a bunch of ponies we had taken from the Crows and told us to make bridles and get on them. When we did they started to buck and throw us off. We kept climbing back on them, and they kept throwing us to the ground and taking a flying kick at us. Our fathers, already mounted with their guns, were all yelling at us:

"*Akakimat! Akakimat!*—Stay with it! Stay with it!"

Ponies were bobbing up and down all over the place, and we boys were hurtling through the air and hitting the ground with a grunt and a laugh. We were having great fun. But the girls commenced to laugh at us and shout: "*Kipitakkieks! Kipitakkieks!*—Old women! Old women!" This angered us —to be called "old women"—and we shouted back to the girls that they were all a lot of "bad puppies." And our fathers got stern at this, and they told us if we did not stop using that language toward our sisters they would leave us all behind, and we would not see the hunt.

"The girls are right," they said, "you are a bunch of 'little old women,' else you would have had those 'stranger ponies' broken in while we were resting on the river."

This quieted us; for we never could be so discourteous as to say anything back to our fathers. So we got mad then—and rode the ponies.

When we got our ponies quieted down, we all gathered in a little group and tied our hair under our chins and looked angrily over at the girls with their mothers. We *looked* angry, but we could hardly keep from laughing when we chanced to glance at one another; for inside us our stomachs were still jumping with laughter at the funny pranks our bad ponies had played on some of us. Young Eagle Talker, sitting over there so stolidly on a mean little flint-eye, had come down the wrong way—in front of his pony on his all-fours—and his mischievous mount had taken a bite at him, relieving him entirely of his breech-cloth, which he was now stolidly trying to adjust without attracting the attention of those bad little girls. Many of us were trying to conceal little trickles of blood from scratches and bruises. My pony had stepped on the middle finger of my right hand and crushed it as flat as a duck's beak; it was numb but bleeding profusely—and it is still flattened and scarred today.

Our fathers were chuckling among themselves—at us—and when the women were all fixed and we were ready to start, the chief said to us so that all of the girls could hear him:

"Come, young braves, and ride up in front with the hunters; and we will show those women how to bring down the buffalo!"

We were so excited at this invitation that we for-

got that we were on wild ponies, and when we kicked
them in the ribs they started bucking again; but we
stuck our mounts this time, and soon we were riding
along proudly with.our fathers.

We went northeast and struck the herd after riding for about an hour.   They were walking fast
when we first saw them, but when they saw us coming they broke into a canter which they quickly
changed to a rolling gallop.   It was then that our
warriors kicked full speed into their mounts and
went racing after them, whooping wildly to strike
terror in the herd and make them break into confusion.

"Therump, therump, therump"—the ground
fairly shook under the beat of our horses' pelting
hoofs.   Our fathers gradually stretched themselves
out into a long, speeding, diagonal line, which began to flank in on the left side of the racing herd.
The heavy, woolly shoulders of the mad-eyed brutes
were bouncing high into the air as they ran, and I
remember wondering how one of them would be to
ride.   We could hear them panting.

When we got close to the herd we youngsters
pulled in our ponies and raced along behind our
fathers, watching every movement they made.   We
saw each of the warriors carefully pick out a fat cow
and then speed up to get as close as he could before firing.   Most of them were using their bows

and arrows first, and they would not pull a string until they were racing along right over the left shoulder of the buffalo. Then, "fluck!"—and a long, steel-tipped arrow would bury itself deep in the shaggy withers of the beast, and it would take a few steps and pitch forward, pierced through the heart. But the buffalo died hard—they rolled and mooed and struggled valiantly for a second or two before shivering and stiffening out under the final thrust of death.

One of our boys, Shakes-the-Other-Fellow, came near losing his life by riding too close behind his father. His father, Pitanina, had picked out a fat cow and was trying to separate it from two bulls, between which it was racing madly for protection. One of the bulls, rather fat and old, became so tired that it suddenly stopped and turned around and lowered its head right in front of Pitanina's horse, which had been galloping directly upon its heels. The horse veered wildly to the left and just missed running into the buffalo. This frightened the buffalo so badly that it turned suddenly to resume its way, when it bumped into the other two buffaloes and in some way tripped them—and all three of them fell sprawling to the ground. This all happened within a second, and Pitanina's son, riding directly behind him, went crashing right into the pile of rolling buffalo.

It was a tense moment: three buffaloes, a horse, and a boy—all lying on the ground rolling frantically in one big pile of wool. Shakes-the-Other-Fellow became so excited as he lay there scrambling amongst the buffaloes that he shoved his hands deep into the wool of one of their backs and took a mighty hold on it. In an instant the buffalo was on its feet again and racing away wildly with the boy sitting upon its back with his hand sunk into its wool. Some of the warriors saw this and they galloped after it, trying to catch the frightened bison. It traveled nearly a half-mile before they could get close enough to it to risk putting a bullet into its head.

They shot it four times before it hit the ground with a terrific bang and sent young Shakes-the-Other Fellow sprawling to the turf with such force that it knocked him completely out of his senses. He came to after a moment or so. He was badly frightened —but he was not hurt. After this occurrence we boys gave him another name in the Sioux language. We called him *Wahsuk-Kiena*—Falling Snow—because he fell so far and hit the ground so lightly.

After this happening our fathers waved us boys to stay back while they galloped on in an effort to bring down the few remaining buffalo.

When we trotted back to where the chase had begun, our mothers were already on the job, carrying out the Indian woman's part of the buffalo hunt.

They were down on the ground skinning the animals and dressing them. Each wife knew which animals had been brought down by her husband, by the arrow which had been left in it. For every Indian had his arrow painted a certain way, so that anything he killed with it could easily be identified. If he shot a buffalo with a bullet he would circle back and hurl one of his arrows into its body, so his wife would know that it was his.

The young son of our late medicine-man was sitting on his pony over among us boys. He was carrying on his back a quiver full of his dead father's arrows, which his mother had given him to play with. One of the women came over to this lad and took out one of White Dog's arrows and walked out on the field, and pulled one of her own husband's arrows out of a buffalo bull and stuck White Dog's arrow in the hole. She said nothing to anyone; but later we saw White Dog's widow squatting over the buffalo, skinning it and sobbing quietly over the bloody pelt.

VIII

The Making of a Brave

WE RETURNED to the place where we had left our old men and women, and there we spent several weeks, curing our meat and buffalo robes, and making pemmican for the winter. Our men cut off the best part of the buffaloes, the breasts, and packed it back to camp and passed it around among the old people, as was the custom in those days. We had a big feast of our favorite dish in those days: buffalo brains and kidneys. We ate most of our meat raw, and if we cooked it, we cooked it very little—usually on the end of a stick.

Always when we had been eating plenty of fresh buffalo meat we would have a craving for some saskatoon-berries—our only fruit—or wild turnips, which might be said to have been the only vegetable we knew, except the small, marble-sized wild potato, which we rarely secured from the interior plateau of the northern Rockies. When we were on the prairies in summer, away from the bush where the saskatoon-berries grew, our mothers would send us boys out to hunt wild turnips. We would find them in mice nests.

We would go along the prairie with a long stick, thumping the ground as we walked. Whenever we came to a hollow sound in the ground we would dig down several inches and find a field-mouse nest full of wild turnips, all peeled and ready for eating. We would get as much as a pailful from one nest. The mice were very clean little animals, and since they never lived in the part of the nest where they kept their food, the small turnips would be as clean and neatly stored as if they had been put away by some cleanly human being.

After we had been at this camp for several weeks, our fathers all got out their "time sticks" one night —calendars—and compared them with one another, to see if they were agreed on "what 'sun' and 'moon' we were living in"; for on a certain "sun" we should have to start north to join the Siksikau band of Blackfeet in the big yearly Sun Dance of all the Blackfoot tribes.

We called a day a "sun," a month a "moon," and a year a "great sun." Our fathers had long sticks on which they kept their calendars. Each day was notched on this stick, and at the beginning of every moon a different kind of notch was made to denote the month; each of the twelve months, or twelve moon periods, had a different kind of notch to identify it. And then at the end of the year another notch would be invented according to what name we had given that year. The years were named according to some great happening during their passing, or numbered from some great happening in the past. We had no weeks.

It was decided at the "Time Council" that we would have to resume our journey northward on the fourth "sun" from that day, in order to reach the Siksikau in time for the Sun Dance, which is always held during the first two weeks of August.

We traveled northeastward for many days, and then one day as we were riding along the Namaka, a river, we looked ahead of us and saw the big Sun Dance camp spread out in a beautiful panorama of color, high up above us on the broad, sunny bosom of the famous Tallow Flats, where for ages past the Blackfeet had sent their young men through the terrible tortures of "brave-making."

The massive camp ahead of us was about two miles long. The hundreds of beautifully painted teepees were thrown in a huge circle about a quarter of a mile around, leaving a big circular campus in the center of the camp, where all of the dances would be held. Away out in the center of the campus we could see the skeleton of the Sun Dance lodge, already thrown up and awaiting the actual day of the dance, when it would be quickly enclosed with evergreens—all but the top, which would be left open so *Natose*, the Sun, could shine down "on its own."

As we looked up at the Sun Dance camp, spread out up there under a bright northern sun, our boyish hearts leaped in anticipation of the fun we were going to have in that camp. There would be hundreds of youngsters there from all of the Blackfoot tribes and other friendly tribes who came annually to camp on the outskirts of the Sun Dance camp to witness this spectacular ceremony of the Blackfeet.

We were now passing through hundreds, literally hundreds, of sleek, wild-eyed Indian ponies which had been turned loose, or hobbled, to graze at will out on the bald prairies surrounding the camp. When they saw us coming they whinnied and kicked their heels high into the air and ran at us and threatened us playfully with their heels. Then they pranced stiff-legged around in a circle, their tails raised and their heads high, vainly showing off their wild beauty to the newcomers. They were just like children: glad to see us. We boys were already picking out the ponies that we were going to trade in some of ours for.

When the big camp saw us coming in the distance some of the braves jumped on their ponies and galloped out to meet us, yelling and shouting as they rode up to us: "Hie, hie, hie, hie, hie"—meaning that they were extremely glad to see us. They led us to the ground that had been set aside for our camp; and when we arrived there and turned our ponies loose, we boys quickly deserted our parents and lost ourselves among the frolicking pageant of children who swarmed the big camp like birds on a berry-bush.

We asked the Siksikau boys if their tribe had had any fights since we saw them, and they said, "Yes, one." And they asked us if we had had any; and we told them about the Crow fight and how our fathers had allowed us to go right up to the camp with them; and also how they had told us to come along with them in the buffalo hunt. And these Siksikau boys said that their chief would not allow them to do anything like that. They were very envious of us, and some of them said that they were going to run away with us when we left. They said that there were some white people coming into their country now, and these people were ruled by a woman chief, whom they called the "Great White Mother"—and these people under the "woman chief" had persuaded the Indians not to fight any more. Their head chief thought this was good for the Indians, said the boys; but their braves did not like it.

They asked us to tell them about the Crow fight. When we had finished our story, they decided that we would have "a big play fight about this fight."

For two weeks we held our contests of strength and skill, played our war games and swapped ponies. All this while our fathers were taking part in the various dances which lead up to the big Sun Dance. Tom-toms were booming every hour of the day. And our fathers were gathered in big groups throughout the campus going through the rhythmic dances of their "secret societies."

At night pairs of warriors would wrap one blanket about themselves and with arms around each other's shoulders, would walk out onto the dark prairies, chanting the dolorous wail of the Sun Dance song. They were "Blood Brothers" and they were praying for one another. Every Indian warrior has a "Blood Brother" whom he adopts as a brother when young, and these brothers stick to one another throughout their lives, on and off the war-path, and each is ready at any moment to give his life for the other. They have absolutely no secrets between them, and they become closer to one another than they are to their own brothers. The "Blood Brother" relationship is perhaps the finest, the most unselfish, the most sacrificing and the cleanest relationship that has ever been developed by the human being.

"Heh-h-h, heh-h-h, heh, hie, ho, hie-h-h!" All through the long, dark, starry night we hear this plaintive wail coming to our ears from away out on the broad depths of the plains—the Sun Dance song. We children sleep little during these nights; for there are all sorts of mysterious rites going on in the camp. Certain rites preceding the Sun Dance can be carried out only after midnight, such as the "fixing" of the great *Saam Okuuinuns*—medicine pipes —big pipes wrapped up in many swathings like a corpse, which have not seen the light of day in more than four hundred years. These pipes must be opened only in the darkest darkness of the night, and no one but the medicine-man can touch them. When they are to be passed on to a new keeper for the year, that keeper must be sneaked up on by the medicine-man and his assistants, while he is asleep, and carried out of the teepee while he is still slumbering, to some mysterious medicine tent, where the ancient pipe is opened and smoked and passed on to him for one year. Fortunate is the person into whose keeping one of these famous pipes is entrusted; for they are said to bring good luck.

All during these nights we hear the padded thud of moccasined feet as these mysterious groups of braves make their way through the darkness to some unknown destination. Never a word. Sometimes we boys would raise the side of the teepee and peer out, and we would see six of these tall, blanketed figures creeping stealthily through the dark camp, bearing some queer-looking object between them. And as a soft wind whistled through the door of the teepee, we would lie on our backs, wide awake, looking up at the stars through the round opening at the top of the teepee—and perhaps become a little scared of great mysterious things that pervaded our life in those days.

But the night that we liked best was the last night preceding the actual opening of the Sun Dance. The big camp would be a blaze of light. Every teepee would have a big crackling fire blazing inside it. To walk outside and look at the camp one would think that it was several hundred huge colored lanterns sitting out on the prairie. Much noise prevailed inside these teepees. Good cheer was everywhere. Everybody was happy. Just like the night before the white man's Christmas.

Our father would come into the teepee and say something cheerful to our mother, and then, as he sat down to get his Sun Dance regalia fixed up for the morrow, he would look at us children and say: "Hah! Tomorrow is the big day. . . . Nobody sleeps tonight in this camp. Hah-h-h. Big day, tomorrow!" Then, his face wreathed with good cheer, he would commence singing his medicine song as he went about the task of dressing, getting our mother to repair his regalia and whiten the buckskin with pumice stone.

We youngsters would keep awake as long as we could, then we would drop off to sleep with the crackling music of the fire in our ears. Daylight would just be peeping into the teepee from above, when we would be awakened by what in those days

was the sweetest music I had ever heard—my father
softly chanting his medicine song. We would turn
on our pallets and look over, half-dazed by sleep, to
see what it was; and there, in front of a cheerful
early-morning fire, would be our father still pulling
at his ermine tails and porcupine quills, and smiling
contentedly to himself. I used to lie and watch him
from under the blanket for several minutes, but that
smile never left his face—not even when he laid
down his regalia and started to dress his long braids
of hair. He was happy.

Then something else would reach us: come to our
noses this time. It would be the fragrant smell of
venison being cooked over the fire by our mother.
Softly she would address an occasional remark to
my father, and he would answer her in the stately
guttural baritone of our language, which has the odd
power to be used very harshly or very softly. But
the gentle modulation of voice and inflection which
my father used with my mother, when alone with
her like this, will never leave my memory.

As we awakened more fully and our ears grew
accustomed to more distant sounds, we would find
that the whole camp was a bedlam of noise. From
every teepee came the rhythmic chant of a medicine
song. In other teepees little groups had already
gathered around a tom-tom and were beating it softly
and singing as the camp was preparing for breakfast.

And through all this noise would come to us the occasional gruff, deep-chested announcements of the "camp crier" as he made the round of the camp, crying out orders from the chief and the medicine-man.

About half an hour before noon we would hear a big commotion, and then we would see twelve young warriors racing into the camp on horseback, dragging behind them the freshly cut evergreens which would be thrown over the skeleton of the Sun Dance lodge at a given signal from the medicine-man. And a little later two men, dressed in special regalia, would come galloping into camp with an eagle's nest, which would be placed at the top of the Sun Dance pole.

At high noon, just as the sun arrived directly overhead, the medicine-man would give the signal for the erection of the lodge.

That was the signal for the cut-loose. Never has one heard such a noise as that which prevails for the next fifteen minutes until the lodge is completed. As fifty men work frantically on the big evergreen enclosure, a hundred warriors come galloping into the campus, shooting, yelling, and racing madly around and around the lodge, while many hundreds of others join in the din with rattles, bells, whistles, and shouting and singing. Children run here and there to dodge the heels of the flying horses. Our parents have forgotten us completely; they have been lost in the excitement of the one big moment of the year. The smell of powder smoke and sweating horses fairly sting our nostrils.

Midst this uproar the Sun Dance woman, who has been fasting in a special teepee for five days, comes out and takes her seat beside the medicine-man just behind the big lodge, which is now going up with startling speed. Before this woman all of the young braves who are to go through the tortures of the Sun Dance come and bow down to be anointed with black paint on their faces and around their wrists.

Then, suddenly, the medicine-man gets up and runs inside the lodge and grabs the eagle's nest. He goes to the foot of the Sun Dance pole, which is still lying on the ground beside a deep hole, and paints a series of black rings around it with the palm of his hand. When he gets up to the top of the pole he draws his blanket completely over him in a squatting position, and thus hidden from view, fastens the nest at the top of the pole. Then comes the final part of building the lodge: five braves rush up and grab the big pole, with the medicine-man still clinging to the top, and set it up in the hole. The medicine-man is now about fifteen feet above the ground, and if he should fall, that would be a sign that the sun did not look favorably upon the dance, and all proceedings would be stopped at once. But we never saw that happen.

MANY SHOTS
Blackfoot Who Has Been Through the Sun
Dance Seven Times

SUN DANCE CAMP
Of the Northern Blackfeet on the Historic Sun Dance Flats,
South of Gleichen, Alberta

Now comes the interesting part of the Sun Dance. All of the young men who are to be made "braves," come walking into the lodge, stripped down to their breech-cloths. The medicine-man drops from his precarious perch at the top of the pole and goes to his medicine paraphernalia and takes out a long, sharp knife and several hundred feet of rawhide thong. He takes up a position beside the small medicine fire, and one by one the young men come before him and kneel.

The medicine-man runs the sharp knife into the left breast of the man in front of him and makes a long, deep gash. Then he pulls it out and makes a similar gash about an inch and a half from the first one. Now he runs the knife under the flesh between these two gashes, and while he holds his finger in the connecting hole, he reaches down with the other hand and picks up a stout rawhide thong about three feet long and draws it through the hole. He then ties the flesh up tightly and with his knife repeats the operation on the right breast, using the other end of the thong to tie it up with. When this is done the young man, who has not yet uttered a sound, has one rawhide thong "sewed" into his chest at both ends. The medicine-man now takes a heavier thong, many feet long, and ties one end to the thong in the young man's chest and the other end to the Sun Dance pole.

And it is now that the young aspiring brave begins his dance. He gets up and starts his dance while the next man comes and kneels before the medicine-man. As the drums boom to the singing of the Sun Dance song, the young man dances and jerks upon the long thong, trying to pull out the flesh which it holds and free himself. He dances on and on, jerking with all his might.

Sometimes they danced many hours without being able to free themselves. If the young man lasted all this time without fainting, the medicine-man would order a warrior to come into the lodge on a pony, and he would untie the thong from the pole and fasten it to the horse. The warrior would then race around and around the lodge, dragging the young man behind him in an effort to release the flesh. We children would run in and jump on and off the young man's back as he was dragged around, to increase the weight. If this did not free him, the warrior would back his horse up several feet and then send it forward with a sudden rush—and "swish"—a sickly sound of rending flesh, and the young man would get up, if he could, with his chest hanging with blood and torn muscles. The medicine-man would "doctor" him for a moment with native herbs, and then the young man went his way —now a brave. He had proved his salt, and the tribe would now allow him to go out on the war-path as a full-fledged warrior. Indians would not permit a young man to go on the war-path against an enemy until he had gone through this ordeal, lest he should disgrace the tribe by showing cowardice. Any man who failed to go through the dance until he pulled the flesh loose or fainted in the attempt was never allowed to rank as a brave, nor to fight as a warrior.

On the day following the Sun Dance—the last day of the camp—a dance was held which was somewhat similar to the I Saw Dance, only on a much larger scale. Two of the greatest warriors of the tribe were asked to reenact their most dangerous encounter with an enemy on the war-path.

A near tragedy followed the above Sun Dance when one of our warriors—the medicine-man Chief Atsistamokon—attempted to add a little too much reality to his enactment.

Among the "foreign" tribes who had come to witness our Sun Dance was a band of Crees under Chief Pretty-Young-Man. Our chief, Atsistamokon, had had a very famous fight with Pretty-Young-Man ten years before while down in what is now Montana, and in this fight they had nearly killed one another. When the head chief of the Blackfeet asked Atsistamokon to reenact this battle, Atsistamokon thought it would be a good idea to get Pretty-Young-Man himself to take the part in it which he had actually played.   When asked about it, Chief Pretty-Young-Man said that he would.   So the Blackfeet invited all of the Crees under Pretty-Young-Man to come over and witness this unique encounter.   The visiting Crees had been camping a little way from our Sun Dance camp, but now they all moved over and pitched their teepees right among those of the Blackfeet.

The fight which Pretty-Young-Man and Atsistamokon were going to reenact was a very famous encounter in the recent history of the Blackfeet and the Crees.   Atsistamokon was leading a Blackfoot war party against the Crees under Chief Pretty-Young-Man.   They met south of the Cypress Hills in Montana.   In the bloody battle that ensued Chief Pretty-Young-Man managed to trap Chief Atsistamokon so that he could neither get out of the pocket that had been prepared for him nor get back to his warriors.

There was only one course left to Chief Atsistamokon and that was to risk a desperate, wild dash straight through the big Cree camp and trust to luck for the safety of his life.   Atsistamokon had already killed two Crees who had come out on horseback and attempted to kill him in his trap, and he well realized the danger of the bold move that he was about to make.

He mounted one of the dead Crees' horses, slung

his bow and arrows over his shoulder, and holding his big battle-ax as a weapon, he gave a war-cry and shot the pony forward as fast as it would go, straight toward the Cree camp. The Cree warriors heard his yell, and when they saw him coming they jumped on their ponies and brandished their weapons in readiness for the slaughter. He rode through a veritable shower of arrows and bullets; and the Crees were so flabbergasted at his failure to fall that they remained in their tracks for a moment, apparently too surprised to grasp the situation and take up the immediate chase of their disappearing quarry.

But Chief Pretty-Young-Man came dashing right on his heels, mounted on the fastest pony among the tribe. He overtook Atsistamokon, rode alongside him, raised his muzzle-loader and fired at him at pointblank range. Atsistamokon ducked and grabbed hold of the muzzle-loader and with the other hand he struck Pretty-Young-Man a terrific blow over the head with his battle-ax. As Pretty-Young-Man sagged and started to drop to the ground, Atsistamokon threw away his battle-ax, caught the mane of his enemy's racing steed, and with one foot pushed the limp form from the back of the horse and vaulted over onto it himself.

He could hear the Crees coming after him. The only defense he had left was his bow and arrows, but he knew that he would not need these; for he was now mounted on the fastest horse the Crees owned.

He left them behind like a dart. And when he returned to his own camp, all of his tribesmen came running out, wanting to know where he got the horse. While they were surging about him, his brother Chief Many Swan walked up to him and pulled three arrows out of his back.

This was the spectacular encounter which Atsistamokon and Chief Pretty-Young-Man were now going to "go over again, to show the people what it was like."

While all of the five tribes present were gathering to witness the spectacle of which they had so often heard, Pretty-Young-Man went over to his teepee to undress for the momentous event.

While he was undressing he said to his wife:

"I have not yet made peace in my heart with Atsistamokon and I am going really to kill him."

And, as he was uttering these words, she saw him take up his muzzle-loader and load it with real lead instead of the wad of buffalo hair which she had laid out for him.

His wife was very frightened, and when Pretty-Young-Man stepped out of the teepee for a moment to go into the bush, she ran up to the head chief's teepee and told him what Pretty-Young-Man had said. The head chief of the Crees returned with her. He went into the teepee and picked up Pretty-Young-Man's gun and took two large round leaden balls out of it, and stuffed in a wad of buffalo hair.

The Blackfeet had known nothing of this.

The Crees all came on over to the Sun Dance lodge, where twenty Cree braves were already on horseback, ready to act out their part of the encounter between Atsistamokon and Pretty-Young-Man.

We boys were all gathered around closely, so that we could get every detail of the famous affair and fight it over ourselves at the first opportunity.

Atsistamokon was sitting on his horse talking with the Cree warriors, when presently Chief Pretty-Young-Man came galloping out into the arena, mounted on a beautiful little piebald stallion, exactly like the one which Atsistamokon had taken from him. When our old warriors saw the resemblance, they uttered a mild exclamation:

"Hanh-h-h-h," they breathed—and placing their two forefingers alongside each other, they looked at their Cree companions and said in Cree: *"Peguin— Tapiskoots—mist-atim!*—Exactly the same—the horse!"

The Crees placed their forefingers together (meaning in the sign language "the same") and looked over at the Blackfeet and nodded their agreement with a broad, friendly smile.

Pretty-Young-Man, without taking any notice of

Atsistamokon, rode over to the mounted Crees and told them how to act—what they were to do; and then, in a manner that indicated that he was anxious to get down to business, he sent a messenger to Atsistamokon to tell him that he could now go down to the far end of the arena, and he would send down the two Cree warriors whom he was to "kill."

Everything went off very well until the battle came to the point where Pretty-Young-Man took up the chase of Atsistamokon as he made his mad dash through their camp—then something happened that made us gasp.

As Atsistamokon raced past Pretty-Young-Man, the latter turned his horse with a jerk and in a moment he was right alongside our Blackfoot hero. As he paced his horse slightly in front of Atsistamokon, he turned in his saddle, raised his gun to a pointblank level with Atsistamokon's face—and pulled the trigger. *"Crack!"* Right into his face he fired!

We saw blood dripping from our hero's features, but to our utter surprise, he went on with the battle as if nothing had happened. He merely turned in his seat, raised his heavy battle-ax and brought it down on Pretty-Young-Man's head with the same terrific force that he had used in the actual battle, and—blunk!—Pretty-Young-Man hit the ground and lay there as numb and still as he had been ten years before.

When we saw this, we thought that we were going to have a big fight. But the Crees all jumped up and shouted:

"*Mewasin! Mewasin!*—It is good! It is good!"

And their head chief came over and shook hands with Atsistamokon and our chiefs; and he told Atsistamokon that he had "done what was right." He then told the Blackfeet that the Crees were going to hold a big dance in their honor that night, and he invited us all to come over.

Atsistamokon's face was only burnt with powder, and though he carried the blue powder marks the rest of his life, he was not injured otherwise.

That night at the Cree dance, Chief Pretty-Young-Man got up and came over to where Atsistamokon was sitting. He stood before him for a moment, then he stuck out his hand and said:

"It seems that we cannot fight any more, now, Atsistamokon; so I suppose we shall have to be friends."

Atsistamokon took his hand, and said, "I suppose we shall."

And that ended the feud.

A small group of friendly Crows had come up from the Missouri River to attend our Sun Dance that year. During the Cree dance that night the chief of our band went over to the chief of the Crows and asked him if he had lately seen what we called

the *Okotoks Isahpo*—the Stone Band of Crows—
our enemy. The Crow chief said that they had just
lately left them camping on the Upper Missouri.
Our chief then asked him if he had seen or heard
them say anything of a Blackfoot warrior named
Roving Night Eagle who was lost to us in our last
fight with the *Okotoks Isahpo*. The Crow chief
said that they had told him all about that fight, but
they had said nothing of taking a prisoner from the
Blackfeet.

Our chief then presumed that Roving Night
Eagle must have been killed, and he notified his
relatives that he was dead.

The next day we had a warrior's funeral for Roving Night Eagle. His wife and brothers were presented with the finest horse in the tribe, to be "sent
to the Spirit World" for the use of our dead brave.
They took this horse a few hundred yards out on the
prairie and shot it. Then they broke up a bow and
a quiver of arrows and a gun, and wrapped them in
a buffalo robe and left them there beside the horse.
We burned some good food, too, so that the spirit
of the food and other destroyed instruments might
go on to the land of the living dead as presents to
our departed warrior.

His widow gashed herself in the thighs with a
sharp buffalo knife, in mourning the loss of her renowned husband; and all of the women painted their

faces black. This meant that we must battle again with the Isahpos, to avenge the death of one of the greatest marksmen our nation had produced. It was an immutable law that all deaths must sometime be avenged by a relative of the deceased, even though that relative might know for a certainty that he would be killed in the effort. We had thought that we had evened up our score with the Isahpos and that perhaps we would never have to fight them again, but the Fates had now decreed otherwise. The death of Roving Night Eagle must be avenged!

IX

White Foreheads

THE Northern Siksikau band of the Blackfeet
said the *Apekwan*—the Hudson's Bay Company—had a post over in the Rockies where they
traded gunpowder and "white man's food" for buffalo robes; and since we had a lot of good robes with
us that we had taken on our hunt, they told us to go
there and "do some trading." Our chief decided
that we would.

So the next day when the big Sun Dance camp
broke up and all of the tribes started for their favorite hunting grounds, we headed west toward the
Rockies, whose snow-covered peaks we could already
see from the Sun Dance flats.

We children looked forward to seeing some white
people. We had seen only a few men, and we had
never been able to go up close and get a good look
at them. And we wondered what their boys would
look like, and their women; for we had never seen
any of these.

Most of the traders who had come to us had been
half-breeds, and we knew them by the Sioux word

Itey-skada, which meant "White Foreheads." That was the name the Indians called them, because their faces were always brown and their foreheads were white. This was perhaps due to the fact that they wore hats, and the sun brought out the Indian tan only in the exposed parts of their faces.

We traveled along the Namaka until we came to the foot-hills of the Rockies, and here we came upon the Suksiseoketuk Indians—the Rocky Mountain Band of Assiniboines—whose hunting-grounds were up there in the foot-hill country. Their chief, Chief Travels-Against-the-Wind, asked us who we were.

"We are roving *Seeha-sapa* from the plains, whose only enemy is the *Okotoks Isahpo*—the Rock Band of Crows," our chief answered.

The Suksiseoketuk chief then said:

"We no longer come down onto your plains to hunt your buffalo. Why do you come into our hills to hunt our mountain-goats and sheep and moose?"

"Our meat for the winter," said our chief, "is already put away in those bags you see the women carrying [pemmican]. We come not to hunt your wild goats. We come to hunt your *wah-shee-chu*— white men—from whom you have secured those fine white blankets you are wearing, with the red and black stripes in them."

"*Ha-h! Neena-washtay—washtaydo. Amba wastaytch, Seeha-sapa!*—Oh! Very good—exceptionally good. Howdy do, Blackfeet," said the Suksi-seoketuk chief.

Then he told our chief to tell his tribesmen to get off their ponies and sit down and he would have the Suksiseoketuk women make us some of the white man's *minne-seeha*—"black water," or tea. And the chief said that while we were drinking of it he would tell us about the white man.

We had never had tea before, and we youngsters did not like it; it was bitter. The chief said that the Hudson's Bay Company had traded it for some of their skins—and they seemed to like this tea. Our old people liked it, too.

But we boys were very interested in what the chief told us about the white man. He told us to beware of his food; as it would make our teeth come out. He told us about the bread and the sweets which the white man ate, and he pulled up his upper lip and said:

"*Wambadahka*—Behold—my teeth are good, and so are the teeth of all our old people; but behold," he said, walking over to a young boy and pulling up his lip, "behold, these teeth of the young people are not good—too much white man's food. Our people, like yours, never used to die until they were over a hundred years old. Now, since we started to eat that white man's food we are sick all of the time. We keep getting worse and soon it will kill us all."

And then the chief reached up and took hold of a shock of his hair at the top of his head, and he said:

"*Payheeh*—hair—the white man has none of this on top of his head. The crown of his head is as slick as the nose of a buffalo. Every time the Indian eats he wipes grease into his hair. White man wash it all out with bad medicine—soap—take all grease out and make all of his hair drop off. Swap your buffalo robes for the white man's blankets and gunpowder, but take not of his food," said the chief, "nor of his 'bad medicine' for washing your hair."

Then, sweeping his hand towards the tall peaks of the snow-capped Rockies, the chief said:

"We Nakota Indians [their own name for themselves, meaning "friends"] were raised on top of these mountains, with the prairies far below us. The Prairie Indians look upon us as the 'High People.' They say, 'The Nakotas are wise like the animals; they stay up in the high mountains where the clear, healthy winds blow.' "

"Ho!" This exclamation was uttered by another Suksiseoketuk chief, who got up and said:

"Though the Nakotas sometimes put fear in the hearts of the Prairie Indians, they are not wise. You Blackfeet are wise. We Nakotas, when we go down on the plains among the enemy, we Nakotas trudge along like this," he said, walking a few steps like a careless individual. "But you Blackfeet, you are wise. You go about like this"—assuming a low, crouching stalk—"just like coyotes," he added with a twinkle in his eye, "you Blackfeet, you see everything, but nobody ever sees you."

Our braves laughed at this—and the Nakotas joined in on a hearty, general laugh at the cunning tactics of our warriors.

The Suksiseoketuk chief told us that if we would camp on the flats across the river that night, he would send a party of his tribesmen along with us the next day, to guide us to the "Long Flagpole," which is the name they had given the trading post on account of a tall pole with a flag at its top that stood in front of it. Our chief accepted this offer, and we pitched our camp there that night.

The next day we started north, accompanied by fifty of the Suksiseoketuk warriors. We traveled for six days, keeping always to the edge of the foot-hills. On the sixth day the Suksiseoketuks told us to pitch our camp at a point we had reached late in the afternoon, and they would send over a messenger to tell the white people at the trading post that we were there to see them.

After we had pitched our camp, several of our warriors went out to see if they could find some otter, which were plentiful in that part of the northland. While they were out they came upon a cabin, and they saw six long-haired people with light skin,

going in and out of this place. Our warriors sat
down and watched them and tried to figure out what
they were; they had never seen any people like them
before. They were not Indians and they were not
white men; so one of our warriors, Big Darkness,
said that they must be the white man's woman—their
wives—white women! They had never seen any
white women before; so they all agreed that that
must be what they were.

But when they came back to camp and told the
others about it, another of our warriors, Sun Calf,
who had seen the woman, changed his mind and said
that he did not believe they were white women after
all; they were "some other kind of people," he said.

This started an argument which became so heated
that our chief was afraid that it would lead to a
fight. So he said the best way to settle the dispute
was for the two warriors to put up a bet, and then go
over and capture one of the "strange beings" and
bring it back, and the camp would decide what they
were.

The men led out five ponies each and bet them on
their respective beliefs. And when darkness came
ten of our warriors, including Big Darkness and Sun
Calf, crept over to the shack and overpowered one of
the "strange beings" and brought it back.

When they returned to our camp, we were waiting
around a big fire singing, so that the disturbance

would not attract the trading post. They led a scared-looking "being" to the edge of the fire, and Big Darkness exclaimed to the throng:

"Now look. Is it not a woman?"

Half of the tribe believed that it was a woman, and the other half said that it was not. The confusion of the argument which followed grew so noisy that it awoke some of the Suksiseoketuk warriors who had their camp about a hundred yards away, and they came over to see what was going on.

They stopped and listened for a moment, and then they began to laugh. They laughed for a long time before they would tell us what they were laughing at. And then one of them said:

"Inexperienced Blackfeet! It is neither a white woman nor any kind of being that you have ever seen before. It is a man from across the *Minne-Tonka*," and he waved his arm toward the Pacific Ocean.

It was a Chinaman! One of the Chinese employed as cooks by some white prospectors.

The next morning the white minister at the Hudson's Bay Post sent word to the Indians that he was coming over to visit them. The Suksiseoketuk told us that he was going to tell us about the white man's *Wahkantonka*, his Great Spirit.

When they received this news of the coming of the minister, all of the Indians painted their faces and put on all of their best medicine clothes. The medicine-man got out his drum, and soon we were all ready to receive him.

When we saw the minister coming, the medicine-man started to beat his tom-tom and sing one of his medicine songs; for he thought that would please the visitor who represented the white man's "medicine" and Great Spirit. Our chief went out and met the minister and shook his hand, and then he took him over to meet our minister, the medicine-man.

After they shook hands, the minister made a speech. He told our medicine-man that he was preaching something not worth while. He said:

"I didn't mean for you people to fix up like this; I meant for you to wash the paint off your faces and put your medicine drums away. There is only one God in Heaven, and I am here to tell you about Him."

Indians never interrupt anyone when he is talking, even if he should talk all day—that is an ancient courtesy among Indians—so everyone stood and listened to the minister while he told us of the white man's God. He made a long speech. He said that the Indians must lay down their arms and live peaceably alongside the white man who was coming into his country.

When the missionary finished his speech, our chief arose and addressed him. He said:

"Why do you tell us to be good? We Indians are

not bad; you white people may be, but we are not.
We do not steal, except when our horses have been
raided; we do not tell lies; we take care of our old
and our poor when they are helpless. We do not
need that which you tell us about."

"But," said the missionary, "there is only one
God, and you must worship him."

"Then if that is true," said our chief, "we Indians
are worshiping the same God that you are—only in
a different way. When the Great Spirit, God, made
the world He gave the Indians one way to worship
Him and He gave the white man another way, because we are different people and our lives are different. The Indian should keep to his way and the
white man to his, and we should all work with one
another for God and not against one another. The
Indian does not try to tell you how you should worship God. We like to see you worship Him in your
way, because we know you understand that way."

"But the Great Spirit you speak of is not the same
one that we worship," said the missionary.

"Then there must be two Gods," said the chief.
"Your God made a land for you far across the 'big
water.' He gave you houses to live in, good things
to eat and fast things to travel in. He gave the
Indian the teepee to live in and the buffalo to feed
on. But you white people did not like the land that
your God gave you, and you came over here to take

the Indians' land. If you did that, how do we know, if we should accept your God, that He won't take everything from us, too, when we die and go to your Hunting Grounds."

"But the Indians must learn how to pray," said the minister.

"We do pray," replied our chief. "This is the prayer that we pray at our Sun Dance (Thanksgiving):

" 'Great Spirit, our Father, help us and teach us in the way of the truth; and keep me and my family and my tribe on our True Father's path, so that we may be in good condition in our minds and in our bodies. Teach all of the little ones in your way. Make peace on all the world. We thank You for the Sun and the good summer weather again; and we hope they will bring good crops of grass for the animals, and things to eat for all peoples.' "

While we were talking like this, a white man came over and said that the trading post was ready for us to come over and trade with them. So our chief and medicine-man shook hands with the minister and thanked him for coming over and talking with us. Then we all mounted our ponies and rode over to the post, about two miles away.

As we rode into the post we passed some stables with some cows in them. We had never been around cows before, and the smell of them made us sick.

We all had to hold our hands over our noses as we rode by this stable. We youngsters had always thought that the cow would smell strong like the buffalo, but they smelled sweet, like milk; and that made us want to vomit.

When we arrived at the post the traders came out to meet us. The white men came up to our fathers and started talking with them through the interpreter, a Suksiseoketuk. We boys had never been close to white people before; so while they were talking with our fathers, we and some of our braves walked up behind them and smelled of them to see what they smelled like. They smelled different from the Indians; they smelled like those cattle, and it made us sick.

Then they invited us to have a big feast with them. They brought out a lot of food. But we could not eat it. Everything they had tasted as those cows smelled. Their tea had cow's milk in it; cow's butter was on their bread, and its cream covered their cakes; and the meat they gave us to eat was cow's meat. Everything cow! Some of our braves got very sick and went out into the bush. We remembered what the Suksiseoketuk chief had told us about keeping away from the white man's food, and we thought at that moment that it was the taste which killed the Indians. It turned our stomachs up, and we could not keep it down.

After the "feast," which did not last long, the white people started to bring out their wares to trade with us for our buffalo robes and ermine. They brought out a lot of things we had never seen before —flour, molasses, bread, axes, tools, and so on. Our chief thought that the molasses was grease, and when a barrel was rolled out in front of him he reached down into it and brought up two handfuls and rubbed it into his hair, saying: "Ah, this will make good grease for the hair." We thought that the flour was snow and that the bread was tree-canker; and we did not care to trade any of our robes for these.

What our braves wanted most of all was ball and powder for their guns. They kept asking for this, but the traders kept bringing out other things. Finally some of our warriors asked the Suksiseoketuk interpreter where they kept their powder and ball, and he pointed to a building. And this brave said, "Come on, we will go over there and show them what we want."

All of the braves went over and crowded into this shed. There was a white man inside, and he got scared; he thought the Indians wanted the ammunition so that they could attack the fort at the post. He walked over to a big pile of black, shiny stuff, and he picked up a handful of it and held it out to our chief and said through the interpreter:

"Do you know what this is?"

Our chief said, "No, what's that stuff?"

"That's gunpowder," said the trader.

"Gunpowder?" queried our chief.

"Yes, gunpowder. Make sure of it; feel of it," he said handing it to the chief.

The chief held out his two hands and it was poured into his palms. As he stood there looking at it, the trader said, pointing to the huge pile of powder on the floor:

"That's quite a lot of powder; isn't it?"

The chief nodded his head.

"You know that one inch of powder will kill a deer; don't you?"

"Yes."

"Well, you can imagine what would happen if I should set that whole pile off. And that is what I am going to do if you try to start any trouble—I'll give one shot and kill the whole crowd!"

"*Tsumahts*," said the chief, looking at the interpreter.

"What did he say?" asked the trader.

"He wants one of your wooden matches," said the interpreter.

"What for?" asked the trader.

"He says he wants to put that handful of powder on the floor and light it and see if it is good powder before giving you any of his robes for it."

The trader's face turned ashen. He threw the box of matches he was holding, at the interpreter and shouted: "Run! And let nothing stop you until you throw them into the creek!"

But before the Suksiseoketuk could make a remark, our chief raised his hand to the interpreter and with a chuckle in his throat, he said:

"Stay! Tell the white man that the Blackfoot likes a little joke, too. Tell him that when the Blackfoot goes on the war-path he pulls off his clothes and paints himself. Now, let him tell us how much of this powder he will give us for each buffalo robe —and we will want some blankets, too."

Summoning a smile, the trader said:

"We heard last night that you were marauding Indians—some prospectors told us that you had raided their cookhouse. But it seems that there is a mistake about this."

Whereupon, the Suksiseoketuk interpreter laughed and told the trader what had happened with the Chinese cook. He laughed hard at this odd happening. And then he said:

"I have had all of this powder put out here for nothing. Come on, friends, with your robes, and we will give you a good bargain."

We left that post with enough powder to kill all of the animals on the prairies. Our spare horses were loaded with balls and powder and blankets.

X

Sheep, Goats, and Mountain-Lions

HAVING traded nearly every one of our buffalo robes for balls and powder, guns and blankets, our chief said that we would soon be facing winter without sufficient furs to keep us warm; and he began to look around for a good hunting-ground. He liked those "white man's blankets" for their looks, but he did not think that they would keep us warm in the severe weather which we should have to face when we got back onto the plains. He asked the Suksiseoketuk braves if there were any hunting-grounds in the Rockies where we could hunt without breaking our word with their head chief. They told us that we could get plenty of mountain sheep and goats, and lynx, bear, fox, wolves and mountain-lions if we would go a little way into the interior of the mountains. They advised him to go down to the Kootenay and Flathead country (north of what is now Idaho), for those tribes were their enemies, and the Suksiseoketuks would not care how much we hunted in those regions of the mountains, they told us.

The Suksiseoketuk lent us two of their guides to take us over the Great Divide in the Rockies; and when they got us over the Rockies and onto a high plateau which ran between the Rockies and the Coast Range, they left us and told us to keep going south, where we would find all of the wild game we needed.

It was the first time we youngsters had been away inside the Rockies, and we marveled at the thousands of feet of solid walls of rock which we saw on all sides as we camped, traveled, and camped. Though it was still late summer, we crossed several high divides where the snow was so deep that we nearly lost some of our ponies. They got stuck to their bellies in the snow, and we had to pull them out by hitching other ponies to them and dragging them over the snow until they could get a footing. But when we got on the plateau it was very hot and dry, and there was plenty of bunch-grass for our ponies to graze on.

One day we forded a mountain river, and when we came out on the other side we were right in the camp of another tribe of Indians. We did not know who they were, and they did not know us. They were not like any Indians we had seen before. They were not tall, compared to our braves, who were six feet and over; and they had large heads and short legs; their clothes were different—no feathers—and they were camping in teepees made of dried grass matting. Their faces were not as dark and red as ours.

When they saw us they did not act like other Indians: they smiled and looked friendly right away. And their children did not stand around aloof and look stolidly at us as the "stranger Indians" on the plains did; they came right up to us and began talking, though we could not understand them.

Our chief started talking to them in the sign language, but one of their men who seemed to be a chief waved that he did not understand that language. But he went into a teepee and came out with a crippled fellow—he had a bent leg—and he led him up to our chief and motioned with his hands for him to talk again. This fellow understood the sign language. He said that this was the camp of the Shuswap tribe, but that he himself was a Kootenay who had married one of their women, and that was why he could speak the sign language. The Kootenays were our enemies whom we had fought many times.

We did not have to tell him that we were Blackfeet from the plains; for he discerned that from our moccasins, which had separate soles unlike the mountain Indian's, and he also noticed how we combed our hair—straight back on top and then braided down on either side. It was by the way we combed our hair that all other tribes knew that we were not Sioux, whom we resembled physically. The difference was that the Sioux warriors parted their hair in the middle like our women, without leaving a roach combed back on top—and for that reason we called the Sioux *Kah-es-pah*, meaning that they "parted their hair in the middle."

This Kootenay said:

"I see you are not Sioux by your hair and moccasins. If you were you would not be welcome here in the Shuswap camp. They are not friends of the Suksiseoketuk." The Suksiseoketuk were an off-shoot of the Sioux.

He asked us what we wanted, and our chief told him that we were out to hunt game. And then this Kootenay turned to the Shuswap chief and said something. Again he turned his address to our chief. He said:

"The chief of the Shuswaps says this: 'We are the allies of the Kootenays. We and the Kootenays control all of the country south of here as far as a man can travel in fifteen days. We ask you not to hunt on our grounds. But we will tell you where to go north of here and get plenty of game. Tell us what you want, and we will tell you where to go.' "

Our chief told him, and then he called our three scouts to listen to the Shuswap chief's instructions.

When this was over, the Shuswap chief told us

that we would all have to have snow-shoes if we
went north; for we would have to travel over deep
snow before we returned. And so a bargain was
made through which we traded some of our fine
ponies for all the snow-shoes the Shuswaps had.

So, after we had rested here for a day, we started
north up the mountainous plateau, into a country
none of us had ever seen before.

After we traveled for about ten days we found
plenty of mountain sheep and goats. The sheep
were easy to hunt and kill, but the goats were almost
impossible to reach. While the sheep grazed in
herds along the slopes of the mountains, the goats
perched themselves singly, away up thousands of
feet above us on the sides of solid walls of rock. To
us, as we traveled along the sides of the mountains,
they looked like little white dots, so high were they
above us. They fed off the moss growing on the
rocks, while the sheep liked to graze from the ground
in the lower levels. The sheep meat was good, but
we were after the pelts of the goats; for the mountain-goat has wool on its pelt while the sheep does
not—just the opposite of the domestic variety of
sheep and goat.

However, we made up our supply of heavy pelts
by getting a number of grizzly bears. They were
easier to hunt at this time of the year; for they were
already getting fat and sleepy for their hibernation.

We made big camps and stayed there for days while our warriors went out to hunt.

While our mothers spent most of their time curing the pelts and making them into robes, clothing, and buckskin, we boys spent our time catching marmots and mountain-gophers. We could run and catch the big, fat whistling marmot, but the gopher, a bigger brother of our prairie-dog, was more wary. We had to set a trap for him. He was so suspicious that every time he came out of his hole he would first stick his head out and peer around in every direction before hopping out. So we made long lariats out of buckskin thongs and left a loose loop at one end. We would place this loop around the top of the gopher hole and lie and wait until he stuck his head out. Then we would jerk the lariat quickly and catch him by the neck in a noose. When we had caught several gophers at the end of these thongs we would drag them back to camp and let them battle with our dogs.

One day we got a big surprise that nearly cost one of our lives. We saw a big hole and thought it was the hole of a marmot. So we laid our noose around it and waited. Presently a large, brown shaggy head came out of the hole, and we gave a quick jerk. There was a terrible yell, which sounded more human than anything I have heard from an animal, and—

When we got our first look at the thing we had pulled from the hole we nearly dropped with fright. It was something we had never seen before. With terrible teeth and claws, a dark brown, shaggy thing came at us like a streak of lightning. Fortunately we had three big wolf-dogs with us, and they made a dash for it. Evidently the dogs had never seen this animal before, either; for it turned from us and went straight at these fierce, gnarling brutes—a thing which we had never seen any other animal dare to do. In a flash the animal had one of the dogs by the throat, and it wheeled over on its back and fairly tore the head off of this dog before the others could reach it.

The other two dogs, *Ponoka* and *Nisitsi-Stumiks* (Elk and Five Bulls), flashed into the fray with their tails lashing the ground, and we stood, too scared to move, and watched the whirling mêlée. It was the most thrilling battle I had even seen—just a whirling mass of tawny hair and brown wool. Blood splattered everywhere, and those unearthly human wails kept coming to us from this terrible demon of the forests, as he rolled and plunged and fought like a dozen wild beasts thrown into one—and yet he was less than half the size of one of our massive wolf-hounds.

When we began to collect our wits we moved backwards and climbed a small cliff and made ready to dash for safety. But we heard something like a man grunting, and we turned and looked and saw Ponoka, the dog that had run down and killed a full-grown elk, sinking his long white fangs into the ruffled throat of the dying beast. With a fierce growl the big wolf-dog, his eyes gleaming vengeance for his slain companion, was swaying wildly from side to side, beating the ground with the thing he had in his mouth.

When finally he shook it and it did not move, he was loath to release it; his vengeance was not yet satisfied. He let it go, seeming to hope that it would move again. When it did not, he made another savage lunge at it and ripped it wide open with one rake of his gleaming teeth. Then he limped over to his dead companion and nosed him and whined and licked the blood from his own dripping legs and whined again. We heard a noise, and saw him leap over a bank out of view. We rushed down, and there in a gully lay Five Bulls, torn and mangled and gone mad with pain.

His eyes were glazed, and as Ponoka tried to approach him he took savage bites at him with his roving head, which looked more like the head of a rattlesnake than that of a dog. Seeming to understand, Ponoka whined and looked at him, and then turned and looked painfully at us. We called him away. He came with us up the bank, but when he saw the ugly, shaggy brute again he grabbed it with a savage growl and tugged and pulled at it until he had drawn it every inch of the way back to our camp.

Consternation swept the camp when they found out what we had brought back with us, unarmed.

It was a wolverine!   The wolverine, the crazy king of the Rockies, the killer of the elk and the bear and the moose—the most dangerous animal known to the Indian.

Our fathers chastised us for pulling things out of holes which we knew nothing about.   And they threatened us with the rawhide lash if we ever went out "hunting" again in that strange region.

North of this place where we were now camping there was a solid wall of rock about two thousand feet high, which began there and ran northwards as far as the eye could reach.   Our fathers said that this massive, grayish-yellow mountain was a mountain-lion range, and they decided to move our camp up near it, where they could bag a few of these big beasts and make themselves some leggings out of their tawny skins.

We moved up there, and remained several days hunting the mountain-lion high up on the dizzy crags of this lofty wall of rock.   Our warriors would climb high up on the narrow paths of the mountain-goat, which had been worn precariously along the side of this perpendicular wall, and along these paths they would seek out the wily mountain-lion as he lay crouched over the path, waiting for a careless goat to come along.

On the second day of the hunt two of our young braves were "working" two goat paths at one time. These two paths ran high up, along the side of the wall, one about fifty feet above the other. One of the braves, Wandering Wolf, was "working" the upper path, while the other, Striped Dog, was stalking the lower one, making it a point to keep in sight of one another at all times. They were several hundred yards apart, with Striped Dog some distance below and ahead of Wandering Wolf.

Once as Wandering Wolf peered down ahead of him to keep his eye on Striped Dog, he noticed something lying just over the path that did not look like a rock—it looked more yellow and brown than the surrounding wall of gray stone. It was lying just a few feet ahead of his companion, and though it did not move he soon perceived that it was an animal. He started to shout a warning to Striped Dog, but before he could catch his ear Striped Dog had approached to within three or four feet of the point over which the strange object was lying. And just as Striped Dog turned his head to look back and up at his shouting companion, Wandering Wolf saw the thing leap down on the path, apparently right onto the shoulders of his unsuspecting comrade.

Summoning all the speed that he could risk along the path of the steep wall, Wandering Wolf hastened to the "switch-back" where the two paths joined in a hair-pin turn, and on to the point where he had last seen Striped Dog. When he reached there Striped Dog was squatted in the path, skinning a mountain-lion.

The lion had jumped down about six feet in front of him, thinking no doubt that he was a goat; and on discovering its mistake was too surprised to move. While it crouched there in front of him Striped Dog had raised his gun and pierced its heart. The lion, a big male, measured about ten feet from the nose to the tip of the tail.

While our mothers were curing the pelts of the few mountain-lions that our braves had been able to kill, a big squall came down from the glacier ahead of us and swept through our camp for fifteen minutes, tearing down our teepees as if they had been made of paper. Trees fell like matches. Two of our teepees caught fire, painfully burning three of our women before they could get out from under them. The poles of our corral were blown off, and our horses stampeded and went careering down the valley in wild confusion. We children were blown about like bits of wood. We would no more than scramble to our feet than the backs of our heads would hit the ground again. At first we yelled and thought we were having a lot of fun, but when we saw the fire and the flying ponies, we got scared and lay on our bellies and kept quiet. The horses came thundering past us, dodging us with the nimbleness of dogs—some of them jumped clear over us, but not one of us was touched.

When the wind had howled for about fifteen minutes, big chunks of wet snow started to splash our faces, and soon a blinding snowstorm was on us. Winter had broken in the Rockies. As the wind slowed up the snow increased.

It snowed all that day and night, and all the next day. Our fathers were out on their snow-shoes, trying to round up the horses, but these had not stopped so soon as the men thought they would. They must have followed the storm with their speed, and kept going until they were exhausted; for not one of them was ever seen again. Perhaps their descendants are still roaming the Rockies among its herds of wild horses.

XI

ROCK THUNDER'S DEATH SONG

NOW, our fathers said, we should have to remain where we were for the winter, or try to reach our distant home on the plains by snow-shoe.

Our women set themselves to work making snow-shoes, copying the type we had secured from the Shuswaps. They made shoes for us boys first, so that we could go out on them and get used to them. This was great fun. Our fathers went out with us to teach us how to walk and run on them, instructing us to keep our knees stiff and move our legs from the hip. Soon we were having snow-shoe races of a hundred yards or more, and were making incredible speed on them, to the great satisfaction of our elders. Then our fathers taught us how to slide down little hills and embankments when we should come to them. We liked this so well that they had to stop us from "practicing" it to excess; for we were wearing out our snow-shoes.

Pretty soon we had all the snow-shoes we needed, with several pairs of spare ones, which our mothers had made with that foresight of preparedness, possessed in the Indian race principally by their women.

We were already thinking of an early moving from this place, when one morning our fathers asked us boys if we had been up during the night on our snow-shoes. We said, "No." And they asked us if we would "swear by the Horn" that we had not. We said that we would. They believed us then and therefore they did not make us go before the Horns; but they were at a loss to find who had been walking about our camp on snow-shoes, on a fresh snow that had fallen in the night. The scouts went out and studied the tracks, and then trailed them for some distance. When they returned they said that the tracks were not made by the kind of snow-shoes we were using; they were longer and more narrow.

While all the camp was still wondering about these tracks, one of our old women, named Wolf's Woman, came running into the camp with her hand over her mouth, which was a sign that she had something bad to tell us.

"*Tsumah-tsi-tsi? Ninow?*—Where is he, the chief?" she was saying under her breath, still holding her hand over her mouth.

All of the women clapped their left hands over their mouths and stood speechlessly waiting for her to speak.

When she ran into one of our minor chiefs, she said with a quivering tongue:

"All are gone in Red Dog's camp—killed!"

"*Hanh-h-h-h-h-h!*" exclaimed our women.

"*Hie-yah-h-h-h-h-h-h!*" A low yelping war-cry from deep down in the chests of our braves, went sounding through the camp like a bugle-call.

We all bent fast steps toward the camp of Red Dog, who with his family of seven, had pitched his teepees down near the mouth of the valley, a little removed from the main camp.

When we arrived there we found five persons, dead. There was no blood, there were no wounds on their bodies, but their throats were blue and swollen. They had been quietly choked to death in their sleep—one by one.

We scurried through the snow, looking for two others, but we could find no sign of them. They were two of Red Dog's daughters, aged about seventeen or eighteen. Hours of search revealed no clue as to their whereabouts.

Finally the chief gave orders to strike camp and take up the trail of the mysterious snow-shoes which had been followed for some distance by our scouts. The chief told the old people and the women and children to follow in the rear and take their time, so that the warriors could travel ahead with all their speed. The warriors took nothing with them—not even food—nothing but their guns and snow-shoes. They left one young scout with us to keep us in their wake; and then they were off at a fast dog-trot.

Fortunately the snow had frozen over with a hard crust, which enabled them to make fast time by sliding their snow-shoes as they pushed them forward. And this crust also made it possible for us to utilize the dogs for pack-animals—keeping their feet above the surface of the snow.

On the evening of the third day out, a swift runner was sent back along the trail to tell us that the enemy we were chasing were *Assinahs*—Northern Crees—who had evidently taken us for Shuswaps. The messenger said that they had come across several of their camp-sites of the night before, and our warriors were gaining time by living off the beaver meat which the Crees were leaving behind them in their camps. They learned that they were Crees from a moccasin they had found, which was beaded in circular figures, according to the fashion of the Northern Bush Crees.

The messenger said it was evident that the Crees little suspected they could be overtaken, because their snow-shoes were known to be the fastest in the entire Northwest. Though the Crees were traveling light and fast, the fact that they were taking time to sleep, showed that they did not think that anyone could overtake them on the slower type of Shuswap shoe.

Living off the pemmican which we carried, we traveled on comfortably in the rear of our pursuing warriors. We were faring well, but our dogs were already suffering. Under the strain of their heavy loads they were beginning to pass blood, and their feet were so cut and bleeding from the icy crust over the snow that we had to stop and make "moccasins" for them. Our women took square pieces of buckskin and filled them with buffalo hair and tied them over their feet. When they were all "shod," the dogs looked as if they were wearing boxing-gloves on their feet.

Although our dogs were more than half wolf— big fellows as large as a two-year-old calf—they taught me something about dogs that day which I never knew before, something that has stuck with me all these years and given me a profound outlook of kindliness on these unfortunate creatures. I never knew before that the dog had a sympathetic nature, nor that he had a sense of gratitude which was more unselfish than that possessed by most human beings.

One of our dogs was undersized because he had less of the timber-wolf in him than the rest. His wild blood was that of the small coyote, and his mother had been a gray mongrel. Because of this every dog in our camp seemed always to pick on him; all but one, and that was a big dark gray stag and timber-wolf, who had more dignity than any dog I have ever seen. This big fellow always "nosed"

friendlily with the little outcast, and he was never too
ill-tempered to allow the little fellow to play
around him, even unto taking playful bites at his
dignified legs. We boys had always noticed this, and
we often threw a chunk of wood at our other dogs
because they bit this little fellow whenever he came
anywhere in their vicinity.

This little mongrel-coyote was so small that the
women could not pack anything on his back, and he
was the only dog in the camp left to run free on
this memorable trek through the Rockies. The day
when the dogs' feet started to go bad the big stag and
wolf, whose name was Bull's Head, was one of the
worst of the lot. His feet were so lacerated that
they had frozen in parts, and he was limping piti-
fully under his load.

We boys were walking behind the dogs, and I had
been watching Bull's Head all day. I was thinking
that if he had been a man he would have been a
great chief; for his dignity was unparalleled in our
big family of camp dogs. While the other dogs
would at times want to frolic under their packs, looking around with flapping tongues on the slightest
cough from the rear, old Bull's Head never once
turned his head nor made an unnecessary movement.
His shoulders hardly moved under a graceful pacing
canter, which he must have maintained with great
difficulty on his swollen feet. But on and on he

paced, his mouth slightly open and his tongue raised high up to the roof of his mouth, and not flapping outside—he was too much timber-wolf for that.

Along toward late afternoon the strain was so great on him that he began to stumble frequently and his big dark gray body was swaying visibly under his heavy load. His frozen feet were bleeding through the buckskin, leaving little red marks in his tracks. The little coyote-mongrel had long since tired himself out running around in big circles on our right and left, looking for some groundling to sniff at; and he was now trudging along with us boys, not daring to walk up with the other dogs.

My attention was drawn to the little fellow when he suddenly stopped and I stumbled over him. He was sniffing at the ground—at the little red splotches of blood. He must have recognized the smell; for he uttered a low, gruff yelp and ran swiftly ahead of us. He ran straight to the side of Bull's Head, and when he reached him he leaned his body heavily against him and pushed forward with all his puny might. One of the women came up and kicked him away, but she had no sooner turned her back than he was again leaning and pushing against the aching body of his one and only friend. When the woman came up again with a stick in her hand, the little fellow looked up at her with a great humble fear in his eyes, but he did not move away. With eyes rolling with fear he stuck to his post and pushed forward all the harder, knowing well he would soon get a savage blow in the ribs.

I could not allow the woman to hit him again. I asked her not to strike him but to watch him and see if she could find out what he was doing. The woman walked along and watched him for a moment, and then she smiled and said, "Anh-h-h!"— and she patted the little fellow on the head and went back with the women. I have never forgotten that dog who stuck to the side of his friend until darkness overtook us and drove us to camp.

Our miserable trek had entered its fourth day when things began to happen ahead of us.

Late in the afternoon of the fourth day two of our warriors traveling at the head of our flying war-party, now miles ahead of us, saw two girls on the trail some distance ahead of them. They ran back and told the chief, and the three of them bent low and sped forward to get a better view of the slowly moving figures. When they had approached to within two hundred yards of the girls, they recognized them as the two missing Blackfoot girls, Ermine Tail and Bird's Skin—and they sped up their pace and approached closer with increasing caution. When they were a few feet behind them the warriors uttered one word under their breath: "*Siksikau!*—Blackfeet!"

The girls turned half startled, and when they saw the warriors they motioned for them to bend close to the ground and walk beside them.

As the warriors half crawled to their side and kept along at their slow pace, the girls told them the Crees were ahead. They said that they were a large party of about seventy. The head party was now about to pitch camp for the night, while the slower ones were just a couple of hundred yards ahead of them.

The girls said that the Crees made them remain up long after the others had retired at night to clean and dry all of their snow-shoes. As the girls were talking to our chief, he was thinking. Finally he said to them: "Tonight when you clean the snow-shoes and dry them, hold them closer to the fire and make sure that each pair is scorched to the breaking-point. Then mix the pairs. Tie a large and a small shoe together." (Unlike the Shuswap snow-shoes, the Cree moccasins were part of their snow-shoes, making them one-piece affairs.)

The girls said that they would carry out the chief's instructions, and our warriors left them.

In the frosty stillness of the following morning our braves crept up close to the sleeping camp of the wily Crees, and lay there on their bellies, completely surrounding the camp, until the first rays of dawn struck the eastern skies.

Then the long, low bellow of a mountain-lion reverberated through the hills—from the throat of a Blackfoot scout—and this was the signal for the war-cry.

"*Hie-yah-h-h-h-h-h—Yeep, yeep!*"—And our "Tigers of the Plains" were once again on the war-path!

They swooped into that camp like so many wolves on a fallen moose. So sudden was the attack that some of the Crees were caught and slashed to death before they could rise from their pallets. Others ran wildly for their snow-shoes; they picked up mis-mated pairs of charcoal and tried to fasten them to their feet—knowing that if they ever got a start on their famous "speed shoes," no one in the Northwest could catch them.

But the Blackfoot girls had done their work too well.

As the confused Crees sat in the snow trying to get a large and a small snow-shoe on their feet, many of them were slain where they sat. Others managed to get the shoes on their feet, but as soon as they stepped on them their feet went through them and on down into the deep, slushy snow. When they got up and tried to run they found that instead of having on a pair of the fastest snow-shoes in existence they had two heavy impediments, resembling tennis rackets, dangling about their ankles. As they struggled knee-deep in the snow, they were shot down in their tracks.

When the short, fierce encounter had ended every Cree, except one boy, had been killed. This boy was left alive and sent back to his people—according to the Indian custom—to tell them the story of the massacre.

Only one of our Blackfeet was wounded. This was Rock Thunder, one of the most renowned warriors in our history. He sustained a severed sinew in the back of his ankle, which made it impossible for him to walk. With his arms about the necks of two fellow warriors, he kept up with the party for several days, while they were trekking back to meet us. But he soon felt that he was a drag on the party, and requested that he be allowed to die in the manner usually chosen by incapacitated warriors. He asked them to burn him on a pyre. The others refused to heed his request. They insisted that he was not a burden on them, and declared that they would gladly carry him back to his people. But Rock Thunder continued to plead with them.

Finally he asked the whole party to halt, that he might talk to them. He said:

"Brothers, our food will be scarce before we get out of the mountains. We have suffered many hardships, and we have many miles yet to travel. If we do not hurry out of here, perhaps larger numbers of Crees may come to seek vengeance on you—and some of you may die. Why allow me to endanger the lives of others? I shall gladly die as the only sacrifice for the many enemies we have killed. I beseech you, build a fire and allow me to die like a warrior, that our success may cost but one life. Brothers, I have spoken."

After much wrangling among the other warriors, during which Rock Thunder renewed his pleading with them, the party finally gathered a number of logs and stacked them in a huge pile. They placed a lot of dry brush in the center of the heap, and bade Rock Thunder to "take his seat."

Without a word, Rock Thunder climbed upon the pile of logs and sat down in the little heap of brush. With his own flints he lighted the brush beneath him. Then, chanting his death-song as the smoke slowly grew into flames, he sat and looked far out over the rolling mountains toward the spot where our victory had been won. He ran the back of his hand across his forehead once, to wipe away the perspiration; and that was the only movement he made —and that only to keep the sweat from running into his eyes.

As the flames began to leap higher he chanted away with increasing fervor. And then, as the choking tongues of fire reached his body, he wrapped his robe around his head—and died.

XII

Wolf Brother

FOLLOWING this terrible battle with the Crees, our chiefs decided that we should pick some quiet place in the Rockies and spend the remainder of the winter there. There were large herds of wild horses running the ranges of the big plateau between the Cascades and the Rocky Mountains—Northern British Columbia—and our fathers decided that we should stay here until spring came, and then go west to this plateau and capture a herd of good horses, before venturing out onto the plains again.

We traveled northwestward through the mountains until we came to the western foot-hills of the Rockies, and here in a deep snow-covered pocket of the Rockies we settled down for the remainder of the winter.

In our band at that time we had a very noted warrior and hunter named Eagle Plume. It was the custom in those days, when the men were being killed so often and the women were growing to outnumber them, for one warrior to have from three to five wives. It was the only way that we could make sure that all of our women would be taken care of when they should reach old age.

But this warrior, Eagle Plume, had only one wife. He was a tall, handsome warrior of vigorous middle age, and but for one thing he was well contented with his pretty wife. She had served him well. She was always busy preparing his meals and waiting upon him; and tanning the hides of the furry denizens of the wilderness, which were killed in large numbers by this famous hunter of the Blackfeet. But she had no children.

Indians are extremely fond of children, and to have no offspring is regarded as a calamity, a curse. Boy children were always preferred; as they could grow up to be hunters and warriors, while girl children could be of little economic use to the family or the tribe.

Eagle Plume thought of adding another wife to his camp, one who might bear him a child; but he loved his faithful young woman and he was reluctant to put this idea into execution. He was unlike many men: he could love but one woman.

However, children were wanted, and Eagle Plume's wife had spent many hours crying alone in her teepee, because the Great Spirit had not given her the power to present him with a baby with which to make their life complete. We heard our old people discuss this, and many times they would send us over to Eagle Plume's camp to play and to keep them company. They would treat us like their own children and give us attentions which we would not receive even from our own parents.

Like all great Indian hunters, Eagle Plume liked most to hunt alone. As we camped in the Northern Rockies that winter, he would go out by himself and remain for days. He would return heavily laden with the pelts of otter, mink, black wolf, marten, and lynx.

It was well through the winter toward spring, and the snow was still very deep, when early one morning he set out on one of his periodic hunting trips into the wild country to the north of where we were camping. That evening as he was making his way down a mountain draw to seek out a camp-site, a wolf came out of the bush and howled at him in the bitter white twilight.

It was a big wolf, not a coyote, but one of the largest specimens of the huge black timber-wolf. With the true curiosity of the wolf, it watched Eagle Plume make camp, then it went quietly away.

"Go now, my brother," said Eagle Plume. "To-morrow I will follow you for that thick fur on your skin."

And so the next morning, running on his snow-shoes, and with a large round ball in his muzzle-loader, Eagle Plume went on the trail of the wolf.

It was easy for an Indian to follow its path, because its tracks were bigger than any wolf tracks he
had ever seen.   It led Eagle Plume a far journey
across a hanging mountain valley and on through a
heavily forested range of low-lying mountains.   The
wolf seemed to be bent steadily on a trail that lay
due north.   Nothing, not even the fresh cross-trails
of caribou, had swerved it from this purposeful
course.   It acted not like a hunted thing evading its
pursuer.

Eagle Plume had traveled all day, and the late
afternoon sun was making long shadows, when suddenly as he peered ahead, he saw the big wolf run
out on a naked ridge that rolled up from a bushy
mountain plain.

It had been snowing for some hours in a quiet,
intense way; and with the descent of the sun, the
wind was rising with fitful whines, making little
swirling gusts of snow-drift on the white surface of
the land, which foretold the approach of a mountain
storm.   The new snow had made the going heavy
for Eagle Plume, and it must have been tiring to
the wolf, too; for it was now sinking to its belly
with each step.

Eagle Plume was a tireless hunter, and he knew
that if the wolf kept to the open country, he, with
the superiority of his snow-shoes, could wear it down.
Already the big, shaggy creature was showing signs

of fatigue, and the intrepid hunter was remorse-
lessly closing up the distance that his quarry was
losing.

After his first view of the wolf on the ridge, Eagle
Plume lost sight of it for a while; then he saw it
again, and when the sun, with its sinister attendants
of two false suns, touched the rim of the mountains
to the west, the wolf remained in plain view all of
the time. The Blackfoot was sweeping forward on
the bumpy surface of the great rolling sea of snow
at a long, tireless lope, while the wolf seemed to be
floundering along in distress.

The wind continued to rise, and soon the country
was enveloped in a stinging, blinding chaos of drifting snow. A blizzard was coming up. And even
the wolf, wild denizen of the region as he was, was
now seeking harborage.

The mountain valley lay flat and expressionless
under its snowy mantle. The only relief to the landscape was a pine grove which stood like an island
straight ahead.

A blizzard had no terrors for a good hunter like
Eagle Plume, when there was wood and shelter in
sight. He knew that the wolf was making for cover,
and he hurried his footsteps so that he might overtake it and make his kill before it escaped into the
pines or became lost in the darkness of the raging
blizzard.

But the storm gathered in strength and violence, and Eagle Plume was forced to summon all of his remaining energies to reach the shelter of the trees before darkness and death should overtake him. When, panting and exhausted, he at last made his objective, he had long since lost all sight and track of his game.

He rested briefly and then began to skirt the lea side of the pines for a suitable place to make fire and camp. As he was doing this he suddenly became aware that the wolf was watching him from a near-by snow-bank. Cautiously he turned in his tracks and leveled the long, cold barrel of his gun straight between a pair of furtive gray eyes—wild, slanted eyes, which looked calmly at him like two pieces of gray flint. He paused for a second and then pulled the trigger. There was a flash in the nipple—but no explosion. The priming had been affected by the drifting snow.

With his teeth he pulled the wooden stopper of his powder-horn and poured dry powder into the pan, keeping his eyes on the steady gaze of the wolf, which made no effort to move or escape. As he deftly reloaded and primed his gun, he spoke softly to the wolf in the manner of the Indian, saying:

"Oh, my brother, I will not keep you waiting in the cold and snow. I am preparing the messenger I will send you. Have patience for just a little while."

As he shook the dry powder onto the pan of his gun, the wolf, without any previous movement of warning, suddenly made a mighty leap—and vanished.

The swift-gathering darkness and the howling blizzard made useless any further effort to capture this remarkable pelt, and realizing for the first time the futility of his quest, Eagle Plume now laid aside his gun and unloosened an ax which hung at his belt, and made hurried preparations to shield himself from the blizzard. He cut down some dead spruce for a fire, and then made himself a shelter of mountain bushes.

During a slight pause in his labor, his ear, keenly attuned to the voices of the wilderness, caught a strange sound. When he listened intently and caught it a second time there was no mistaking what it was. It was the wail of a child.

Throwing down his ax and wrapping his blanket about his head and body, he stumbled out into the darkness and hurried blindly in the direction whence the wail had come. As he jogged along through the swirling snow, his ears alert to hold the wailing sound above that of the screeching wind, one of his snow-shoes caught in something and he fell faceforward into the snow. As he got up and reached down to pick up his blanket, his hand touched the heavy object which had tripped him. He kneeled

WOMAN OF THE BLOOD BAND OF BLACKFEET,
With Child in Moss-Bag Carrier, the Indian Youngster's Cradle

down and looked at it—and it was a woman—an Indian woman—a dead Indian woman.

Still the wailing continued. He walked around and around trying to locate it. It seemed to come from the air, not from the ground. From point to point he walked and stopped and listened. Finally he walked up to a tree, and there, hanging high out of the reach of prowling animals, he found a living child in a moss bag—a baby a few months old.

Snug in its native cradle, packed with dry moss and rabbit skins, it had suffered none from the cold.

He built a great fire and made a camp, and slept that night with the foundling wrapped in his arms.

In the morning he snared some rabbits, and slitting the throat of one with his hunting knife, he pressed the warm blood into the mouth of the hungry infant.

With his ax and some saplings it did not take him long to knock together a rough sleigh. And so he came back to our camp in the valley, dragging the unknown dead woman behind him; and underneath his capote he carried the child in its moss bag.

When the people of our camp came out to meet this strange company of two living and one dead, he handed the baby to his wife and said:

"Here is our child; we will no longer have need for a strange woman in our lodge."

Eagle Plume's wife cradled the child in her arms and warmed it to her bosom; and our old people said that the fires of maternity kindled in her at the touch of the infant, and that milk for its sustenance flowed in those breasts that for so long had been dry.

That night as we sat around the camp fire and Eagle Plume told his story with all the graphic detail of an Indian recital, a big wolf cried its deep-throated howl from a high butte that overlooked our camp.

"*Mokuyi!*—It is he, the wolf!" cried Eagle Plume. Then raising his hand, he declared: "I shall never kill another; they are my brothers!"

And on the instant he turned to the child and christened him, *Mokuyi-Oskon*, Wolf Brother, and he was known by this name until he was eighteen.

The child grew and flourished. He became a great chief; and his name is today graven on a stone shaft which commemorates the termination of inter-tribal Indian wars in the Northwest.

XIII

The Ghost Horse

WITH the first touch of spring we broke camp and headed southwest across the big bend of the upper Columbia, toward the plateau between the Rockies and the Cascades. It was on this lofty plateau that the world's largest herd of wild horses had roamed during the last hundred and fifty years. Several hundred head of them are still there, where every summer efforts are being made to exterminate them by the provincial government of British Columbia. It was these horses that we were after, to replace the herd which the storm had driven away from our camp.

We struck the herd in the season of the year when it was weakest: early spring, after the horses had got their first good feed of green grass and their speed had been slowed by dysentery. Since these wild creatures can run to death any horse raised in captivity, it is doubly a hard job to try to ensnare them on foot. But, like wolves, wild horses are very curious animals; they will follow a person for miles out of mere curiosity. And, when chased, they will invariably turn back on their trails to see what it is all about; what their pursuers look like; what they are up to.

The big timber wolves would do the same, when we were traveling in the North Country. They would trot along behind us all day. When we would stop, they would stop, and stand motionless and look at us with one foot raised; and when we would start again, they would continue to follow us. If we made a noise at them they would jump back and hide behind the nearest bush. From then on, they would keep out of sight, but whenever we looked back we would see them peeping at us from behind the farthest bush.

They used to scare us children, but our fathers told us not to be scared; the wolves would not hurt us; they were just curious about us—although, they said, if the wolves followed us all day they might try to snatch off our dogs when we camped that night. So they told us boys who were traveling in the rear to keep trying to "shoo" them away before we should make camp for the night. Wolves like dog meat better than any other, though male wolves will never harm a female dog.

But with the wild horses it was different. They always traveled ahead of us, but they had a way of turning back on their own trails and coming upon us from the side or the rear, to keep watch on us. It was this never-satisfied curiosity of the wild horse that enabled our braves to capture them on foot.

The method of our warriors was to locate a herd and then follow it unconcernedly for hours, and maybe for days, before making any attempt to round it up. This was to get the horses used to us and to show them that we would not harm them.

We had been trailing fresh manure for five days before we finally located our first herd away up on the expansive Couteau Plateau of central British Columbia. There they were: a herd of about five hundred animals grazing away over there on the side of a craggy little mountain on top of the plateau. Their quick, alert movements, more like those of a deer than those of a horse, showed they were high-strung beings that would dash off into space like a flock of wild birds on the slightest cause for excitement. There was one big, steel-dust stallion who grazed away from the rest and made frequent trips along the edge of the herd. It was obvious to our braves that this iron-colored fellow with the silver manes was the stallion who ruled the herd, and our warriors directed all of their attention to him, knowing that the movements of the entire herd depended on what he did.

When we had approached to within about five hundred yards of the herd, our braves began to make little noises, so that the horses could see us in the distance and would not be taken by surprise and frightened into a stampede at seeing us suddenly at closer range.

"Hoh! Hoh!" our braves grunted softly. The steel-dust stallion uttered a low whinny, and all the herd raised their heads high into the air and, standing perfectly still as though charmed, looked intently over at us with their big, nervous nostrils wide open. They stood that way for moments, without moving a muscle, looking hard at us. Then, as we came too near, the burly stallion tried to put fear into us by dashing straight at us with a deep, rasping roar.

Others followed him, and on they came like a yelling war party, their heads swinging wildly, their racing legs wide apart, and their long tails lashing the ground like faggots of steel wire. But before they reached us the speeding animals stiffened their legs and came to a sudden halt in a cloud of dust. While they were close they took one more good look at us, and then they turned and scampered away with the rest of the herd, which had already begun to retreat over the brow of the mountain.

But the big steel-dust stood his ground alone for a moment and openly defied us. He dug his front feet into the dirt far out in front of him, wagged his head furiously, and then stopped long enough to look and see what effect his mad antics were having upon us. Around and around he jumped gracefully into

the air, swapping ends like a dog chasing its tail.
Then again he raised his head as high as his superb
stature would carry him, and with his long silver
tail lying over his back, he blazed fire at us through
the whites of his turbulent flint-colored eyes. Having displayed to us his courage, his defiance and his
remarkable leadership, he now turned and pranced
off, with heels flying so high and so lightly that one
could almost imagine he was treading air.

Our braves laughed and said:

"Ah, *ponokamita*, vain elk-dog, you are a brave
warrior. But trot along and have patience. We
shall yet ride you against the Crows."

For five days we chased this huge herd of horses,
traveling along leisurely behind them, knowing that
they would not wander afar; that they would watch
us like wolves as long as we were in their vicinity.

By the fifth day they had become so used to us that
they merely moved along slowly when we approached them, nibbling the grass as they walked.
All during this time our braves had been taming
them by their subtle method. At first they just
grunted at them. But now they were dancing and
shouting at them. This was to let the horses know
that although man could make a lot of noise and act
fiercely, he would not harm them; that no injury
could come to them through closer contact with man.

Nothing scares a horse quicker than a quiet thing

that moves toward him and makes no noise. He will jump and break his neck at the noiseless movement of a rodent in the grass or a falling twig, while a roaring buffalo or a steaming train will pass him unnoticed. That is because he has the same kind of courage that man has: real courage; the courage to face any odds that he can see and hear and cope with, but a superstitious fear of anything ghostlike. The mountain-lion and most other animals of prey, have courage of a different kind. A slight, unexplained noise will bring them to a low, crouching, waiting position, while a loud noise will send them scurrying for cover. They have more discretion and less valor than man or the horse.

On the tenth night of our chase our warriors made their final preparations to capture the herd. They had maneuvered the horses into the vicinity of a huge half-natural, half-artificial corral which they had built of logs against the two sides of a rock-bound gulch. From the entrance of this corral they had built two long fences, forming a runway, which gradually widened as it left the gate of the corral. This funnel-shaped entrance fanned out onto the plateau for more than a half-mile, and it was covered over with evergreens to disguise its artificiality. It was a replica of the old buffalo corral which we used to build to round up the buffaloes when they were plentiful on the plains.

The mouth at the outer end of this runway was about one hundred yards wide. From this point on, the runway was further extended and opened up by placing big tree tops, stones and logs along the ground for several hundred yards. This was to direct the herd slowly into the mouth of the fenced part of the runway, where, once wedged inside, they could neither get out nor turn around and retrace their steps. They would be trapped; and the only thing left for them to do would be to keep on going toward the corral gate.

Subdued excitement reigned in our hidden camp on this tenth night of our chase; for it was the big night, the night that we were going to "blow in" the great, stubborn herd of wild horses. No one went to bed that night. Shortly before nightfall more than half of our braves, comprising all of our fastest-traveling scouts and young men, quietly slipped out of our camp and disappeared. According to prearranged directions, they fanned out to the right and left in a northerly route and crept noiselessly toward the place where the herd had disappeared that afternoon. All during the early night we heard wolves calling to one another; arctic owls, night hawks and panthers crying out moanfully in the mystic darkness of the rugged plateau. They were the signals of our men, informing one another of their movements.

Then, about midnight, everything became deathly quiet. We knew that they had located the herd and surrounded it, and that they were now lying on their bellies, awaiting the first streaks of dawn and the signal to start the drive.

One of our subchiefs, Chief Mountain Elk, now went through our camp, quietly giving instructions for all hands to line themselves along the great runway to "beat in" the herd. Every woman, old person, and child in the camp was called up to take part in this particular phase of the drive. We children and the women crept over to the runway and sprawled ourselves along the outside of the fence, while the men went beyond the fenced part of the runway and concealed themselves behind the brush and logs—where it was a little more dangerous.

Thus we crouched on the ground and shivered quietly for an hour or more before we heard a distant, "Ho-h! . . . Ho-h!" It was the muffled driving cry of our warriors, the cry which for ten days they had been uttering to the horses to let them know that no harm could come to them from this sound. Thus, the horses did not stampede, as they would have done had they not recognized this noise in the darkness.

We youngsters lay breathless in expectancy. We had all picked out our favorite mounts in this beautiful herd of wild animals, and to us as we lay there, it was like the white boy lying in bed waiting for Santa Claus. Our fathers had all promised us that we could have the ponies that we had picked, and we could hardly wait to get our hands on them. My favorite was a beautiful calico pony, a roan, white, and red pinto—three different colors all splashed on his shoulders and flanks like a crazy-quilt of exquisite design. He had a red star on his forehead between his eyes, and I had already named him, *Naytukskie-Kukatos*, which in Blackfoot means One Star.

Presently we heard the distant rumble of horses' hoofs—a dull booming which shook the ground on which we lay. Then, "Yip-yip-yip, he-heeh-h-h," came the night call of the wolf from many different directions. It was our braves signaling to one another to keep the herd on the right path. From out of this medley of odd sounds we could hear the mares going, "Wheeeeeh-hagh-hagh-hagh"—calling their little long-legged sons to their sides that they might not become lost in the darkness and confusion.

Our boyish hearts began to beat fast when we heard the first loud *"Yah! Yah! Yah!"* We knew that the herd had now entered the brush portion of the runway and that our warriors were jumping up from their hiding-place and showing themselves with fierce noises, in order to stampede the horses and send them racing headlong into our trap.

Immediately there was a loud thunder of patter-ing hoofs. Horses crying and yelling everywhere, like convulsive human beings in monster confusion. Above this din of bellowing throats and hammering feet we heard one loud, full, deep-chested roar which we all recognized, and it gave us boys a slight thrill of fear. It sounded like a cross between the roar of a lion and the bellow of an infuriated bull. It was the massive steel-dust stallion, furious king of the herd. In our imagination we could see his long silver tail thrown over his back, his legs lashing wide apart, and stark murder glistening from the whites of those terrible eyes. We wondered what he would do to us if he should call our bluff and crash through that fence into our midst.

But, now, here he came, leading his raging herd, and we had no further time to contemplate danger. Our job was to do as the others had done all along the line: to lie still and wait until the lead stallion had passed us, and then to jump to the top of the fence and yell and wave with all the ferocity that we could command. This was to keep the maddened herd from crashing the fence or trying to turn around, and to hasten their speed into our trap.

"*Therump, therump, therump.*" On came the storming herd. As we youngsters peeped through the brush-covered fence, we could see their sleek backs bobbing up and down in the starlit darkness like great billows of raging water. The turbulent steel-dust stallion was leading them with front feet wide apart and his forehead sweeping the ground like a pendulum. His death-dealing heels were swinging alternatingly to the right and left with each savage leap of his mighty frame.

Once he stopped and tried to breast the oncoming herd, but these erstwhile slaves of his whims struck and knocked him forward with terrific force. He rose from his knees, and like something that had gone insane, he shot his nostrils into the air and uttered a fearful bellow of defiance at any- and everything. He seemed to curse the very stars themselves. Never before had he tasted defeat, utter helplessness. The loyal herd that had watched his very ears for their commands was now running wildly over him.

I believe that, if at that moment there had been a solid iron wall in front of that stallion, he would have dashed his brains out against it. I remember looking backwards into the darkness for a convenient place to hop, if he should suddenly choose to rush headlong into the noise that was driving him wild with helpless rage. But, even as I looked back, I heard a whistling noise, and my eyes were jerked back to the runway just in time to see the steel-dust king stretching himself past us like a huge greyhound. With each incredible leap he panted a breath that shrieked like a whistle.

No one will ever know what was in his brain; why he had so suddenly broken himself away from his herd. But on he went, leaving the other horses behind like a deer leaving a bunch of coyotes. A few seconds later the rest of the herd came booming past us. As we went over the fence, shouting and gesticulating, we looked into a blinding fog of sweat and breath, which fairly stung our nostrils with its pungency.

I thought that herd would never stop passing us. I had never seen so many horses before, it seemed. We stuck to our posts until it was nearly daylight, and still they came straggling along; now mostly colts limping and whining for their mothers.

When we climbed down from the fence and went down to the corral at daylight, the first thing we saw was four of our warriors lying on pallets, bleeding and unconscious. They were four of the best horsemen in our tribe: Circling Ghost, High Hunting Eagle, Wild Man, and Wolf Ribs. When our mothers asked what was the matter, someone pointed to the corral, and said: *"Ponokomita—akai-mahkah-pay!"* ("That very bad horse!")

We looked and saw a dozen men trying to put leather on that wild steel-dust stallion, who, with his heavy moon-colored mane bristling belligerently over his bluish head and shoulders, looked now more like a lion than a horse. He was splotched here and there with his own blood, and his teeth were bared like a wolf's. Four men had tried to get down into the corral and throw rawhide around his neck. While the other wild horses had scurried away to the nethermost corners of the corral, this ferocious beast of a horse had plunged headlong into them and all but killed them before they could be dragged away.

He had proved to be one of the rarest specimens of horse known to man—a killer—a creature that kicked and bit and tore and crushed his victims until they were dead. One might live a hundred years among horses without ever seeing one of these hideous freaks of the horse world, so seldom are they produced. He had already killed two of his own herd, young stallions, right there in our corral. Little did we wonder, now, that he was the leader.

Our braves were taking no more chances with him. They were high up on top of the seven-foot corral fence, throwing their rawhide lariats in vain attempts to neck the murderous monstrosity. But this devil disguised as a horse had the reasoning of a human being. He would stand and watch the rawhide come twirling through the air, and then just as it was about to swirl over his head he would duck his shaggy neck and remain standing on the spot with his front feet spread apart, in devilish defiance of man and matter. None of our oldest men had ever seen anything like him.

It was finally decided to corner him with fire-brands and throw a partition between him and the rest of the herd, so that our braves could get busy cutting out the best of the other animals, before turn-ing the rest loose. This was done, and by nightfall we had captured and hobbled two hundred of the best bottoms anywhere in the Northwest.

The next day our braves began the arduous task of breaking the wild horses to the halter. They used the Indian method, which is very simple and methodical. While four men held on to a stout rawhide rope which was noosed around the animal's neck, another man would approach the horse's head gradually, "talking horse" to him and making many queer motions and sounds as he went nearer.

"Horse talk" is a low grunt which seems to charm a horse and make him stand perfectly still for a moment or so at a time. It sounds like "Hoh—Hoh," uttered deep down in one's chest. The horse will stop his rough antics and strain motionless on the rope for a few seconds, while he is doing this and looking straight at the approaching figure, the man will wave a blanket at him and hiss at him—"Shuh! Shuh!" It takes about fifteen minutes of this to make the horse realize that the man is harm-less; that no motion which he makes, no sound that he utters, will harm him in any way.

It is a strange fact that a wild horse, of either

the ranch or the open ranges, will not react to quiet kindliness at first. He must first be treated gruffly —but not harshly—and then when he is on a touching acquaintance with man, kindness is the quickest way to win his affections.

When the man has reached the head of the horse his hardest job is to give him the first touch of man's hand, of which the horse seems to have a deathly fear. He maneuvers for several minutes before he gets a finger on the struggling nose, and rubs it and allows the horse to get his smell or scent. When this has been done, the brave loops a long, narrow string of rawhide around the horse's nose and then carries it up behind his ears and brings it down on the other side and slips it under the other side of the nose loop, making something like a loose-knotted halter, which will tighten up on the slightest pull from the horse.

This string is no stronger than a shoe-lace, yet, once the warrior has put it on the horse's head, he tells the other men to let go the strong rawhide thong, and from then on he alone handles the horse with the small piece of string held lightly in one hand. The secret of this is that whenever the horse makes a sudden pull on the string it grips certain nerves around the nose and back of the ears, and this either stuns him or hurts him so badly that he doesn't try to pull again.

With the horse held thus, the warrior now stands in front of him and strokes the front of his face and hisses at him at close range. It is the same noise that a person makes to drive away chickens—"shuh, shuh"—and perhaps the last sound an untrained person would venture to use in taming a wild, ferocious horse, yet it is the quickest way of gaining a horse's confidence and teaching him not to be afraid.

When the warrior has run his fingers over every inch of the horse's head and neck, he now starts to approach his shoulders and flanks with his fingers. The horse will start to jump about again at this, but a couple of sharp jerks on the string stop him, and as he stands trembling with fear, the warrior slowly runs his hand over his left side. When this is finished he stands back and takes a blanket and strikes all of the portions of his body that he has touched, and shouts, "Shuh!" with each stiff stroke of the blanket.

When he has repeated these two operations on the other side of the horse, he now starts to do his legs. Each leg, beginning with his left front leg, must be gone over by his hand, with not an inch of its surface escaping his touch. This is the most ticklish part of the work; for his feet are the horse's deadly weapons. But two more jerks on the string quiet the horse's resentment, and within another fifteen minutes every square inch of the horse's body has been touched and rubbed, even down to his tail and the ticklish portions of his belly and between his legs.

Now, the job of breaking the horse is all but finished. There is just one other thing to do, and that is to accustom the horse to a man hopping on his back and riding him. This is done very simply, and within about five minutes.

The warrior takes the blanket and strikes the horse's back a number of blows. Then he lays the blanket on his back very gently. The horse will at first start to buck it off, but another jerk on the string, and he is quieted. The warrior picks the blanket up and lays it across his back again. The horse will jump out from under it perhaps twice before he will stand still. When he has been brought to this point, the man throws the blanket down and walks slowly to the side of the horse and places both hands on his back and presses down lightly. He keeps pressing a little harder and harder, until finally he places his elbows across his back and draws his body an inch off the ground, putting his full weight on the back of the animal. A horse might jump a little at the first experience of this weight, but he will stand still the next time it is tried.

After the warrior has hung on his back by his elbows for several periods of about thirty seconds each, he will now very gradually pull himself up, up, up, until he is ready to throw his right foot over to the other side. It is a strange fact that few horses broken in this manner ever try to buck. He will stand perfectly still, and the man will sit there and stroke him for a moment and then gently urge him to go; and the horse will awkwardly trot off in a mild, aimless amble, first this way and that—so bewildered and uncertain in his gait that one would think it was the first time he had ever tried to walk on his own feet.

The reason a horse can be broken in the above manner is that he is a remarkably intelligent being with rationality. A chicken has no reason; therefore it goes through its life running away from "shuhs" that never harm it. This keeps it from getting many extra crumbs that it could leisurely eat if it only had the reason to learn from experience as the horse does.

Four months later we were again back on our beloved plains in upper Montana. Our horses were the envy of every tribe who saw us that summer. They all wanted to know where we got them. Our chief told the story of this wild-horse hunt so many times that it has since become legend among the Indians of these prairies.

But at the end of the story our venerable leader would always look downcast, and in sadly measured words, he would tell of the steel-dust stallion with the flowing moon-colored mane and tail, which he had picked out for himself. He would spend many minutes describing this superb horse, yet he would never finish the story, unless someone should ask him what became of the spectacular animal.

Then he would slowly tell how our band had worked all day trying to rope this beast, and how that night they had decided to leave him in the little fenced-off part of the corral, thinking that two or three days' contact with them might take some of the evil out of him. But the next morning when they visited the corral he had vanished. The horse had literally climbed over more than seven feet of corral fence, which separated him from the main corral, and there, with room for a running start, he had attacked the heavy log fence and rammed his body clear through it. Nothing was left to tell the tale but a few patches of blood and hair and a wrecked fence.

That should have ended the story of the steel-dust beast, but it did not. On our way out of the camp on the wild-horse plateau we had come across the bodies of seven wild stallions and a mare, which this fiend of the plateau had mutilated in his wake. He had turned killer through and through, even unto the destruction of his own kind. Our old people said that he had been crazed by the fact that he had lost control of his herd in that terrible dash

down the runway. This blow to his prowess and
pride of leadership had been too much for him; it
had turned him into a destructive demon, a roaming maniac of the wilds.

This horse became famous throughout the Northwest as a lone traveler of the night. He went down
on to the plains of Montana and Alberta, and in
the darkest hours of the night he would turn up at
the most unexpected points in the wilderness of the
prairies. Never a sound from him; he had lost his
mighty bellow. He haunted the plains by night,
and was never seen by day. His sinister purpose in
life was to destroy every horse he came across.

This silent, lone traveler of the night was often
seen silhouetted against the moon on a butte, with
his head erect, his tail thrown over his back like a
statue, his long moon-colored mane and tail flowing
like silver beneath the light of the stars. Owing to
his peculiar nocturnal habits and to the fact that his
remarkable tail and mane gave off in the moonlight
something like a phosphorescent glow, he became
known throughout the Northwest as the *Shunka-
tonka-Wakan*—the Ghost Horse. The steel-blue
color of his body melted so completely into the inky
blueness of the night, that his tail and mane stood
out in the moonlight like shimmering threads of
lighted silver, giving him a halo which had a truly
ghostly aspect.

XIV

THE WHITE MAN'S BUFFALO ROBE

WHEN we got back down on the Milk River that fall, near the northern border of Montana and the Northwest Territories, some white men came into our camp and wanted to treat with us; to buy our land for dollar bills and put us on reservations with other Indians. They came over to our camp and told us that all of the tribes to the south and east of us had signed treaties with the governments of the United States and Canada, and were living on reservations and getting along well. And they advised us to give up our roaming existence and settle down in our place. They spread their one-dollar bills on the ground, and said:

"This is the white man's 'buffalo robe'—money." (The Indians had used buffalo robes for their money.) "The Sioux Indians," they said, "call this money *maza-ska*—white metal—because they know that they can exchange it for metal money that will buy anything the white man has. It is of much value, and you must use it from now on."

Our chief picked up one of the dollar bills, and

there was a picture on it of a man with a bald head. Our chief looked at the other members of our tribe and said: "We will call this *Stikikikinasi*—Bald Head." And from that day on the dollar bill has been known among the Blackfeet as "Bald Head."

When the white chief had laid all of his money down on the ground and shown how much he would give all of us for signing a treaty with him, our chief took a handful of clay and made a ball of it and put it on the fire and cooked it. And it did not crack. Then he said to the white chief:

"Now, give me some of your money; we will put the money on the fire and the clay alongside of it, and whichever burns the quickest is the cheapest."

The white chief said:

"My money will burn the quickest, because it is made of paper; so we can't do that."

Our chief then reached down into his belt pocket and took out a little buckskin bag of sand, and he handed it to the white chief, and said:

"Give me your money. I will count the money, while you count the grains of sand. Whichever can be counted the quickest will be the cheapest."

The white chief took the sand and poured it out into the palm of his hand, and as he looked at it, he said: "I would not live long enough to count this, but you can count the money quickly."

"Then," our chief said, "our land is more valu-

able than your money. It will last forever. It will
not even perish by the flames of fire. As long as
the sun shines and the waters flow, this land will
be here to give life to men and animals. We cannot sell the lives of men and animals; therefore we
cannot sell this land. It was put here for us by the
Great Spirit, and we cannot sell it because it does
not belong to us. You can count your money and
burn it within the nod of a buffalo's head, but only
the Great Spirit can count the grains of sand and
the blades of grass on these plains. As a present to
you, we will give you anything we have that you can
take with you; but the land, never."

The white chief then said:

"I was sent here by the Great White Mother who
rules over all the country from *Kewatin*—North
Wind—across the *Kisisaskatchewan*—Swift Current,
a river of the North—on to the Western Sea. She
invites you to join your brethren of the North in
treaty with us, and to come and live under our flag
in peace. You will never get along with the Blue
Coats—Americans. If they are not looking after
you well, look up into our country. Whenever you
look northwest and see the Red Sun, that will be
my sun, my 'Red Coats'—Northwest Mounted Police. Whenever you come inside, then you will live
with us and your brothers, the Northern Siksikau."

That ended our first treaty parley.

Rich with skins and furs from our winter's hunting in the Northern Rockies, our chief decided late that summer that we should journey on down to Fort Benton in Montana, and trade in our catch for the white man's wares: steel arrowheads to replace our flint heads; colored beads to replace our colored porcupine quills; more blankets to replace our diminishing supply of buffalo robes; powder and balls and guns; knives and tools to replace our bone implements, and sail canvas to replace our heavy skin teepee coverings.

North of Fort Benton we ran into a huge camp of friendly Crows and half-breed buffalo-hunters, camping in two large adjacent camps on the upper Missouri River. The half-breed hunters had come out from the land of Kewatin in Manitoba, to trade their robes at Fort Benton.

We were invited to pitch our camp among them, and that night the Crows and the half-breeds held two big dances, to celebrate the meeting of all of these stranger Indians and the half-breeds.

While they were dancing we boys noticed two older boys with long hair dancing with the Indians. They acted like Indians and talked only Indian, yet they were white. We youngsters watched them, and we noticed that one of them was with the Crows and the other with the half-breeds, and that they were both watching one another. We boys were interested in this unusual thing; for they were about the first white-skinned boys that we had ever had a good look at. We never took our eyes off them, and soon we discovered that they did not know one another; we could tell by the shy way in which they kept glancing at one another during the dance.

After a while, when one of the long dances ended, we saw the white boy who was with the Crows walk over to the other white boy and say something to him, and the boy answered him in the sign language, which we could all understand. By this time we had interested our mothers in these two boys, and they, too, watched them.

In the sign language, the boy with the half-breed hunters, replied to the white boy of the Crows:

"I do not understand your language; I speak Cree."

"Who are you, then; why are you with the Cree half-breeds? Are you not a white boy like myself?" asked the Crow white boy.

"Yes," replied the other, "I am white, but I do not know who my parents are. I have never seen them. I was captured by the Sioux in the Minnesota Massacre when I was a baby, but when I grew up and found out that I was different from the Indians, I ran away. I may have been about ten or eleven when I did this; anyway, I was so small that I could hide in badger holes in the daytime. That is how I got away. I ran off one dark night. I knew the Sioux would come after me when they found out I was gone; so I walked all night and hid by day in badger holes on the prairie. I did that for five nights before I ran into some half-breed buffalo-hunters; and I have been with them ever since. I am seventeen now. How old are you? Who are you?"

This white boy who had been talking was a tall, slim lad. The boy with the Crows was a chunky, heavy-set lad who was always smiling.

The Crow white boy said:

"I have a name that is in the white man's language, and I cannot say it in the sign language. I am sixteen. I come from across the big water [England]. But I have been with the Crows since I was ten. I came over to this country with my mother and aunt, who were going to join my uncle, who was rich, in the Gold Country to the west [California]. We traveled from the east in wagons. When we got to Fort Benton my mother caught the 'Black Curse,' smallpox, and died; and the next day my aunt died, too. I was left with no one to look after me; and so the Crows adopted me and raised me. They have been good to me. Have you been treated well?"

"Yes, I have been treated all right," said the quiet-mannered fellow of the half-breed band. "I

do not remember much of my life with the Sioux.
I remember that I had a lot of brothers. I mean,
the Sioux woman who had me had a lot of boy children, and we used to play and have a good time.
But we all had to work hard."

By this time half of the Indians were standing
around the two white boys "looking-in" on their
conversation. And the tall lad was shy; but he
went on:

"There was a white girl, older than I, maybe
about sixteen, in another band of the Sioux who had
gone up into Kewatin from the massacre. I used to
see her once in a while, when we were camping close
together, and I used to try to get a chance to talk
to her and find out who we were, but they watched
her too close.

"One day I saw her go down to a water-hole that
both of our bands were using, and I slipped away
from our camp and went down, too. I asked her
who she was. She said she did not know. She was
captured in the massacre, too. She said that she was
being raised in the chief's family, and they watched
her all the time; for the chief was going to marry
her when she was old enough. She had red hair
and was pretty good-looking. I never had another
chance to talk to her. I do not know what became
of her. That is all I know about myself. They
say that my parents were killed in the massacre, and

one of the Indian women snatched me up out of the mud and saved me. But I wish I knew who my relatives are."

Years later I visited the Minnesota Massacre Sioux, now living in refuge in Western Canada on two reservations: the Standing Buffalo band at Fort Qu'appelle, Saskatchewan; and the Akisa band at Oak Lake, Manitoba. I remembered this incident on the Upper Missouri, which was still being talked about by our old people, and I asked them what they knew about the white child they had brought up from the massacre when they fled into this country for refuge from the American troops. I found that the woman who adopted and raised the child was Mrs. Akisa, wife of the chief.

Mrs. Akisa said that there was so much blood in the streets of Redwood, Minnesota, that day that the earthen road-bed had turned to red mud. In this mud she had seen a little white baby lying kicking and crying, as the battle proceeded and the Indians and white citizens were trampling other youngsters under their feet in the excitement. To save this little fellow, whose upturned face had appealed to her, she had reached down and snatched it up and wrapped it in a buffalo robe.

On their flight into the Northwest Territories, as western Canada was then known, they, the Sioux, were attacked by the Mandan Indians, and a running battle lasting several hours brought down many victims on both sides. Holy Flying, another of the Massacre Sioux, told me that all during this running fight Mrs. Akisa had held the little white baby behind her own body, to protect it from the flying bullets and arrows.

Mrs. Akisa had kept the baby and raised him as one of her own children until he was a sizable boy; then one night he had disappeared. She had heard that he was still living, now a middle-aged man, somewhere in Manitoba. She loved this child as one of her own, and she had spent many of her aged hours brooding over its loss.

I went down to Winnipeg and put an article in the Winnipeg Tribune, under date of February 24, 1923, asking this Sioux white boy to get in touch with me through the Tribune. Five months later, on June 13, 1923, a gaunt, raw-boned man of the plains went into the Tribune office at Winnipeg, and told the managing editor Vernon K. Knowles that he could not read or write, but a woman on the plains had just told him that "somebody had asked for him in that paper a few months before."

He said:

"It was the Sioux Indians who brought me up from the massacre when I was a baby. Where are these Indians now? I would like to find out who my folks are."

Recognizing who he was, Mr. Knowles wired me, and I returned to Winnipeg and told Ross Tanner—that is his name—all about himself. We spent all that day together. We powwowed about the old days, and he told me that he had raised two families since that day, down on the Missouri River, both by Indian wives; and he now had twenty-one half-breed children. His home was, and still is, at Amaranth, Manitoba, a short distance from Winnipeg.

But the most peculiar sequence of this strange meeting followed an article about Mr. Tanner which the managing editor placed on the front of the Tribune that day.

The same afternoon, another white man who looked and acted like an Indian came into the Tribune office and asked where he could find Ross Tanner, explaining that the last time he had seen him was in an Indian camp down on the Missouri when they were boys. And this man was John Philips, now living on Pacific Avenue, in Winnipeg —the white boy who had been adopted and raised by the Crows!

The managing editor Mr. Knowles phoned me and Ross Tanner to come to his office, and then he put us in his car and drove us out to the address which Mr. Philips had left.

When the three of us walked into John Philips' modest home, we found him sitting there with his

Cree Indian wife and seven half-breed children. The two men recognized one another immediately, though now on the threshold of old age, and their greeting was rather touching.

They grabbed hold of each other's shoulders with both hands, and stood looking at one another with a broad grin on their faces and tears in their eyes. They did not speak for a minute; then both of them said: "Well, well, well!" And we all sat down and powwowed over the old days for the rest of the afternoon. Mr. Knowles, the managing editor of the Tribune, thought that the occasion was so unusual and interesting that he would remain with us and not return to his office that afternoon.

As far as Tanner and Philips and I were concerned, this was only the beginning of many interesting and prolonged chats which we enjoyed during the next couple of weeks.

Ross Tanner got in touch with the Sioux and learned that a half-breed interpreter who had come up with them from the massacre, and who had formerly known the white settlers at Redwood, Minnesota, by name, had later joined the half-breed buffalo-hunters; and it must have been this interpreter who gave him the name of Ross Tanner. They, themselves, did not know his name, but they thought that this half-breed might have known who his parents were.

As if the chain of coincidence had not already run itself out, that same year, 1923, the editor of the Mentor asked me to write an article for his magazine on the Indians of the Far Northwest. I wrote this article, and in it I casually mentioned Ross Tanner's mysterious identity; how he had been brought up from the massacre and how he was now a man who had never known who he was. It came out in the March number of the Mentor, 1923. And five months later I received a letter from Mr. Louis C. Tanner, member of the Liberty County School Board, Liberty, Texas, informing me that Ross Tanner was the son of his uncle, who, badly torn and mangled, had escaped from the massacre, and was then living at Detroit, Michigan.

And that ended the strangest chain of coincidences I have experienced.

XV

The Passing of the Medicine-Man

WHEN we boys began to be old enough to fend for ourselves in the open, we wanted to become toughened like our braves; and so early in our youth we would start to run away from our homes and stay away for days at a time. We would steal away an extra gun or arrow set, owned by our father or one of our uncles, and, taking a small hunting teepee along with us, would leave our camp in the darkness of night, to seek adventure on our own. We even aspired to meet some of the enemy sometime and give them a battle—but the Great Spirit only knows what would have happened to us if we ever had come across any of the fighting Crows. Fortunately, we did not.

But we did come across some Crow boys one day, and I shall not soon forget it. Five of us youngsters had left our camp and gone over to a coulée with underbrush growing in it, and pitched our little camp. We never went so far away that we could not always see the smoke from our main camp, but on the prairies this meant that we could go as far out as ten or twelve miles, and still see the smoke and glow from our camp by both day and night.

On this particular trip we were cooking some prairie chickens one day, when we heard boys talking a strange language across a small creek that ran by the mouth of our coulée. We all grabbed our weapons—real guns and arrows—and sneaked down to the spot where this little stream could be forded easily, knowing that the stranger Indians were going to cross here. We could see them through the brush, coming along the creek on the other side, making for this fording point.

We all lay down and concealed ourselves carefully at the place where the boys would come up after they had crossed. They were talking away in Crow and picking saskatoon-berries, putting them into the large skin pails which they carried.

One, two, three, four—four Crow boys, one by one, came up out of the water right over where we were lying, and when the last had made his appearance, we all jumped up with our war-cry and jabbed our weapons into their faces with a sharp command:

"Stop, Sparrowhawks! We are Blackfeet, and we are going to kill you!"

It was a bad trick to play on boys like ourselves; but I shall not forget what happened. The Crow boys uttered a frightened exclamation and threw their hands up into the air with such force that it fairly rained berries for the fraction of a second. The berries stung us in the face and head so sharply that we thought that we were meeting a charge of buckshot; and, we, too, became momentarily frightened.

When it was all over we stood and looked at one another for a moment, and then we burst out laughing. The humor of both sides of the situation seemed to strike us the same instant. The Crows were laughing at us, and we were laughing at them. We all had such a good laugh that we decided to forget the enmity of our fathers and play together for a while.

We invited the Crow boys to run away from home, too, and to stay with us till next day. They did. And we had a great time sitting around our small camp-fire that night, talking in the sign language and telling of our experiences. We never hated the Crows after that.

One of the greatest medicine-men the Blackfoot nation has produced "came to his 'medicine' " on one of these runaway trips which we boys used to make. The name of this remarkable mystic is *Mo-kuyi-Kinasi*—Wolf Head. Wolf Head is living today (1928) on the Blackfoot Indian Reservation at Gleichen, Alberta. The story of how he "came to his 'medicine' " is the most remarkable that I have known among many renowned medicine-men of the Northwestern Plains. Wolf Head is now eighty-three years old, and he is still more powerful among the Northern Blackfeet than their head chief.

Head Chief Running Rabbit, of the Blackfeet, the son of Atsistamokon, said this to me in recent years: "Wolf Head holds far more power among the Blackfeet than I do. But I do not mind it. I like it, because it was Wolf Head who made me what I am. I owe to him everything I have accomplished."

That Wolf Head has a unique power that is unexplainable even to a highly educated white man is admitted by the present Blackfoot Indian Agent George H. Gooderham, a graduate of Toronto University, a white man who was born among Indians and has no queer notions about what they can, or cannot, do.

The remarkable power of Wolf Head's medicine is said to be due to the fact that it came from the elements themselves. He is said to have the "Power of Thunder." However that may be, the story of how he came into this uncanny medicine is known, and was witnessed, by every surviving Blackfoot warrior. And here is how it happened:

When Wolf Head was seventeen, he, like all other Blackfoot boys, decided one day to run away from his people and seek new adventure in the wil-

derness of the northwestern prairies. The tribe was
at that time camping on the Red Deer River in the
Northwest Territories—now Alberta. He took three
young companions with him, all of whom, like himself, aspired to become great warriors on their own
merit. They set out in the middle of an August
night, on foot and with nothing but their buffalo
robes and their firearms.

The next day was very hot. Shortly before noon,
when the heat was most intense, a terrific thunder-
storm burst upon them from the west without a moment's warning. The storm was accompanied by a
driving wind of hurricane velocity and a startling
display of lightning. The four boys were traveling across an open stretch of prairie-land, but when
the storm struck them they broke and ran as fast as
they could toward a clump of bush a few hundred
yards away. When Wolf Head and one of his companions made the bush, they threw themselves to a
squatting posture, drew their blanket around their
heads and bound themselves tightly together under
the same blanket to withstand the pressure of the
wind.

The last thing Wolf Head remembers was an
amazing display of blue and red lightning which
flashed through the air with blinding intensity.
. . . Nothing more.

Many hours later, just as the sun was going down,

he awoke from a peculiar dream and tried to pull himself to his feet.

"I did not have my senses with me," he said. "I was like a crazy man. Blood was running from my mouth and nose and ears. I was in great pain when I got up, and I could not walk straight. I just ran around and around in a circle. I wondered what had happened, and what was the matter with me.

"While I was running around like this I saw one of our Blackfoot hunters coming my way. I yelled to him for help, but when he saw me he turned and ran as fast as he could back toward our camp. That was Chief Weasel Calf, there," said Wolf Head, pointing to this renowned Blackfoot as he was sitting by the Sun Dance fire while Wolf Head was relating this remarkable happening.

"Yes," said Chief Weasel Calf. "That was I. When I saw him I thought he was a ghost, and it scared me. I ran back to the camp and told the others about it. And when we returned Wolf Head was still running around and around in a circle. He had no clothes on, and his body was all cut up down the left side, and bleeding hard all over. He did not look like a live man. We thought he had been killed and it was his ghost. More than a thousand of us went out to him from the camp, and when we went up close to him and saw that he was not a ghost, we told him what had happened. We told him that he had been struck by lightning. Two of his runaway companions had come back to our camp and told us about the two who had been killed and whose bodies were lying out there, burned. That was why the hunter ran when he saw him.

"Some of our braves took him and carried him back to our camp, and the rest of us started to look for the other boy. We found him lying dead about four hundred yards away from where Wolf Head had been thrown; and we found his blanket two hundred yards east and his rifle two hundred yards west of where they were sitting when the lightning hit them. It must have been a hard piece of lightning."

Then Wolf Head continued:

"All I remember of this thing was that after we saw the lightning I went to sleep and dreamed that I was in a teepee. I was sitting with a woman, and she was the one who tried to kill me. She said she was the Woman Thunder. She sang several different songs and gave them to me for my medicine songs. After a while the woman's boy, Boy Thunder, came in; and he sang my war-song, and gave it to me. The woman then told me not to be scared in war, because I was going to live to be an old man. And she said that I was going to do many things that would surprise my people. She said: 'I am going to give you seven rifles' "—meaning that he was going to kill seven of the enemy on the war-path. "I had taken five of these rifles when we signed peace with the Canadian government, and I could not fight any more.

"When the sun was going down she gave me my sun song, and then I woke up. And I was just like a crazy man.

"After they took me back to the camp that night I was in great pain. I went off into a dream. Boy Thunder came to me in that dream and said: 'I am the fellow that strikes. I am going to make a great medicine man of you. You will do things that will astound your people. I shall come to you many times when you are asleep, and each time I come to you I shall teach you something new.'

"As the years passed Boy Thunder kept coming to me when I was asleep, and every time he came he would tell me how to do something that I never knew about before. He taught me all about Indian medicine, and soon I became a great medicine-man.

"After I had grown up and become a man, a white medicine-man came among us to tell us about the white man's Great Spirit. He was the first white man who had ever come among us, and he took our language and made a writing for it."

(I, Chief Long Lance, might explain that this first white man was the venerable Archdeacon Tims, who, now aged, is still living on the Sarcee Indian

Reservation at Calgary, Alberta, where he is the missionary to the Sarcee tribe.)

"One night after this white medicine-man had come to us," continued Wolf Head, "Boy Thunder came to me in my sleep, and spread a large tanned buffalo skin on the ground. Then he picked it up and hung it on the wall of the teepee, so that it was all stretched out with the legs hanging down. On this side there were a lot of markings, which looked peculiar to me. Boy Thunder said to me, pointing to these queer drawings:

" 'Do you know what these are?'

" 'No,' I said.

" 'They are different languages,' he said. 'Each line you see is a different language written out. Do you recognize any of them?'

" 'No,' I said.

" 'Look hard,' he told me.

"I looked for a long time, but I could see nothing that I knew. So I told him no again.

" 'Keep on looking hard,' said Boy Thunder.

"I looked hard and long, and then down on one of the legs of the buffalo skin I did see something that I could read. I pointed to it, and said:

" 'I know what that is; I can understand that.'

" 'What is it?' he asked.

" 'It is the Blackfoot language put into writing,' I told him.

"He said: 'That is right, and from now on you will be able to read this language.'

It is a strange fact that Wolf Head did get up the next morning and astound Archdeacon Tims and the entire tribe by writing in the Blackfoot syllabarium, which was invented by the archdeacon and which he had not been able to teach any of the Indians yet, owing to their lack of education. This venerable missionary of the Anglican Church marvels today over this weird occurrence.

On another occasion Boy Thunder came to Wolf Head and told him how to take and develop photographs with a little camera which a later missionary, Canon Stocken, now retired and living at Victoria, B. C., had brought onto the reserve with him. The next day, much against Canon Stocken's wishes, Wolf Head borrowed his camera, and that afternoon he came back with a fully developed photograph of White-Headed Chief sitting on his horse. There was no one on those miles upon miles of prairies but Canon Stocken who owned or had ever seen a camera. Canon Stocken retains today this remarkable photograph taken by Wolf Head before the white man came.

Wolf Head's next phenomenon occurred when he went to sleep one night and awoke the next morning with the powers of a sculptor. He set to work that day and carved out of stone two life-sized

WOLF HEAD
Famous Blackfoot Medicine-Man, Standing in Front of His
Yellow Medicine Teepee

busts of King Edward and Queen Victoria, whose
likenesses he had seen on two medals presented to
the head chief by a Hudson's Bay Company official.
The present Indian Agent of the Blackfoot Reservation at Gleichen, Alberta, Mr. George Gooderham,
has these two busts sitting on the mantelpiece of the
agency office.   He has been offered considerable
money for them by various museums and the Canadian government, itself, but he has refused to part
with them.   They are both perfect likenesses of their
Majesties, and are declared by sculptors to be works
of genius.

Wolf Head's last curious exploit was performed
about ten years ago.   He went to sleep one night,
and Boy Thunder came to him and told him "how
to be an engineer."   The next morning he journeyed
over to the coal mines on the Blackfoot Indian
Reservation, and after several days' work, con-
structed a complete operating coal-mining system.
The agency and government authorities declare that
it could not be improved on by the best modern mining engineers.   Working alone in this remarkable
mine, Wolf Head mined twelve dollars' worth of
coal every day until he got tired of it.

After much persuasion on the part of the missionaries, Wolf Head a few years ago gave up his practices as the tribal medicine-man and accepted the
religion of the white man.   Since that date, he says,

he has lost every one of his powers as a medicine-man.

"Boy Thunder never came to me again after that," he told me. "I was a rich man when I changed my religion; I had many horses. Now I have nothing. I am poor, and I have no medicine powers left—they all flew from me that day when I gave up my old religion."

Though Wolf Head is as he says he is, the tribe nevertheless still looks up to him as its greatest man. Knowing his past as it does, it will never cease to do that.

Wolf Head is still the possessor of a medicine tee-pee which would bring him a fortune in horses if he would sell it. But he will never part with that teepee. It was given to him, together with one other medicine teepee, by Boy Thunder, who gave him his life's medicine, the Thunder Bird—Eagle—and told him how to paint it on these two teepees. One of the teepees is blue and the other, yellow; and both of them bear a huge painting of the Thunder Bird. The South Blackfeet at Browning, Montana, after much beseeching finally persuaded Wolf Head to sell them the blue medicine teepee for their band of the nation, and they have it at Browning to-day. But Wolf Head will never part with the yellow teepee. It is his home—the only reminder of his days of marvelous glory as the greatest medicine-man in the Northwest. The photograph reproduced is one which I took of Wolf Head standing in front of his famous yellow medicine teepee, with the painting of the Thunder Bird—Eagle—showing over his shoulder.

XVI

The Carnival of Peace

IT WAS two years since we had had our last trouble with the Crows. It was late autumn, and we were camping one night on the fringe of the Cypress Hills near the Montana-Alberta border when something strange happened.

We had been some hours in bed and it must have been near midnight, when out of the inky blackness of a starless night, we heard a rustling among our horses which stirred us to our elbows. No one spoke a word. In this breathless silence I heard a "click," and I knew that my father had slipped his arm under his muzzle-loader, and had cocked it to fire.

Our horses, too, had remained silent for an instant after their first startling jump, but now they broke again, and we could hear them trying to gallop with their hobbled feet. Now our dogs became aroused! One hundred shaggy giants, who could not bark because they were half wolf, sprang as one into a howling, yowling fury—"rrrrrooo-eeeyow-wah-wah-wah-oooweee!" Above this savage medley we were startled by three terrible screeches. It was the noise of a ghost! We knew it; for it was the yell of—Roving Night Eagle!

Roving Night Eagle—our warrior who had been killed by the Crows!

My father dashed out of the teepee door like a hurtling black shadow. "Thump-thump-thump"— moccasined feet rushing—where, we did not know. We heard this, in Blackfoot—it came to us from out among the horses:

"I am a Blackfoot. I am the enemy of no living person!"

"Hanh-h-h-h-h," groaned my mother. "It is the voice of Roving Night Eagle!" She clapped her hand over her mouth and sat motionless. We youngsters hugged to her side and shivered with fear.

Then we heard voices, and strained our ears to catch what they were saying. We must have sat that way five minutes before our father swept back the teepee door and shouted:

"All to the big lodge.—It is Roving Night Eagle!"

We threw our blankets about us and rushed out behind our mother. When we got outside we could see the big lodge already lighted with a fire. Everyone was rushing toward it.

When we got inside, there was a whole crowd of

expectant people like ourselves, but we did not see Roving Night Eagle anywhere. While we were looking around for him we heard a commotion at the door. We turned and saw two big braves holding up a ghost. That is what we children thought it was—a ghost. It was tall and pale and crippled. One knee was bent hard and stiff, and when it walked slowly between our two braves it bobbed up and down on this short bent leg. When it came nearer the fire it began to look a little like Roving Night Eagle. And when we asked our mothers if it were he or his spirit, they told us to keep quiet; it was Roving Night Eagle.

They sat him on a pile of buffalo robes close to the fire, for he was shivering and twitching from exposure.

Soon food came in, and we sat silently and watched him eat. A pipe was lighted and handed to him after he had eaten. He sat a long while and smoked. Then he straightened his back and looked around at us for the first time, and said, "Hanh!"— which meant that he was going to talk.

"Brothers," he said, "it makes my heart glad to be back with my own people. Two years I have been among strangers who spoke not our language.

"You did not know that you had left me among the *Isahpos*—Crows. You all remember the second fight we had with the Crows, the next day after we crept into their camp and took their horses while they were sleeping.

"It was my fault that I was hit by the Crows. When we ambuscaded them and they ran toward the river, some of us wanted to go after them, but our medicine-man White Dog would not allow us to. I wanted a Crow scalp of my own, for the scalp which they had taken from my brother, and so I slipped away from the rest when you were talking there, and went on after the Crows, down to the river.

"When I came upon them they were throwing off their blankets and jumping into the river, to swim across to the other side. I ran up to one fellow and struck him with my battle-ax, and as I sat down on his chest to scalp him I saw six others coming toward me. When I jumped up they fired on me. One of their bullets struck me in the knee and tore it off. I crawled into the bush and then slid my body down into the water, and held to a branch with only my nose sticking out of the water. They looked for me a long time before they left.

"When they had gone I crawled back into the bush, and kept crawling until daylight.

"I was sitting in the middle of a field resting the next morning when I saw three Crows coming toward me out of the underbrush. They had come back to search for me. I threw myself on my stomach and began firing at them. I shot two of them, and the other fellow ran back into the bush. [Roving Night Eagle was the best sharpshooter in the Blackfoot nation.] They had been firing at me, too, and when I looked at my right leg now, I found that it had been shot twice again. It was now broken in three places: here, here, and here," he said, baring his grotesquely scarred limb and pointing to his thigh, his knee, and his shin-bone.

"I knew that I would be killed if I did not quickly get out of this country. So I took my gun and put the butt of it against my stomach, and I grasped the stock with both hands and used it for a stick [crutch]. In this way I went along on one foot and the gun, and dragged my left leg along the ground. It was limber in three places.

"I traveled five days this way without food. On the fifth day I killed a badger and a duck, and ate them. My moccasins had worn out and my feet were bare in the snow; so I made myself a pair of moccasins from the badger skin, and kept going.

"Late afternoon of the next day, I heard someone yell, and I looked about and saw two men coming toward me on horses. They were white men—American traders in Assiniboia—Saskatchewan.

"These men took me to their shack at Wood Mountain. They kept me there two years, trying to cure my wounds. I learned their language.

"Eight days ago I heard one of them say that they were going to cut off my leg. That night I ran away barefoot and without moccasins in a big blizzard. I made up my mind that I would rather die in the blizzard than lose my leg.

"I knew that you, my own people, would be somewhere down on our river here at this time of the year; so I came down to look for you. Some Crees told me where you were, and I saw your camp early today, but I could not reach it until now—I was too weak and lame. Our own dogs nearly ate me before I got in tonight, but I am here—and I give thanks to the Great Spirit."

Then drawing himself painfully to a half-standing position on his one good leg, he raised his hand and said: "I pray that the Great Spirit will be as good to all of you as he has been to me."

Our chief arose and said:

"White Dog was never wrong in his life. He is dead now, Roving Night Eagle; but he told us the spirits never spoke falsely to him. And if we had had sense enough to read his words, we would have known that you were alive all this time. His spirit sees you here tonight, and I know his heart is glad. Bring the drums!"

The big medicine drum was brought into the lodge. It was the same big drum that our renowned White Dog had so many times awed us with

during his weird career as our medicine-man. We
had guarded it above all things throughout our ca-
lamitous days in the Rockies, but never once had it
been removed from its covering of skin, put on there
by the mystic hands of White Dog himself.

"Boom, *boom* — boom-*boom* — boom, *boom*."
Everyone sat still as the thundering notes of this
drum came to us for the first time since that fateful
night over the buffalo head, when White Dog was
making his last bid to the Spirits to get the outcome
of our impending battle with the Crows. No one
sang—just the drum.

Presently, in a voice ever so low, White Dog's
widow chanted one verse of his famous medicine
song—the song he had sung the night he died. Then
we relapsed into silence again.

A freezing wind howled fitfully through the flaps
of the lodge. Aroused and made uneasy by the
sound of the tom-tom at this strange hour of the
night, some of our dogs shoved their noses high into
the heavens and howled the plaintive call of the
timber-wolf. Now and then a muffled grunt from
some corner of the lodge—and then nothing but the
drum, the whining winds, and the baying dogs.

The first to break the long silence was our chief,
who had been sitting with a misty glint in his eye,
gazing into space. With a sad smile on his face,
he said:

"White Dog is with us tonight; I can feel him here." And we all believed him; for there was something in the air that said it.

In the days succeeding Roving Night Eagle's return to us, our medicine-man broke his leg in two places and set them in splints, and after a few months had passed, he was entirely well, with only a stiff knee to remind him of his harrowing adventure.

Our chief was so elated over his return and the vindication of White Dog's "medicine," that he called a council and said that he was going to make peace with the Crows. He dispatched a runner to the Crow chief, who was coming with his band more than one hundred miles away, with a present of Indian tobacco—*kinikinik*. The messenger was to present this tobacco to the chief of the Crows, and if he accepted it, was to invite him to meet us half-way on the journey and "smoke the pipe with us."

Six days later the runner returned with a present of "Eastern Indian tobacco"—tobacco like that used by the white man today—which the Crow chief had sent to our chief, with a word of peace. A week later we all met out on the plains, the Crows and the Blackfeet, and we gave peace to one another.

In his speech before the big gathering of Crows and Blackfeet, our chief said:

"We have been foolish people, the Crows and

the Blackfeet. We have fought all of our lives. We fought one another only because we had the same color of skin and were the same people. That must never be again. As long as the sun shines, grass grows, and men walk on two feet, we must be friends, the Crows and the Blackfeet. If you were not a brave people like ourselves, I would want to go on and fight and kill you all. But you are too brave to kill. We want to honor you as we would our own brave warriors. Let us smoke!"

Our medicine-man "made" the pipe—filled it and lighted it—and handed it to our chief. He smoked it for a moment and then started it on its course through the two tribes. When this was over we all sat down to a big feast which our women had been preparing—and never again were the Blackfeet the enemy of the Crows.

We camped together for five days, during which we boys and the Crow boys contested our skill with one another in games and mimic battles. We fought over all of the battles that our fathers had waged against each other, and it was the best time we had ever had. We youngsters were glad to be at peace with the Crows; for we had liked them ever since we met some of their boys and played with them that day and night on the river-bank, months before. We exchanged many presents before we parted, and some of us adopted "brothers" among the Crow boys.

XVII

Outlaw

WHEN we came out of our winter camp in the foot-hills of the Rockies two years later, other Indians told us that there was what the white man would call today a big settlement boom on in the Northwest, and that the white man was pouring into our hunting grounds by the thousands.

It seemed that our days as rovers of the plains were now to come to an end. The Indians everywhere we went were uneasy. Our chiefs and councilors began to hold frequent councils to decide what we should do about it. Should we make one last stand against this race that was coming in and taking our country away from us? Or should we subscribe to the peace treaty which the head chief of the Blackfoot nation, Niokskatos, had already made with the white man in Assiniboia?

Government agents of the great white chief were already coming to our chief and telling him that we must stop our roaming about and put our children in the schools of the missionaries, that they might learn to work with their hands and become as white men.

Missionaries were everywhere, telling the Indian about the white man's God and asking him to cut his hair off and wash the paint off his face and dress himself in the queer-looking clothes of the white man. Our long hair was our most highly prized physical possession. We spent more than an hour every day dressing it carefully and braiding it over the smooth surface of some little pool of water, which we used as a looking-glass.

And the white missionaries said that we must stop painting our faces, too. An Indian without paint! We could not imagine that. They might as well tell us to stop singing. We had a different kind of paint for every mood we found ourselves in. No Indian was ever without some sort of paint on his face. When we got up in the morning we painted our faces the way we felt. If we felt angry, peaceful, in love, religious, or whatever the mood was, we painted our faces accordingly, so that all who should come in contact with us would know how we felt at a glance. It saved a lot of useless talking. And when I was a youngster the Indians did not like to talk very much. They used to like to go about quietly and think a lot. We would sometimes sit in our teepees for hours at a time without saying a word, yet we were all enjoying ourselves. It was just our custom—and it made us feel good inside.

We thought that the Indian looked funny in

white man's clothes, with his hair short and without paint, and I remember that whenever we youngsters saw an Indian like this we used to laugh at him. The Indian never has looked well in white man's clothes, because he does not take the pride in them that he does in his native dress, which he fusses with a lot and keeps immaculately clean and neat.

Our very God existed in the plains and forests that we had known and which were now to be taken away from us forever. Our Indian religion taught us that the Great Spirit existed in all things: in the trees, the animals, the lakes, rivers, and mountains. And when we wanted to get close to the Great Spirit and pray, we went out alone and got close to the things in which he lived. Now we were being told about a new God. Where he lived, no one knew; and it made us youngsters feel uneasy. Our old people nightly called upon the Great Spirit to help us and to show us the truth.

As we boys played about the camp, some old warrior whom we looked upon as a great hero of bygone days would come up to us and place his arm around our shoulders and walk along with us, praying out aloud for our future in this period of great uncertainty.

Other old warriors would go about our camp, each with one hand over his mouth, talking and praying to themselves.

"Natose, what are we coming to? Where are our warriors of bygone days? Where are our buffalo? Natose, are we no longer men?"

During this turbulent period of uncertainty we boys used to go up on a big butte every evening at sunset, and we would sit down up there and talk things over.

"Our parents have raised us to be warriors," we would say, "and now the white man wants to put those funny clothes on us and make us do the work of women."

All of our training had suddenly been upset. Our religion had taught us to give good for good and evil for evil. Now, the missionaries were telling us to give good for good and good for evil. "What does that mean?" we asked ourselves. If a man shot at us and missed us, were we to give him another ball so that he could shoot at us again? We could not understand this. What were we to do about the settlers who were squatting on the lands that the government was setting aside for us? Were we to invite them to take more of our land?

We could not figure this out. And sometimes, as the sun was setting and it started to get cold on the butte, we would all huddle close together in the gathering darkness—and just sit and think. Though powerless little children, we, like all youngsters, felt a great responsibility in the things that were going on about us. We felt that if our old people would let us fight we could soon clear up the situation. I suppose all boys are like that.

We would go back to our camp and ask our fathers if there was going to be a war. And they would say:

"No, we are going to try to eat cows." Which meant that they were going to try to eat the white man's food and live peaceably. The mention of the sweet-smelling cow made us all sick. We had been used to the strong, goatlike smell of the buffalo, and we could not imagine eating meat which smelled so sweet and sickly as the cows we had passed with our hands over our noses.

While we were still marking time like this, something happened north of us which brought great excitement among the Indians and caused considerable alarm among the white settlers of this region.

Indian runners came into our camp and told us the Indian outlaw Almighty Voice had come out of his two years of hiding in the northern wilderness, and that he was now going to "fight it out" with the Royal Northwest Mounted Police, who for twenty-four months had been scouring every nook and cranny of the Northwest for his whereabouts.

Scarcely did we think, on that bright day in 1897 when this news reached our camp, that this young Indian was destined soon to make the greatest single-handed stand in all the history of the North American West.

Almighty Voice, giant young son of Sounding Sky and Spotted Calf, had two years before been arrested for killing a range steer that belonged to the government of the Northwest Territories. He had thought that it was one of a small herd that had been given to his father. This occurred on the One Arrow Indian Reserve, fourteen miles from Duck Lake, Assiniboia, now Saskatchewan, where there was a large settlement of half-breeds and a mounted-police post.

Almighty Voice had been taken to Duck Lake and placed in the mounted-police guard-house. One of the mounted police in charge of the Duck Lake Post, Corporal Casimar Dickson, jokingly told Almighty Voice, through an interpreter, that they were "going to hang him for killing that steer." The corporal did this "to scare him," he said. Hardly did he realize the terrible effect which this innocent little joke was going to have on this untutored young Indian.

Almighty Voice was the grandson of Chief One Arrow, who led the Duck Lake Indians in the Northwest Rebellion of a few years before, and the son of Sounding Sky, one of the most redoubtable fighters in this last rebellion against the whites, who was still looked upon by the mounted police as the most dangerous Indian of that part of the North-west.

Reared in the primitive adventurous environment of the Indian of that day, Almighty Voice had become famed throughout the region as a runner, a hunter, and a man of indomitable courage and independence. Altogether, he was dauntless, resourceful, physically powerful, and enduring; a young warrior who could well justify the alarm which his reappearance had now aroused throughout the white settlements of that vast open territory.

It was in the afternoon when Corporal Dickson told Almighty Voice that "he was going to be hanged." That night in the little mounted-police guard-house, which still stands at Duck Lake, Saskatchewan, the mounted police chained Almighty Voice to a heavy iron ball and left him to roll up in his Indian blanket and go to sleep on the floor of the guardroom. Corporal Dickson was on duty to guard him until midnight; then he was to be relieved by another "mountie" who was sleeping upstairs.

Shortly before eleven that night Corporal Dickson decided that he wanted to go off duty a little early, so he got up from the dimly lighted table at which he was sitting in the guardroom and took the butt of his rifle and banged the ceiling with it to awake his relief man.

"Come on down!" he shouted up. "I want to go

a little early tonight. Want to get over to Mac's
before he closes."

"All right," answered the other mountie. But instead of coming down he went back to sleep again.

After waiting impatiently for a few minutes, Corporal Dickson got up again and banged the ceiling,
shouting to his companion to make haste. Presently
the other mountie came down the stairs and sleepily
took over the midnight vigil. The relief policeman
walked over to a dark corner of the guardroom and
looked carefully at the long blanketed form of Almighty Voice. He was lying there with his blanket
wrapped around him from head to foot, apparently
sound asleep.

The mountie went back to the table with the oil
lamp on it and sat down. Neither of the policemen
knew this, but all during these proceedings Almighty
Voice had been lying there with his blanket wrapped
half around his head, with the exposed eye shut and
the other peering out at them from beneath the fold
of the blanket. He had seen everything that they
had done; he was watching their every movement.

When the relief mountie went back to the table,
he sat there sleepily for a while, and then his head
started to droop. Down, down, down it sank,
until finally his face keeled gently forward to the
top of his folded hands—and he was fast asleep,
face-down on the table.

This was the opportunity Almighty Voice had been waiting for.

He picked up the heavy ball to which he was chained, and slowly tiptoed over to the table. Stopping just behind the sleeping mountie, he reached over his shoulders and picked up the bunch of keys lying beside his hands, and stooped forward and unlocked the heavy manacle around his ankle. With short, quick steps he made for the door.

Once outside of that door, he knew that he was safe; for no one, white or red, had ever beaten him in a foot-race.

He sprang across the back yard of the guardhouse, and with a mighty leap cleared the high fence without touching it. He sped like a doe toward the Saskatchewan River. Six miles of incredible running brought him to the western bank of this broad, swift-flowing stream. Without stopping to get his breath, he broke off several heavy saplings and lashed them into a three-cornered raft. He stripped and threw his blanket and clothing onto this raft, and pushing it ahead of him, he swam a half-mile to the other side of the river. He resumed his long, fourteen-mile run, and before it was yet daybreak he arrived panting and sweating at the door of his mother's lodge.

His mother Spotted Calf is also my adopted mother, and that is why I am able to record the inside story of this famous man-hunt, which today is so amply dealt with in history and in all books on the Northwest Mounted Police. Spotted Calf and her husband Sounding Sky are still living on the One Arrow Indian Reserve, at Duck Lake, Saskatchewan —mother and father of Almighty Voice.

When Almighty Voice threw back the door of his mother's lodge his first words were these:

"The mounted police told me today that they were going to hang me for killing that steer. They will never hang me—I will die fighting."

Then he asked his mother for his father Sounding Sky; he wanted to ask his father's advice before taking his stand against the mounties. His mother told him that the mounted police had arrested his father and taken him to Prince Albert, where he was being kept under guard. Knowing his warlike history and the power which he held over his people, the mounted police thought that Sounding Sky might start an Indian uprising if he were allowed to remain among his people.

Early the next morning the mounted police came galloping in from Duck Lake, to search the camp for Almighty Voice. They went into Spotted Calf's lodge and searched every inch of the place—but one —for their escaped prisoner. In a corner of the lodge was a pile of provisions covered over with blankets and buffalo robes. Almighty Voice was lying concealed beneath these robes with his eye beaded down the barrel of a rifle that barely pointed from one of the folds of the blankets. Not once did the mounted police go near this pile of blankets, which was fortunate.

After the mounted police had departed Almighty Voice left the One Arrow camp with his fifteen-year-old wife and made for the Kenistino Reserve in the North. He took with him a muzzle-loader and two horses.

The mounted police, world-famous for their unrelenting efficiency as man-hunters, immediately dispatched Sergeant C. C. Colebrook and a half-breed scout to retake their prisoner, cost what it might.

North they went, along a fresh trail which they presumed Almighty Voice and his young wife had taken.

One morning, as they were riding through a lonely stretch of the North Country, they heard a gunshot. Spurring their horses forward and rounding a bush into a little clearing, they suddenly came upon Almighty Voice in the act of picking up a prairie-chicken that he had just shot. His girl-wife was holding their horses a few feet away. When Almighty Voice looked up and saw the policeman approaching he quickly reloaded his gun and stood waiting. At twenty yards he ordered a halt.

"Stop, or I'll shoot," he hissed in Cree.

This was interpreted to the sergeant by the half-breed scout.

"No," said Sergeant Colebrook, "I'm going to do my duty."

Again Almighty Voice sent forward a command to halt. "Another step forward, and I'll shoot!" he warned. The sergeant rode on. "Crack!"—a bullet came tearing into his neck; and he fell forward in his saddle, dead.

Turning his gun on the half-breed scout, Almighty Voice said: "I'm not going to kill you, but I am going to mark you."

"Crack!" barked his gun again—and a bullet shattered the half-breed's elbow.

The half-breed turned his horse, and as he dashed off, Almighty Voice shouted after him: "And if I ever see you again I'll kill you!"

The half-breed stopped at the mounted police at Duck Lake barely long enough to acquaint Inspector Allen with what had happened, and then he spurred his horse forward. No one in this country has ever seen him since.

The killing of Sergeant Colebrook marked the real commencement of this, the greatest man-hunt in all the history of the West. Almighty Voice was now outlawed with a big price on his head, dead or alive.

From this time on, until May 24, 1897—nearly

two years later—he is dropped into mysterious ob-livion by all books dealing with his career. The mounted police force scoured the northern wilder-ness for him in vain. Not once, during this time, were they able to pick up a sign of his trail.

"The Riders of the Plains," the official history of the Royal Northwest Mounted Police, says: "During this period Almighty Voice never showed himself among his people, nor did he apparently hold any communication with them."

But the inside story of these two mysterious years is well known by his father and mother, who are still living at Duck Lake (1928). And here, for the first time in any book touching upon this notorious episode, I shall give this story.

As a matter of truth, Almighty Voice hid out in the wilds of the northern wilderness and made many secret visits to his parents during these years. For months at a time he would disappear from all human habitation and merge himself with the track-less wastes of the northern wilds; then on some dark night, like a ghost from another world, he would appear silently at the door of his mother's teepee. He would peer cautiously through the flap of the door and then enter without a word, his silent young wife always entering behind him. After inquiring for his father, who was still being held by the mounted police, he would drop off into a deep sleep.

Tired and worn by the ceaseless, ever-moving vigil of the hunted wolf, he would remain in slumber for perhaps two days under the constant watch of his faithful mother. Then he would awake, eat a lot, talk a little—and then vanish again.

Once when he came in from the depths of the wilds, his wife carried a little moss bag strapped over her back, and in it was a tiny brown baby. Almighty Voice, Jr., had been born to them in the wilderness. He is today an upstanding young Indian more than six feet tall, and the photograph reproduced here is of him and his twin babies, born to his young wife during my last visit with him on the One Arrow Reserve, at Duck Lake, Saskatchewan.

Finally, in the early spring of 1897, the mounted police suddenly changed their tactics. In some way they sensed that there was a strong tie between Almighty Voice and his father Sounding Sky; and so they decided to send Sounding Sky back to the One Arrow Reserve and see if they could not use him as a decoy to catch their quarry.

When a short time later Almighty Voice returned to the camp on one of his periodic visits and found his father there, the two of them went into secret conference. His father told me that when this conference was over, "Almighty Voice did not want to hide any more." He went out and said to his mother:

SPOTTED CALF AND SOUNDING SKY
Parents of the Historic Indian Fighter ALMIGHTY VOICE

"The next time the mounted police come into this camp, I am going to show myself and fight it out with them."

The mounted police had been right in their supposition; for a week had not passed when one of their half-breed informers saw Sounding Sky crossing a certain corner of the reserve at an unusual time of the day, and he knew that Almighty Voice was in the vicinity. He went back and tipped off the police.

The next morning Inspector James Wilson, in charge of the Duck Lake Post, dispatched two mounted police constables and a half-breed scout, named Napoleon Venne, to ride out to the reserve and take their man.

Venne, the half-breed scout, told me that they rode up to the big Indian camp in the Minnechinas Hills, and stopped in the trail in front of it and got off their horses. They made believe that they got off to roll a cigarette, but in reality they were scouting their eyes through the Indian camp for some clue of Almighty Voice.

While Venne was rolling his cigarette with his bridle-reins thrown over his arm, his horse started to jerk excitedly. He pulled him up with a sharp command, and started to roll his cigarette again. Again the horse jumped and snorted uneasily, and as he was about to give him another welt over the head, he heard a slight rustling in the bush beside the trail. But just as he turned to see what it was, a shot split the air, and Venne fell to the ground with a bullet in his chest.

Constable Beaudridge and the other mountie picked Venne up and rushed him back to Duck Lake.

When they had gone, Almighty Voice and two Indian boys who had joined him in his last stand against the mounties crawled out of the bush and walked across the trail into the camp. He was angry because Venne had not been killed. He told his father and mother all about it. He said:

"We were lying there when they rode up and stopped. When they got off their horses I crawled a little closer to the trail and had my gun leveled at Venne's heart, when my cousin here, Going-Up-to-Sky, said: 'Let me shoot him.' I wanted to try him out because he was so young [he was only fifteen], and I lowered my gun and said, 'Go ahead, but take your time and aim well.' I wanted to get Venne because he is a half-breed and has not business mixing himself up in this fight. I shall get him yet."

Venne, who lived in a little half-breed settlement on the edge of Almighty Voice's reserve, heard this, and he fled the country and remained in exile in the Yukon for fourteen years. But he is back now, living in his old home, with his wife, son, and daughter. And he still carries the large round bullet embedded deep into his chest.

By a strange trick of fate, Venne now lives less than a mile and a half from the camp of Almighty Voice's father and mother. One day I was sitting in front of their teepee eating with them, when Mr. Venne's son rode by on a horse, driving some of his father's cattle. Almighty Voice's mother said simply and without any feeling or animosity: "It is a good thing for that boy that my son did not fire the bullet that struck his father, or he would not be living now." That is a well-known fact; for it is recorded in the records of the mounted police that Almighty Voice himself never wasted a shot. Until his final stand, he never fired a shot without killing.

The shooting of Venne aroused genuine alarm throughout the country; for everyone knew now that Almighty Voice was in the neighborhood again, and they knew that he was on the war-path in deadly earnest. In addition to his boy cousin Going-Up-to-Sky he now was also accompanied by his brother-in-law Topean. He had assumed the offensive and become a killer, and these two boys, according to an Indian tradition of loyalty, had chosen to make the stand and die with him. With an Indian, this means that he intends to get as many as he can before he is killed.

The news of Almighty Voice's sudden reappearance after two years of baffling evasion was received with grave concern at Prince Albert, forty miles away. At midnight that same day twelve mounted policemen under Captain Allan (who died in Vancouver, August, 1927) set out on horseback for the Minnechinas Hills. At the same time another mounted police force under Inspector Wilson was dispatched from Duck Lake.

Captain Allan's party, riding past Bellevue Hill the next morning, noticed in the distance three objects moving toward a small thicket of trees. "I see three antelope over there," one of the constables reported. But when they approached closer they were surprised to discern the naked forms of three young Indians, stripped for battle, with their bare, slick bodies glistening in the sun like the smooth brown coat of the antelope.

Captain Allan knew instantly that he had located his quarry, and he gave quick orders to charge.

The three Indian boys stopped dead in their tracks. Almighty Voice stood and waited until the charging mounties had advanced to firing range; then he opened up. The first burst of Indian fire brought down the two officers commanding the detachment. Captain Allan's right arm was smashed with a bullet, and Sergeant Raven sagged forward in his saddle with his thigh crushed and dangling uselessly over the side of his horse. Corporal C. H. Hockin now assumed command of the detachment.

Almighty Voice had now counted his fifth "coo"

—one killed and four wounded. As the mounted police halted to take care of their wounded and reorganize their forces, Almighty Voice and his two companions disappeared into a small thicket, a clump of bush about a half-mile through, now famous as the "Almighty Voice Bluff." His people knew that he had selected this bluff in which to make his last, desperate stand against the mounties, and that he had no thoughts of ever coming out of it alive.

Corporal Hockin's detachment, which stood guard awaiting the reenforcements that had been summoned, was soon joined by the detachment from Duck Lake. That afternoon this combined force was further reenforced by a command consisting of every spare man from the Prince Albert barracks of the Northwest Mounted Police.

At six o'clock that evening Corporal Hockin called for volunteers to charge the thicket. Nine mounted policemen and civilian volunteers answered this call.

This was the most disastrous movement of the day. The Indians, perceiving their intention, were on the edge of the thicket awaiting their onslaught. Scarcely had the fringe of the bush been reached when Corporal Hockin received his death wound, a bullet in the chest.

The rush continued, both Indians and raiders firing as fast as their guns would shoot. Ernest Grundy, postmaster of Duck Lake, was the next to fall dead, with a bullet through his heart. An instant later Constable J. R. Kerr went down to his death with a ball in the chest.

One of the Indian boys, Topean, had been killed on the edge of the brush, and Almighty Voice had received a bullet which shattered his right leg.

Almighty Voice had now counted his eighth "coo" —four killed and four wounded. Five of the Royal Northwest Mounted Policemen had answered the call to duty; two mounted police scouts and one civilian volunteer. All of these fine fellows of the Northwest Mounted Police had gone to their Maker through an idle joke which a thoughtless fellow who had crept into their force had carelessly perpetrated on a young Indian, who, according to some of the mounted policemen themselves, had in him the makings of a good red citizen of the early West. In justice to the mounted police, it must be said that the man responsible for this, Corporal Dickson, was immediately stripped of his uniform, dismissed from the force, and under guard was made to dig the grave of Almighty Voice's first victim Sergeant C. C. Colebrook.

But the real battle of this famous episode had not yet begun.

The tragic consequences of these two disastrous charges brought about a retreat of the attacking party, without time to remove their dead. That night, however, the besiegers tried to burn the Indians out of the bush by setting fire to it. But the attempt was a failure.

Not until then did the mount d police realize the size of the job they had undertaken. A third call for reenforcements was sent out. A cordon of pickets was thrown completely around the thicket, to prevent the escape of the Indians in the darkness.

That night in the Regina Mounted Police Headquarters, two hundred miles to the south, a big mounted-police ball, celebrating the sending to England of the Queen's Jubilee contingent of mounted policemen, was at its height when suddenly the band struck up, "God Save the Queen." Men and women looked at one another in amazement. When the national anthem ceased, Colonel Herchimer, the commanding officer of all the mounted police, announced that the sending of the Jubilee Contingent to England had been canceled; that grave news had just been received from the North Country. Whereupon, he issued orders that every available mounted policeman was to start north at once.

This force consisted of twenty-five men, a nine-pounder field gun and a Maxim gun under Assistant-Commissioner McIlree and Inspector McDonnell— now General Sir Archibald McDonnell, of Calgary, Alberta, Commissioner of Boy Scouts for Western Canada. Another detachment of reenforcements left Prince Albert the next day under Inspector Gagnon. This brought to the field practically the entire mounted police force of Assiniboia.

Added to this, hundreds of volunteers had been recruited and rushed to the scene. A transport was recruited at Duck Lake, equipped with picks and shovels and sent out to dig trenches and throw up earthworks, to enable the troops to advance on the bluff under cover—this, in case they should not be able to exterminate the Indians by shell-fire. So disastrous had been the first two attacks on the thicket that orders were issued from mounted police headquarters forbidding the mounties from making any further raids. Enough lives had been lost, and it was realized that field operations must now be adopted.

As the stillness of night crept over the field on that fatal Friday evening, Almighty Voice shouted out of the bluff to the troops:

"We have had a good fight today. I have worked hard and I am hungry. You have plenty of food; send me some, and tomorrow we'll finish the fight."

When this message was interpreted to the mounted police they were amazed. But it expressed the Indian's code: fair fight, fair game, no bad feeling in the heart. It may be hard to believe, but Almighty Voice admired the dashing courage of the mounted police fully as much as he did that of his two boy companions. The Indian loves the brave, strong-fighting opponent and hates the weak, cowardly adversary.

Early the next morning a crow flew over the thicket in which the three Indians were hiding. . . . "Tang!" went Almighty Voice's gun, and the crow dashed headlong into the bush, to be devoured raw by the hungry Indians. One of the mounties remarked: "Isn't it queer? That fellow never wastes a bullet—something falls every time he fires."

Almighty Voice's old mother Spotted Calf had stood on top of the rise just back of the thicket all night, shouting encouragement to her son. Through the chilly darkness she stood on her little pinnacle and recounted to him the brave exploits of his father Sounding Sky and his famous grandfather Chief One Arrow; and she urged him to die the brave that he had shown himself to be.

"Don't weaken, my son," she shouted. "You must die fighting them!" From time to time the mounted police would search and find her in the darkness, and gently try to get her to go home.

"They said to me," she told me, " 'You must not stay here; you will get hurt!' And they would try to lead me off the field. But I could not go home and sleep when I knew my boy was in there."

Now and then Almighty Voice would answer his

mother through the darkness, informing her how he was faring.

After the two attacks on Friday, he said, he and his remaining boy relative had dug a hole and got into it and covered it over with brush. They were lying under this brush with their deadly rifles poking out to kill anyone who attempted to come into the thicket after them. Two mounted police lay dead ten feet from his pit, he said; and he had taken their rifles and ammunition and thrown away his clumsy old muzzle-loader.

"I am almost starving," he said. "I am eating the bark off the trees. I have dug into the ground as far as my arm will reach, but can get no water. But have no fear—I'll hold out to the end."

Excitement had become intense in the surrounding countryside, as all day Saturday fresh troops were arriving on the field from Regina, Prince Albert, and Duck Lake. The whole population of Assiniboia (now Saskatchewan) seemed to have flocked there overnight.

My friend Dr. Stewart, who still practices at Duck Lake, and who owns the last gun used by Almighty Voice, was one of the two men who rescued the dying body of the gallant Corporal Hockin from the very edge of the deadly bluff. Constable O'Kelly, the "Fighting Irishman," discovered the body with his field-glasses, and he believed that he had seen it move. He called for a volunteer to make a dash with him down the hill and across the lowland to attempt a rescue. Jumping into a buckboard, Dr. Stewart, the volunteer, and Constable O'Kelly tore down the hill as fast as their horses could pull them.

They stopped right on the edge of the thicket, and Constable O'Kelly piled the limp form of Hockin in the back of the buckboard while Dr. Stewart jumped out and held the horses. Then they whirled around and beat a galloping retreat. Constable O'Kelly had kept jumping to avoid the rain of bullets that were directed at him, and was hit only in the shoe. But not a bullet was fired at Dr. Stewart as he stood still holding the horses, in easy range of Almighty Voice's deadly weapon. The doctor attributes this to the fact that Almighty Voice knew him very well.

"He could have made quick work of me if he had wanted to," Dr. Stewart said to me, "but he knew I was there only as a medical attendant, and he was sport enough not to take a pot at me."

By Saturday evening the field guns were well in place—a nine-pounder and a seven-pounder—and at six o'clock the first shells were sent thundering into the thicket.

The second shot got the range, and the next landed plump into the spot where the fugitives were known to be ensconced.

The heavy barrage of bursting shells lasted for some time. When it finally ceased and every one of the one thousand mounties and volunteers stood breathless, wondering what had happened to the fugitives, a voice came out of the brush. It was the voice of Almighty Voice. It said:

"You have done well, but you will have to do better."

Darkness settled quickly over the landscape, and a silence as sickening as the whining, thundering shells of a few moments before bored itself into the very souls of the besieging troops. "Men heard one another breathing," one of them once remarked to me. Creeping in behind the thoughts of their own dead comrades, came the half-sad realization that tomorrow would spell the eternal end of the two creatures in the bush below, who had partaken of neither food, water, nor sleep during the last three days. Right or wrong, they had displayed a quality which all brave men admire.

One of them also confided to me that he secretly hoped that the Indians would escape during the night and never be heard from again.

No one will ever know what was in the heart and mind of Almighty Voice during that gruesome, black stillness.

The night wore on, interrupted only by one mysterious rifle shot, which clipped the hat off the head of one of the pickets while he was lighting his pipe. The queer part of it was that the shot did not come from the direction of the thicket, but from behind the picket line, which will be explained later by a most unusual happening.

Along in the midnight a group of coyotes, attracted to the vicinity by the odor of the dead bodies, set up a dolorous chorus of baying; and their "yip, yip, yip, hoo-h" only added to the uncanniness of the situation.

Then another sound floated from the opposite hill —the hill just back of the place in which the Indians lay. "Hi-heh, hi-heh, heh-yo, heh-yo." It was Almighty Voice's wrinkled old mother chanting her son's death song.

"I wanted to go in that bluff and take my son in my arms and protect him," she told me, sweeping her arms through the motion of a motherly embrace. Again and again she had tried to slip into the brush all during the four days' vigil, but each time she was intercepted by the mounted police.

"They told me," she said, " 'You must not go in there; it would not be nice for us to have to kill a woman.'

"I was very weak that night," she continued. "I had had nothing to eat for three days and no sleep. I did not want to eat while my son was starving."

Presently a deep-toned echo of the old woman's

song came thundering out of the thicket. It was Almighty Voice answering his mother's death song to him. That was the last time his voice was ever heard. . . .

At six o'clock the next morning the big guns began belching forth their devastating storm of lead and iron in deadly earnestness. It was obvious that no living thing could long endure their steady beat.

At noon the pelting ceased. At one o'clock volunteers, led by James McKay (now Justice of the Supreme Court of Saskatchewan) and William Drain, decided to make another raid on the bluff. The mounties themselves had been refused permission to make another raid, owing to their heavy casualties.

On the first rush the volunteers were not able to locate the hiding-place of the Indians. Well, indeed, had they concealed themselves beneath their covering of brush. A second charge, however, brought them upon the gun-pit.

Here, lying in the brush-covered hole, was the dead body of Almighty Voice.

His boy cousin Going-Up-to-Sky was lying in the hole wounded and alive.

According to old Henry Smith, the half-breed who removed Almighty Voice's body to his mother's teepee, as he had promised her he would, one of the mounted policemen walked up to the hole and put a finishing bullet through the wounded lad's head. Perhaps it was for safety, but some of the other mounties grew angry at this hasty act, and one of them said aloud: "A man who could do that has no heart in him at all, and should be shot himself."

Almighty Voice was shot in seven places, but his death missive was a piece of shrapnel which had split open his forehead. In the bottom of the gun-pit there were two holes, the depth of a man's arm, which had been dug by the fugitive in an effort to reach water. The bark on the surrounding trees had been stripped off and eaten.

The bodies of Constable Kerr and Postmaster Ernest Grundy were lying about ten feet from the hole. The dead body of Almighty Voice's brother-in-law Topean, who had been killed in the first day's fighting, was lying on the fringe of the thicket, about twenty yards from the pit.

The startling revelation that Almighty Voice had got completely out of the bluff on Saturday night, and succeeded in working his way clear through the pickets to a point some one hundred yards beyond the mounted-police lines, was brought to light by the finding of one of his blood-soaked moccasins at this outlying point. A crude crutch which he had made to support his shattered ankle was also found where he abandoned it on his return trip. How he got away and why he returned, no one will ever know.

But this surprising discovery explained that mysterious shot which had clipped the hat off the head of one of the volunteers during the uncanny lull on Saturday night.

On a tree near the spot where the bodies of three mounties had fallen, there were some peculiar characters which had been cut into it with a knife. When an interpreter was called to examine it, it was found to be a sentence written in Cree syllables. It said:

"Here have died three braves."

Almighty Voice, before he was killed, had crawled out of his hole and carved this tombstone to his three last victims. It was a noble tribute to the courage of the three dead mounted policemen.

Today this tree marks the spot where the North American Indian made his last stand against the white man.

Almighty Voice was named by his grandfather Chief One Arrow. When he was a little boy Chief One Arrow called him *Gitchie-Manito-Wayo*—Almighty Voice—because his voice was so loud and deep, sounding, as Chief One Arrow said, like the voice of the Great Spirit.

Not so long ago I took my adopted mother Spotted Calf out to the Almighty Voice Bluff, to let her look at the hole in which her son was killed. Though she was right on the edge of the thicket when he was killed and had spent all of her life just six miles

ALMIGHTY VOICE, JR.
And His Twin Babies

from it, yet she had never in her life seen that hole before. She said just before we started:

"I have never wanted to see that hole, but I think I will let you take me out today." We walked the whole distance from her camp, six miles.

With us was the old half-breed Henry Smith, who had taken Almighty Voice's body back to his mother's teepee. With us also was Almighty Voice, Jr., son of the outlawed Indian who was born in the wilderness during the two years of refuge. Now he was a tall, powerful young man of twenty-eight. And walking along beside him was his girl-mother, who still looked young and pretty though her husband was killed nearly twenty-eight years before. Then there was Prosper, Almighty Voice's brother, a giant Indian standing six feet six inches in his moccasins— one of the highest types of the present-day Indian in the Northwest.

When we reached the bluff, a half-mile clump of bush lying on a rolling, open prairie-land, we had some difficulty in finding the hole. And though she had never seen it herself, Almighty Voice's mother seemed to know more about it than any of the rest of us. It was she who finally got the bearings by standing on a low hill behind the bluff, and then directing us where to enter the bush. She came on in behind us, but when we found the hole she never came up to it; she stood some distance away.

There the old hole was, about the size of a bath-tub—trees around half torn off by shell fire—bark which Almighty Voice had eaten still missing from some of the trunks—a short undergrowth starting to grow inside the hole—and the famous tree, still uttering its mute sentence: "Here have died three braves."

We hardly spoke; we just went around from place to place, examining this and that, and thinking.

It was a beautiful, bright northwestern summer day. Under its peaceful quietness, broken only by the occasional short, gruff cough of a wolf-dog some-where in the distance, it was hard for us to realize that this fine, picturesque stretch of bush and prairie-land once echoed the thunder of the Northwest Re-bellion and the cannon which wiped out Almighty Voice.

I stood at the pit and gazed thoughtfully across the broad stretch of lowland at the rising hill be-yond, where the field guns were put in position. Then I turned in the opposite direction and looked up the abrupt west slope of the rise on which the bluff is situated. I could see the spot about a hun-dred yards above, where the old mother stood shout-ing and singing to her son during the four long days and nights of the siege.

This reminded me to look toward this wonderful old woman, to see how she was reacting to her first visit to the scene since she was carried away exhausted on the tragic morning of May 28, 1897.

I shall never forget the pathetic figure which met my eyes. With a sleeping grandchild strapped over her back, she was standing a little way back from the hole, soaking her tears in the corner of a crimson-and-yellow blanket. She never once looked toward the hole, nor did she approach it nearer than ten feet. She just stood there with her face turned slightly to the side and toward the ground, with one hand quietly mopping her eyes and the other picking aimlessly at the little twigs of red willow which crept up to her waist-line. Her head was bent as if she were ashamed of the emotions which she could not control. Wonderful woman—I am proud to bear the name of this lovable character who long ago adopted me as her son. And my highest hope in the new life that I have adopted from the white man is that I shall never do anything to bring shame upon that name—Spotted Calf.

XVIII

No More Roving

ALL during the Almighty Voice episode messengers from other tribes had been coming into our camp to hold secret conferences with our chief. Some of the tribes wanted to rebel and try to drive the white man off the plains. These messengers asked our chief to journey to a certain point and meet the other tribes in a secret council of war. One of these councils was held. It is well known to the Assiniboines and Northern Blackfeet, but it has never been known or recorded by the white man. And since some of the principals are still living, I shall not comment upon it further. However, some day, when these old warriors have gone on, I shall write and leave the story for history. It will surprise many to learn by just what hair's-breadth the Northwest escaped what would have been the most terrible massacre in the history of America.

But it was the influence of Niokskatos, head chief of all the Blackfeet, which persuaded the other chiefs to lay down their arms and let Almighty Voice's stand be the last.

Our day as free rovers of the open plains had ended. A few years later we boys were in mission schools, learning our A B C's and how to hoe with our hands. How this shamed us: to have to work like women, when we had thought that we were going to be warriors and hunters like our forefathers. This manual labor so humiliated us that whenever we looked up and saw any of our old warriors passing the school, we would lay down our hoes and stand still until they had passed.

I used to go to my room at night and lie and think of the old days when there were buffalo and plenty of animals everywhere. . . . At that time there were a lot of old men, and it was nice to be around. . . . Then I would think of what my grandfather used to tell me when I was a small child. He said that some day the white men would be everywhere on the plains. I did not believe him. He said that some day they would drive all of the animals away; they would put up fences everywhere, and the Indian would have to camp in one place all of the time. I did not believe him. But now I was beginning to realize that everything my grandfather had said was coming true—and I wondered if he could see it.

But the new day is here: it is here to stay. And now we must leave it to our old people to sit stolidly and dream of the glories of our past. Our job is to try to fit ourselves into the new scheme of life which the Great Spirit has decreed for North America. And we will do that, keeping always before us the old Blackfoot proverb: *Mokokit-ki-ackamimat*—Be wise and persevere.

THE END